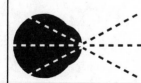

This Large Print Book carries the
Seal of Approval of N.A.V.H.

MacCallister:
The Eagles Legacy:
Kill Crazy

MacCallister:
The Eagles Legacy:
Kill Crazy

William W. Johnstone
with J. A. Johnstone

THORNDIKE PRESS

A part of Gale, Cengage Learning

GALE
CENGAGE Learning

Farmington Hills, Mich • San Francisco • New York • Waterville, Maine
Meriden, Conn • Mason, Ohio • Chicago

GALE
CENGAGE Learning®

LIBRARY OF CONGRESS CATALOGING-IN-PUBLICATION DATA

Johnstone, William W.
  MacCallister : the eagles legacy /kill crazy by William W. Johnstone with J. A. Johnstone.
    pages cm. — (Thorndike Press large print western)
    ISBN 978-1-4104-7251-9 (hardcover) — ISBN 1-4104-7251-5 (hardcover)
    1. Western stories. 2. Large type books. I. Johnstone, J. A. II. Title.
PS3560.O415M33 2014
813'.54—dc23   2014020280

Published in 2014 by arrangement with Pinnacle Books, an imprint of Kensington Publishing Corp.

Printed in the United States of America
1 2 3 4 5 6 7 18 17 16 15 14

MacCallister:
The Eagles Legacy:
Kill Crazy

CHAPTER ONE

The sound of a shot rolled down through the gulch, picked up resonance, then echoed back from the surrounding walls. Emile Taylor, who was holding a smoking pistol, turned to the others with a smile on his face. He had just broken a tossed whiskey bottle with his marksmanship.

"I'd like to see somebody else here who can do that," he snarled.

Emile was one of six men who had made a temporary camp in an arroyo that was about five miles west of the town of Chugwater.

"Emile, there ain't nobody said you wasn't good with a gun, so there is no need for you to be provin' yourself to us," Johnny said. Johnny was Emile's brother. "Anyhow, that don't really matter all that much."

"What do you mean, it don't matter?"

"Hopefully, we ain't goin' to be gettin' into no gunfights. The only thing we're goin' to do is ride into town, rob the bank, then hightail it out of there before anyone knows what hit them. And if we pull this off right, there won't be no shootin'."

"What if someone tries to shoot at us?" Emile asked.

"Then you can shoot. But I don't want no shootin' unless we absolutely have to."

Emile was about five feet four inches tall, with ash-blond hair and a hard face. Johnny was two inches taller, with darker hair. Johnny was missing the earlobe of his left ear, having had it bitten off in a fight the last time he was in prison. Although the two men were brothers, they didn't look anything alike until one happened to look into their eyes. Their eyes were exact duplicates: gray, flat, and soulless.

"After we do the job I think we ought to split up . . . ever' man for hisself," Al Short said. "That way, if they put a posse together they won't know which one to follow."

"No, but they might choose to follow just one of us," Julius Jackson pointed out. "And whoever the one is they choose to follow is goin' to be in a heap of trouble."

"Besides which, if we do that, where at will we divide up the money amongst us?" Bart Evans asked.

"I don't know," Short said. "I didn't think

about that."

Evans chuckled. "You didn't think about it? Hell, man, the money is what this all about. How can you not think about it?"

"What we ought to do is, once we leave town, just wait behind a rock and shoot 'em down," Clay Calhoun suggested.

"You mean you'd shoot them from ambush?" Emile asked. "That ain't a very sportin' thing to do."

"Hell yes. I ain't like you, Emile. I ain't tryin' to build myself no reputation. If someone is comin' after me, I don't need to kill the son of a bitch fair and square. . . . I just want to kill him."

"Clay has a point," Evans said. "The best way to handle a posse would be to set up an ambush. Besides which, most of 'em will be nothin' but store clerks and handy men anyway. Prob'ly ain't none of 'em ever used a gun more 'n once or twice in their life anyway, so even you faced 'em down there wouldn't be nothin' you could call sportin' about it."

"Well, then if we're goin' to do that — ambush 'em, I mean — maybe it would be better for us to all stick together," Jackson said.

"No," Short replied. "I still think it would be best if we split up. I think we'll have a better chance that way."

"All right," Calhoun said. "How about this? Instead of all of us separatin', what if we was to break into two groups? That way the posse will still have to make a choice as to who to follow. And if they decide to split and follow each group, it will cut their numbers in half, which means we would have a better chance."

"Yeah, that sounds like a pretty good idea," Short said.

"No need for any of that," Johnny said. "I've got an idea that will throw them off our trail, once and for all, so that we all get away clean. Only we're going to need different horses."

"What do you mean, we are going to need different horses?" Jackson asked. "We got horses already. We got good horses."

A big smile spread across Johnny's face. "Yeah," he said. "But these ain't the horses we're goin' to use when we hold up the bank. These horses ain't even goin' to get close to town."

"That don't make no sense to me a'tall," Evans said.

"Then let me explain it to you," Johnny said. "The way I got it planned out, we're goin' to steal us some horses from several different places. Then, just before we go into

10

town to hold up the bank, we'll hobble our horses in some place out of the way, and when we go into town to rob the bank, we'll be ridin' the stolen horses."

"I don't understand," Jackson said. "Why would we take a chance on ridin' stoled horses when the ones we got is perfectly good? What if we have to leave town at a gallop? We won't know nothin' a'tall 'bout the mounts we'll be stealin'."

"All they have to do is get us into town and out again, and any healthy horse can do that," Johnny said. "Then when get to a place that we will have picked out, we'll dismount, take off our saddle and harness, then send the stolen horses on their way."

"Why would we do that?" Short asked. "I mean, if we go to all the trouble to steal 'em, why would we just turn 'em a' loose?"

"You said it yourself, Al. Like as not after we rob the bank, the marshal will be rounding up a posse," Johnny said.

"I reckon he will, but what does that have to do with stoled horses?"

"The posse will be trailin' us by followin' the tracks and such we leave when we ride away from the bank, right?"

"Yeah."

"All right, now follow me while I try to explain. When we turn them horses loose,

11

where do you think they will go?" Johnny asked.

"Well, I reckon they would —" Short started. Then he stopped in midsentence as a huge smile spread across his face. "Son of a bitch! They'll more 'n likely go back wherever it was we stole 'em from."

"Yes," Johnny agreed. "And if we steal each horse from a different place, then the horses will lead the posse all over hell's half-acre. And while the posse is followin' them, we'll be takin' off on our own horses."

"Yeah!" Short said. "Yeah, that's real smart. Did you come up with that all by yourself?"

"Ha!" Emile said, hitting his fist in his hand. "I may be the best shot in the family, but there can't nobody say Johnny ain't the smartest. And that's why he is in charge."

"You need to get on into town now, little brother," Johnny said. "Look around, see what you can see. But don't get into no trouble."

"I'll have a drink for all you boys," Emile said as he started toward his horse. "One for each one of you."

"Just don't get drunk and foolish," Johnny cautioned.

Duff MacCallister's ranch, Sky Meadow,

was fifteen miles south and slightly east of where Johnny Taylor and the others were plotting to hold up the Chugwater bank. Duff MacCallister had left Scotland four years earlier, and shortly after arriving in the United States he'd moved to Wyoming. Here, by homesteading and purchasing adjacent land, he'd started his ranch. Since that time, he had been exceptionally successful, and Sky Meadow now spread across some thirty thousand acres of prime range land lying between the Little Bear and Big Bear creeks.

Little and Big Bear creeks were year-round sources of water, and that, plus the good natural grazing land, had allowed Duff to try an experiment. The experiment had been to introduce Black Angus cattle. He'd been well familiar with the breed, for he had worked with them in Scotland. His experiment had been successful, and he now had ten thousand head of Black Angus cattle, making his ranch one of the most profitable in all of Wyoming.

Duff's operation was large enough to employ fourteen men, principal of whom was Elmer Gleason, his ranch foreman. In addition to Elmer, who had been with Duff from the very beginning, there were three other cowboys who had been with him for a very long time. These three men, Al Woodward, Case Martin, and Brax Walker, not only worked for him, but also were extremely loyal and top hands, occupying positions of responsibility just under Elmer Gleason.

Though the relationship between Duff and the three men was solid now, it had not gotten off to a very good start. Their first encounter had been at a community dance that had been held in the ballroom of the Antlers Hotel. The hotel was on the corner of Bowie Avenue and First Street in the nearby town of Chugwater.

On that night, Duff had escorted Meagan Parker to the dance, but Woodward, Martin, and Walker had shown up without women. Given the general disproportionate number of single men to single women in the West, it was not all that unusual for young cowboys to come alone. But Woodward, Martin, and Walker spent the first half hour getting drunk on the heavily spiked punch.

"I got me an idea," Woodward said. "Martin, let's me 'n' you join one o' them squares."

"We can't. We ain't got no woman to dance with us."

"That don't matter none," Woodward

explained. "Once we start the dancin' and the do-si-do'n and all that, why, we'll be swingin' around with all the other women in the square."

"Yeah," Martin said. "That's right, ain't it?"

"No, it ain't right," Walker said.

"What are you talkin' about? What do you mean it ain't right?" Woodward asked.

"Well, think about it. Whichever one of you takes the woman's part will be do-si-do'n with all the other men when you get to swingin' around."

"Yeah, I hadn't thought about that," Martin said.

"Hell, that ain't nothin' to be worryin' about," Woodward said. "Next dance, why, we'll just switch around. Martin, you'll be the woman on the first dance, then I'll set the next one out, and Walker, you can come in and let Martin be the man. Then on the third dance, why, I'll come back in and be the woman. That way, all three of us can do-si-do with the other women."

"All right," Martin said. "But let's pick us a dance with some good-lookin' women in it."

When the next sets of squares were formed, Woodward and Martin joined the same square as Duff MacCallister and

15

Meagan Parker.

"Well, lookie here, Martin," Woodward said, pointing toward Duff. "Looks to me like you won't have to do-si-do with all men. You'll get one man that's wearin' a dress. That ought to count for somethin'."

The "man in a dress" remark was prompted by the fact that Duff MacCallister had arrived at the dance wearing a kilt. But it wasn't just any kilt; it was the green and blue plaid, complete with Victoria Cross, of a captain of the 42nd Regiment of Foot, better known as the Black Watch, the most storied regiment in the British Army.

"Man in a dress," Martin said derisively, laughing just as the music started.

As the couples broke apart to swing with the others, Martin made a round with the men, including Duff. But on the next round he rebelled. Pushing one of the men aside, he started swinging around with all the women until he got to Meagan. That was when Duff stepped out into the middle of the square and grabbed him by the arm.

"Get out of my way, girlie," Case Martin said to Duff. He reached for Meagan, but as he did so, Duff, using his thumb and forefinger, squeezed the spot where Martin's neck joined his shoulder. The squeeze was so painful that Martin sunk to his knees with his face screwed up in agony. The other squares, seeing what was happening in this one, interrupted their dancing. Then the caller stopped, as did the band — the music breaking off in discordant chords.

"If you gentlemen are going to dance in our square, you'll be for doing it correctly," Duff said, talking quietly to the man who was on his knees in pain.

"Missy, you done started somethin' you can't finish," Al Woodward said, throwing a punch at Duff.

As gracefully as if he were performing a dance move, Duff bent back at his waist and allowed Woodward's fist to fly harmlessly by his chin. Duff counterpunched with one blow to Woodward's jaw, and Woodward went down to join Martin, who was still on the floor.

Walker, who had been sitting this dance out, pulled his pistol and leveled it at Duff.

"No!" Meagan shouted.

Duff reacted before anyone else did. Pulling the *sgian dubh,* or ceremonial knife, from its position in his right kilt stocking, he threw it in a quick, underhanded snap, toward Walker. As he had intended, the knife rotated in air so that the butt, and not the blade, hit Walker right between the eyes,

17

doing so with sufficient force to knock him down.

Marshal Ferrell and his deputies took charge then, escorting all three of the troublemakers out of the dance hall and down to the jail.

CHAPTER TWO

Within three months of that unpromising beginning, Woodward, Martin, and Walker had begun working at Sky Meadow. On this day, almost two years after the three had been hired, they were working the south range of the ranch. They weren't herding — they were just making certain that the cattle, which had a tendency to wander about as they were grazing, stayed within the confines of the ranch. As they were riding up a long, low hill, they heard a cow bawling.

"Listen to that," Woodward said.

"Listen to what? It ain't nothing but a bawlin' cow," Martin replied.

"That ain't no ordinary bawlin'. That's a-scared bawlin'," Woodward insisted.

The three cowboys urged their horses into a rapid lope up the rest of the rise and, when they crested the ridge, saw that a pack of wolves had brought down one of the animals.

"The sons of bitches! Look at that!" Martin said. He pulled his rifle from the sheath.

"No," Woodward said, holding his hand out to stop Martin. "You can't hit the wolves from here. We need to get closer."

Thinking the newly killed cow would keep the attention of the wolves, the three men rode down the hill as fast as they dared across the uneven ground, hoping to close the distance so they could come within range of the wolves.

Just before they got into range though, the wolves sensed their presence and darted off.

"The bastards are getting away!" Martin said, angrily. Pulling his rifle, he began shooting, though the range was too great and the bullets did nothing but kick up little dust clouds where they hit. The wolves escaped easily.

Dismounting, the three cowboys walked over to the steer. It was lying on the ground now, still alive, even though the wolves had already begun to eat him. Too weak to make any sound, the animal looked up at the three men with big, brown, pain-filled eyes.

"Damn," Woodward said. "Look at the poor bastard."

Pulling his pistol, he shot the animal in the head, putting it out of its misery.

"This is the third one we've found like

this," Walker said.

"Yeah, well, now we know for sure what's causing it, 'cause we actual seen the wolves while they was doin' it," Martin said.

Woodward chuckled. "What did you think was doin' it, Case? Prairie dogs, maybe?"

"No, but I thought it maybe could have been a cougar or somethin'."

"Yeah, I guess it could have been. All right, come on, let's see if we can find them wolves before they get 'em another one."

The three cowboys hunted the wolves for the next two hours, but without success.

"What do we do now?" Martin asked.

"We need to tell Elmer," Woodward said.

"I ain't lookin' forward to tellin' him about a problem that we ain't took care of yet," Walker said.

"I know what you mean, but it's got to be done."

Back at the ranch, Elmer was supervising the half dozen or so men whose duties this day had not taken them out on the range. Cowboys — as Elmer explained patiently, almost patronizingly, anytime he hired a new hand — had to be jacks-of-all-trades.

"You got to be part carpenter so's you can keep the buildings up, and part wheelwright so as to keep the wagons repaired. You need to be some veterinarian too, so's you can take care of the animals, and even a little bit of a doctor to take care of wounds and such, seein' as we're so far from town that it ain't always that easy to get to a real doc."

At the moment, a couple of the cowboys, Ben and Dale, had one of the ranch wagons jacked up with the left rear wheel off. They were packing the hubs with grease, a job that was so dirty and unpleasant that it was passed around among the men so that one person didn't have to do it all the time. Elmer approached the two men, carrying two glasses of lemonade.

"I thought you boys might like this," he said, offering a glass to each of them."

"A cold beer would have been better," Ben said. "But this will certainly do. Thanks, Elmer."

The two men wiped as much grease from their hands as they could before they took the glasses.

"How is it goin'?" Elmer asked.

"This here is the last wheel on the last wagon," Ben replied. "What you got in mind for us after this?"

"I don't have nothin' more in particular for you, today. Why don't you boys just look around and see if you can find somethin' that you know needs doin'. If you do find something needs done, just go ahead and take care of it."

"All right. Hey, Elmer, after we're done for the day, you don't mind if we run into town, do you? They say there's a new girl at Fiddler's Green," Ben said.

"I don't mind, if all your work is done," Elmer said. "New girl, huh?"

"Yeah, and they say she's really a looker," Dale added.

"She'll just be one more way Biff has of getting money from you boys," Elmer said. "By the way, have either of you seen Simon Reid?"

"Reid? Ain't he mucking stalls today?" Dale asked.

"He is supposed to be. But he ain't there."

"He ain't? You mean he's left Earl to muck the stalls all by his ownself?"

"It sure looks like that," Elmer said.

"I don't like to tell tales on others," Dale said. "But if you got three men workin' and one loafin' on a job, you can bet the one loafin' will be Reid."

"I tell you what," Ben added. "If that son of a bitch ran out on me like he did to Earl, I'd near 'bout lay an axe handle up alongside his head next time me'n him seen each other."

23

"And I'd hand you the axe handle," Ben added.

"If you see him, tell him I'm lookin' for him," Elmer said.

"Will do," Dale promised.

Elmer left the two men, mumbling to himself as he started back toward the ranch office. The ranch office was a relatively new addition to the Sky Meadow compound, a small building that sat between the "big house," as the cowboys called Duff MacCallister's residence, and the bunkhouse. Duff was in the office tallying the latest numbers, compiled from the count the cowboys gave him almost daily.

"Elmer, you're looking a bit peeved," Duff said when Elmer came into the office and sat down at his own desk, with a disgusted sigh. "Would you be for tellin' me what has you in such a state?"

"It's Simon Reid, again," Elmer replied. "That son of a bitch is as worthless as tits on a bull. I thought I was a better judge of men than that. I shoulda known from the time I hired him that he wasn't worth a cup of warm piss."

Duff laughed. "Elmer, 'tis no one I know with a more colorful grasp of the English language than you. Sure 'n' sometimes I wonder if 'tis English at all that you speak."

"Damn it all to hell, Duff, I'm tryin' not to cuss, I really am. But Reid absolutely makes my ass knit barbed wire."

Duff laughed again. "Och, mon, now your language has gone from colorful to incomprehensible. How does one's arse knit barbed wire? Never mind, I know the answer to my own question. One's arse would knit barbed wire very painfully."

At that moment there was a knock on the door.

"Maybe that's Reid," Elmer said, getting up to answer the door.

It was Woodward, Martin, and Walker.

"We need to talk," Woodward said.

"Duff is cipherin' an' such. Let's talk outside, so's not to disturb him," Elmer responded, stepping out of the office, then shutting the door behind him.

"We've got problems, Elmer," Woodward said. "Big problems."

"What kind of problems?"

"Losing-beeves kind of problems," Woodward said. "We found three of 'em down half eaten."

"Half eaten?" Elmer replied, confused by the comment.

"By wolves," Walker added.

"You're sure it's wolves?"

"Yeah, hell, they was still workin' on one

25

of the beeves when we seen them," Woodward said. "Five of the critters they was."

"Why didn't you shoot 'em?"

"We tried to shoot 'em, but we can't get close enough to the bastards to hit 'em," Martin said.

"They're too damn smart. They either see us or hear us or somethin'. But we can't get no closer 'n about two or three hunnert yards from 'em before they start runnin'. And you can't hit no wolf from three hunnert yards away. Hell, you can barely see the sons of bitches from that far," Walker said.

"The bastards started eatin' on that last poor critter even before it died. We had to put it out of its misery," Woodward said.

"Good, that was the right thing to do," Elmer said. He sighed. "All right, thanks for tellin' me about it. I'll let Duff know."

"I agree, Duff needs to know," Woodward said. "But for the life of me, I don't know what he will be able to do about it."

"This is Duff MacCallister we're talking about, remember?"

Woodward laughed. "Yeah," he said. "Now that I think about it, I have no doubt but that he will take care of it."

"Listen, you boys haven't seen Simon Reid, have you?"

"Reid? No, not since this mornin'," Woodward said. "Didn't you toll him out for workin' in the barn today?"

"Yeah, I did. But he ain't there, and accordin' to Earl, he ain't seen hide nor hair of him since just after lunch."

As Elmer, Woodward, Martin, and Walker were having their impromptu conference, Simon Reid, the subject of their conversation and the man who had been the cause of Elmer's earlier agitation, was having a business meeting with three men. The meeting was being conducted five miles away from the ranch compound. It was at the extreme west end of Sky Meadow, and its remote location was by design, for the business at hand was cattle rustling. The cattle being rustled belonged to Duff MacCallister.

"As you can see, I've cut out ten of 'em," Reid said, referring to the cattle that stood stoically nearby. "They're Black Angus, which is the finest and most expensive cow in the country. Do you have any idea how much these here cows is bringin' at the Kansas market?"

The three men Reid was making his pitch to weren't Sky Meadow cowboys. They weren't even local men. Creech, Phelps, and a third who called himself Kid Dingo, were from Bordeaux, a town that lay twelve miles north of Chugwater.

When none of the three answered him, Reid continued his pitch. "Right now, these cows, at the Kansas City market, is bringin' forty dollars a head."

"Yeah, well that's interestin' an' all, but you may have noticed that we ain't exactly the Kansas market," Creech replied.

"And I ain't askin' for no forty dollars, neither," Reid said. "I'm just tellin' you that so's that you know what a good deal I'm givin' you. I'm only askin' twenty dollars a head."

"We'll give you five dollars."

"Five dollars?" Reid replied, reacting sharply in response to the low offer. "What do you mean, five dollars? Come on, Creech, are you out of your mind? I'm takin' a hell of a risk by sellin' these cows to you in the first place. I stole these here cows from Duff MacCallister's herd, and if you don't know much about him, well, let me tell you, he ain't somebody you cross. Besides which, I know you're goin' to get at least thirty dollars a head for 'em, when you get 'em back to Bordeaux."

"What we sell 'em for ain't no concern of your'n," Phelps said.

"Come on, fellers, me 'n' you've know'd each other a long time," Reid said, continuing to plead his case. "You ain't got no call to try and cheat me like that."

Creech, Phelps, and Kid Dingo moved away a few feet so they could talk privately. They consulted for a moment; then, nodding, Creech turned back to Reid.

"All right, we'll give you ten dollars a head for 'em, but that is as high as we are goin' to go. That's a hunnert dollars for you, and we'll take it from here. All you got to do is put the money in your pocket and ride away," Creech said.

"A hunnert dollars," Phelps added, with a smile. "Think of the whiskey and the whores you can buy with a hunnert dollars."

"All right," Reid said. "Give me the hunnert dollars and the cows is yours."

The transaction made, Reid pocketed the money and started back toward the barn. He was supposed to be mucking out the stalls. That was a job he hated, but he smiled as he thought of the one hundred dollars riding in his pocket right now. Having that much money would make the job bearable.

Chapter Three

At the butte where Woodward and the others had told him they had seen the wolves, Duff MacCallister reined up his horse, Sky, then sat in the saddle for a moment as he perused the range before him. Except for roundup, and cattle drives, such as when he would drive a herd down to the loading pens and rail head in Cheyenne, the cattle were never in one, large herd. Rather, they tended to break off into smaller groups, bound to each other within those groups as if they were family units.

Duff saw one such group now, gathered near the water and standing together under the shade of a cottonwood tree.

With a pair of binoculars hanging around his neck, Duff dismounted, then walked out onto a flat rock overhang. Lifting the binoculars to his eyes, he studied the open range below him. That was when he spotted them — at least eight wolves, sneaking up on the cattle.

Duff walked back to his horse, then pulled a Remington Creedmoor rifle from his saddle sheath. The rifle, a recent purchase, had been developed especially for the Creedmoor Marksmanship Club. It had a well-deserved reputation for accuracy, featuring a telescopic sight as well as a device that would allow the shooter to compensate for range and wind.

Woodward had reported that when anyone tried to get close enough to the wolves to shoot them, the crafty creatures would see, smell, or hear them, then dart quickly out of the way. That meant that the only way the wolves could be eliminated was if someone could shoot them from a standoff position that was so far away that the wolves would not even realize they were in danger.

Such a feat would take a rifle with extreme range, as well as a marksman who was skilled enough to take advantage of that superior range. The scoped Creedmoor was that rifle, and Duff MacCallister was that marksman.

Lying down on his stomach, Duff took up a prone firing position on the rock. He cranked in the range, then picked up a few grains of grass and dropped them to estimate the windage. That done, he sighted in on the wolves. The wolves were at least five hundred yards away, so distant that without the magnification of the scope, they could barely be seen.

Because of the great distance, the wolves were totally unaware of Duff's presence. They approached their prey with the extreme confidence of predators who knew that, collectively, they were superior to any creature that might be near.

But Duff was not near, and they were not superior to him.

Duff squeezed the trigger; the gun boomed and kicked back against his shoulder. One and a half seconds later, the lead wolf was sent sprawling by the impact of the heavy bullet. A tenth of a second after the strike of the bullet, the sound of the shot reached the remaining pack, but it came from so far away that they were unable to connect that sound to what had happened to the leader of the pack.

A second shot killed a second wolf, and within less than a minute, Duff had killed every one of them. His work done, he picked up the remaining shells, returned to his horse, replaced the rifle in its boot, mounted Sky, and started back home.

When Duff returned to the compound, he

could hear the blacksmith's hammer ringing, and outside the machine shed, he saw Ben and Dale painting a wagon. He could also hear his foreman's voice coming from the barn. The voice was loud and angry, and Duff heard Reid's name being spoken.

"I gather Elmer has found the errant Mr. Reid," Duff said to the two men who were painting.

"It ain't as much Elmer findin' him as it is Reid just come ridin' back in without so much as a by-your-leave," Ben said.

"He told Elmer he thought he was finished with the work he was give to do," Dale added.

"And Elmer took issue with that, did he?"

"Yes sir, he sure did, an' ol' Elmer's been givin' Reid hell ever since."

"Keep the damn stalls clean!" Elmer's voice said loudly. "You wouldn't want to be sleeping ankle deep in horse shit, would you?"

"They're horses," a voice replied. "This is only natural for them. Horses is supposed to live in shit."

"It ain't natural at all," Elmer said. "If we was doin' things natural, the horses wouldn't be in stalls in the first place. They'd all be runnin' free. We're the ones that's got 'em all cooped up, so the least we can do is give 'em a clean place to be. Now get it done."

"I didn't sign on to clean horse shit out of a stall," Reid said. "You want the shit cleaned, you clean it yourself."

"I've had about enough of you, Mr. Reid," Elmer said. "You've been slacking off way too much here, lately. You lollygagged around all mornin' long, and after lunch you wasn't nowhere to be found. You left Earl to do the work all by himself."

"I told Earl where I was goin'. Yesterday, my rain slicker fell offen' my saddle, and I went back to look for it. Then, while I was lookin' for it, I seen some cows drifting off the ranch. I figured savin' them cows was more important than cleanin' up horse shit."

"Did you now? Well, here is the thing, Reid, how do I know you was actually roundin' up wanderin'-away strays? Or even lookin' for your rain slicker for that matter? I mean, you lied about greasing the wheel on the hay wagon last week, and because it didn't get no grease, the axle got so wore down that it's out of round and we're goin' to have to put on another one."

"Then why don't you have me doin' somethin' important like that, instead of shovelin' shit out of a stall?"

"I tell you what, Reid. You don't have to

worry about cleaning out no more shit because you ain't a-goin' to be working here no more. Get your tack and get out of here. You're fired."

"You can't fire me, old man. The only one who can fire me is the man that owns this place."

Duff had been just outside, listening in on the discussion, and he chose that moment to walk in to the barn.

"That is where you are wrong, Mr. Reid," Duff said. "Elmer Gleason is the executive administrator of this operation, and as such, has full authority to fire anyone he deems needing fired."

"He's the what?" Reid asked.

"I'm the ramrod," Elmer said. "Now, get."

"Someday you are going to regret this," Reid said.

"That wouldn't be a threat now, would it, Reid?" Elmer asked. "Because if it is, well, by God, me 'n' you can just settle this out here and now."

"I'll leave, but I ain't goin' nowhere without drawin' my pay," Reid said.

"How much are you owed?" Duff asked.

"I'm drawin' forty dollars a month."

"Reid, you do know that Mr. MacCallister is payin' more than any other rancher in the valley, don't you? Most anyone else is paying is thirty dollars and found."

"Here's twenty dollars," Duff said.

"You're bein' awful generous, Mr. Mac-Callister," Elmer said. "The most we owe him right now is ten dollars, and we don't even have to settle up with him for that until the end of the month."

"If I am for understanding the way you feel about him, Elmer, the more distant he is from Sky Meadow, the better things will be."

"I guess that's true, all right.

Duff smiled. "Then let's just say he can get farther away on twenty dollars than he can on ten."

Reid took the twenty-dollar bill, then glared for a moment at both Elmer and Duff.

"You got your money, Reid. Now get," Elmer ordered.

Reid walked outside where his horse, still saddled, stood tied to a hitching rail.

About half the cowboys employed by Duff owned their own horses, while half rode horses that belonged to Sky Meadow. Reid was one of the cowboys who owned his own horse, and from the very first day that had given him an attitude of superiority over those who did not. Now, as he rode away from the compound, a few of the other cowboys turned out to watch him leave.

Reid's air of superiority and his lack of cooperation with the others who worked on the ranch, as well as his general laziness, had not engendered strong friendships. As a result, those who had turned out to watch him leave did so with a sense of satisfaction that he was gone. A few even called insults out to him.

"Ha! I'll bet this here is the first time anyone ever seen a bag o' shit ridin' a horse before," one of the cowboys called.

"Look there, boys. That's somethin' you don't see all that often," another said. "Two horse's asses at the same time, one at the horse rear end, and the other sittin' in the horse's saddle."

There were other insults and derisive comments shouted until Reid, who urged his horse into a gallop, moved out of range.

"It looks as if your decision to fire Mr. Reid is being well received by the others," Duff said.

"It looks like it, don't it?" Elmer replied. "It turns out there didn't nobody like the son of a bitch. So tell me, Duff, did you see any wolves?" he asked.

"Aye, eight of the creatures I saw," Duff said.

"Good. I'll get someone out there to bury them."

"Sure now, 'n' how is it that you know I killed them?" Duff asked.

"How do I know? Because you seen 'em, that's how I know. You ain't a' goin' to tell me they run off now, are you?"

"They're dead," Duff said.

"Uh-huh. Like I said, I'll get someone out there to bury 'em. If we leave 'em to lay around and rot, next thing you know the water could get bad."

"I'm going into town this afternoon to check the mail and collect a few items at the store," Duff said. "Would you be for wanting me to pick something up for you?"

"Better get some coffee," Elmer said. "You bein' an Englishman, you always remember tea, but don't always remember coffee."

"Och, 'tis a Scotsman I am, and nae an Englishman," Duff corrected. He smiled. "Sure now, and have you nae corrected me anytime I refer to you as a Yank?"

"Lord, no, don't do that," Elmer said with a wince. "You know damn well I ain't no Yankee."

"Aye, I know well, Elmer Gleason. 'Tis a pair of rebels we both be, but in differing ways."

■ ■ ■ ■

When Elmer walked back out to the barn, he saw the wagons painted and glistening, with the wheels greased and reattached.

"Good job, men," he said.

"Al, Case, and Brax are goin' into town. Since all the work you give us to do is done, can we have the rest of the afternoon off to go into town with them?"

"I reckon so," Elmer said.

Ben smiled, broadly. "Come on, Dale. Let's get washed up some."

Ben, Dale, Woodward, Martin, and Walker lived in the bunkhouse. Long and relatively narrow, the bunkhouse was one of several buildings that now occupied the compound. It had seven beds on either side. Each individual bed, and the area immediately around it, became the personal domain of the cowboy who slept there, his space as inviolate as if it were his home. And, in fact, it was his home.

The cowboys used different forms of expression to personalize their "homes," which not only established them as their private areas, but gave them a sense of belonging and identity.

Dale had a picture of a fancy saddle that he had cut from a Sears and Roebuck catalogue pinned to the wall above his bed. Ben had a blue ribbon he had won in a foot race in Cheyenne the year before. There were other pictures and bits of memorabilia tacked to the wall above other bunks, from a calendar featuring a picture of a passenger train roaring through the night, to more than one "lucky" horseshoe.

Ben and Dale filled a number-two washtub with water, then flipped a coin to see who got to use the water first.

Ben won the coin toss and was now sitting in the tub in the middle of the floor, scrubbing his back with a long-handled brush.

"Dale, you ever been to a big city?" Ben asked.

"I been to Cheyenne."

"No, I mean a big city, like maybe Denver, or San Francisco, or St. Louis, or someplace like that."

"Well, I was borned in St. Louis, but I don't remember it."

"I ain't never been to no big city either, but I'd dearly love to go someday."

"Why?"

"I've heard tell that in San Francisco they got a whore standin' on near 'bout ever' corner."

"They got whores in Chugwater."

"Yeah, but most of the whores in Chugwater are so ugly they'd make a train take five miles of dirt road. The ones in the city is all real pretty, and 'cause they got so many, it don't cost you hardly nothin' at all to go to bed with 'em."

"Maybe someday me 'n' you can go to San Francisco," Dale suggested.

Ben climbed out of the tub then and started toward his bunk.

"The water is all your'n now," he said.

Dale walked over to look down into the tub. "What water?" he asked. "Looks to me like I'm about to climb into one of them bog holes we sometimes got to pull the cows out of."

CHAPTER FOUR

There were two saloons in Chugwater. One was the Wild Hog. It made no pretensions and existed for the sole purpose of providing inexpensive drinks to a clientele who didn't care if the wide plank floor was unpainted and stained with spilled liquor and expectorated tobacco juice. The Wild Hog did offer a limited food menu, but the biggest thing that set it apart from Fiddler's Green, the other saloon in town, was its women. While the girls who worked the bar at Fiddler's Green provided pleasant conversation and flirtatious company only, the women who worked at the Wild Hog were soiled doves who, for a price, would extend their hospitality to the brothel that was maintained on the second floor of the saloon. Nippy Jones, who owned the Wild Hog, made it very clear to the girls he hired that they would be expected to offer that service.

Because the evening rush had not yet started, Nippy was working the bar himself when Simon Reid came in.

"What are you doin' here, Reid?" Jones asked. "I thought all you Sky Meadow boys was connected to the Fiddler's Green by the hip."

"They might be," Reid said. "But not me, seein' as I don't ride for Sky Meadow."

"What do you mean you don't ride for Sky Meadow? You been with Duff MacCallister for near 'bout a year."

"I ain't with him no more," Reid said without any further explanation. "Let me have a beer."

Everyone agreed that the other saloon in town, Fiddler's Green, was an establishment that was equal to anything you could find between St. Louis and San Francisco. Fiddler's Green was owned by Biff Johnson, a retired army sergeant who, while he was with the Seventh Cavalry, had served with Custer, Reno, and Benteen.

Fiddler's Green was practically a museum to the Seventh Cavalry in general, and to Custer's last battle in particular. The walls were decorated with regimental flags and troop pennants, with arrows, lances, pistols and carbines picked up from more than a dozen engagements. He had one of Custer's hats. Libbie Custer had personally given it to him when he'd escorted her back to Monroe, Michigan, after George A. Custer was killed.

Even the name "Fiddler's Green" was indicative of Biff's service in the cavalry. Cavalry legend has it that anyone who had ever served as a cavalryman would, after they died, stop by a shady glen where there was good grass and a nearby stream of cool water for the horses. There, cavalrymen from all wars and generations would drink beer, chew tobacco, smoke their pipes, and visit. They would regale one another with tales of derring-do until that last syllable of recorded time, at which moment they will bid each other a last good-bye before departing for their final and eternal destination.

Emile Taylor was one of the customers in Fiddler's Green this afternoon. He was sitting at a table with Cindy Boyce, one of the bar girls, and Francis Schumacher, a local citizen. Cindy was a very pretty young woman, with red hair, blue eyes, a peaches-and-cream complexion, and a slender body with womanly curves. Schumacher was rawhide thin, with a handlebar moustache and hair that hung to his shoulders. Until recently, he had been a deputy. A month earlier Marshal Ferrell had fired him for beating up a drunk that he had brought into jail. Now, Schumacher was working at the livery stable, a position he considered a come-down.

At the moment, Emile was giving Schumacher tips on how to make a fast draw.

"What you have to do is always keep your holster and your pistol well oiled," Emile said. "That way when you go to draw your gun, it won't get hung up on you."

"How many men have you killed?" Schumacher asked.

Emile chuckled. "That's not somethin' you ever actually want to ask someone," Emile said. "Let's just say that I've seen the elephant a few times."

"Can't you two find something better to talk about than guns and killing?" Cindy asked.

"Ha!" Emile said. "I suppose the only thing you want us to talk about is how pretty you are."

Cindy smiled. "That wouldn't be a bad subject," she agreed.

When the five Sky Meadow cowboys came into town, the first place they visited was Fiddler's Green. As soon as they pushed in through the swinging batwing doors, they were greeted by two of the bar girls, one blond and one brunette.

"Hello, boys," the brunette said.

"Hello, Nell, hello, Mattie," Woodward said.

"Hey, Mattie, is that the new girl over there?" Ben asked, pointing to the redhead who, instead of wandering around the bar pushing drinks, was sitting at a table with two men.

"Yes, that's Cindy," Mattie said. "She just started working here last week."

"Folks have been talking about her, and they are right. She's a pretty thing," Martin said. Then, realizing that he may have committed a faux pas, he added, " 'Course, she ain't no prettier than you two are, though."

Both Nell and Mattie laughed. "Don't worry about it, honey," Nell said. "I know she's younger and prettier than I am. But I ask you this. Who is it that came over here to talk to you?"

"You did," Ben said, smiling at her, grateful for the way she handled it.

"Who's the man she's sitting with? I know Francis Schumacher — he's been around a long time. I mean the other one."

"His name is Emile, but I haven't heard anyone say his last name," Mattie said.

"She sure seems to be friendly with them," Walker said.

"Would you like me to ask her to come visit with you boys for a while?" Nell asked. "I'm sure she would be happy to."

"Why would we want to talk to her when we have you two girls?" Woodward said.

Smiling, Mattie removed Woodward's hat and ran her hand through his hair.

"Now isn't that a smart thing to say?" she asked. "Oh, there are some new customers. We have to go talk to them for a while, but don't you boys leave. We'll be back," Mattie promised.

The five cowboys, who had stopped by the bar to get their beer when they came in, watched Nell and Mattie walk over to greet the new men. Then they found a table that would accommodate all five of them, and started rehashing the day's events.

"I guess you heard about the wolves," Woodward said.

"Yeah," Ben replied. "We spent the whole day workin' on wagons, tightening spokes in the wheels, greasing hubs. We even painted a couple, but we did hear about the wolves. Someone said that Mr. MacCallister shot five or six of 'em."

"Eight of them," Martin corrected. "I don't know how he done it. We couldn't

47

none of us get close enough to the damn things to hardly even get a good look at 'em. But Mr. MacCallister went out there, and I swear, no more 'n an hour later he come back in, leavin' eight of them critters lyin' dead in the dirt."

"Folks say he is as good a shot as there is in Laramie County," Woodward said.

"Laramie County? Huh! I'll bet there ain't no better shot in all of Wyoming," Walker said. "Al, I'm sure you mind the time he shot an apple off Miss Parker's head from a hundred feet away. And it wan't no ordinary apple, neither. It wan't no bigger 'n a plum."

"We had a little excitement of our own today," Dale said.

"What was that?" Woodward asked.

"I reckon you fellas heard what happened to Simon Reid, didn't you?" Dale asked.

"No, what?" Martin replied.

"I heard," Walker said. "Reid quit, didn't he?"

"Quit, my ass," Dale said. "He got hisself fired is what happened."

"What did he do to get hisself fired?" Woodward asked.

"He got to mouthin' off to Elmer, and Elmer up and fired him. That's what he done," Ben said, stepping in so that Dale didn't get to tell the entire story.

"Elmer ain't the kind of person you want to get mad at you," Woodward said. "I reckon Reid is lucky that fired is all that got done to him."

"Elmer's sort of strange duck," Ben said.

"What do you mean, he's a strange duck?"

"Most of the time he's kind of quiet. But when you are around him, you always get the idea that he's sort of like a stick of dynamite, just waitin' to explode."

CHAPTER FIVE

Elmer Gleason, the subject of their conversation, had a most interesting background. In a way, one could say that Duff had inherited Elmer with the ranch, because when Duff had come to develop the land he had filed upon, Elmer had already been there.

"They say the place is hainted," R.W. Guthrie had told Duff when he'd first arrived in the territory. He had been talking about Little Horse Mine, a worked-out and abandoned gold mine that was on the land Duff had just taken title to.

" 'Course, I ain't sayin' that I believe in haints, you understand. But that is what they say. Some say it wasn't the Spanish, that it was injuns that first found the gold, but they was all kilt off by white men who wanted the gold for themselves. But what happened is, after the injuns was all kilt, they become ghosts, and now they haint the mine and they kill any white man who comes around tryin' to find the gold. Now, mind, I don't believe none of that. I'm just tellin' you what folks says about it."

As it turned out, the "haint" Guthrie had spoken of had been Elmer Gleason. Elmer had located a new vein of gold in the mine and, unable to capitalize on it, had been living a hand-to-mouth existence in the mine, unshaved and dressed only in skins.

Then Duff had discovered Elmer in the mine, and because the mine was on the property Duff had just filed upon, everything Elmer had taken from it so far had actually belonged to Duff. Duff had had every right to drive Elmer off, but he hadn't. Instead, he'd offered Elmer a one-half partnership in the mine.

That partnership had paid off handsomely for both of them. Now, Elmer was Duff's foreman and closest friend. And Duff's half of the proceeds from the mine had built Sky Meadow into one of the most productive ranches in Wyoming.

Before going into the mine, Elmer had lived for two years with the Indians. He'd married an Indian woman who had died while giving birth to their son. He didn't know where his son was now, and he didn't care, even though he knew that he probably should. He had left him with his wife's sister, and had not seen him since the day he was born, nor did he have any plans to.

As a part of Quantrill's irregulars during the Civil War, Elmer had taken part in the raid at Lawrence, Kansas.

From the *Leavenworth Daily Conservative* of August 23, 1863:

150 MALE CITIZENS OF LAWRENCE SLAUGHTERED
TOTAL LOSS $2,000,000, CASH LOST $250,000

The scene along Massachusetts Street, the business artery of Lawrence, is one mass of smoldering ruins and crumbling walls. Only two business houses are left upon the street — one known as the Armory, and the other the old Miller block. About one hundred and twenty-five houses in all were burned, and only one or two escaped being ransacked, with everything of value carried away or destroyed.

After the war, Elmer had ridden for a while with Frank and Jesse James. Separating from the James gang shortly after the disastrous Northfield, Minnesota raid,

Elmer had cut a swath of lawlessness through the West. Then, leaving the outlaw trail behind him, he'd become a sailor, and later an armed mercenary fighting in Afghanistan during the British-Afghan war.

Elmer had never told Duff about his time in Afghanistan because, as a mercenary, he had been fighting for the Afghans against the British. He knew that Duff had not been there, and he was glad that he hadn't been. But this was a part of Elmer's history that he had no intention of sharing with his friend.

It was raining hard as Elmer waited on the Khyber Pass Road in Afghanistan, in the shadow of the Hindu Kush Mountains. He had information that a British pay officer would be coming this way, accompanied by a small guard detail. Elmer's men were hidden in the rocks completely out of sight, whereas the British soldiers and the stagecoach were on the road, in plain view.

As the pay detail approached, Elmer held his hand up, preparing to give the signal. He held back though when, unexpectedly, the British officer in charge of the guard rode to the front, stopped, then looked down the road.

The officer in charge, a captain, sent two of his soldiers down the road ahead of them, and Elmer turned in his saddle to make certain

that his men were well concealed. He mo-
tioned for Sajadi to get out of sight. At his
signal, the Afghan slipped back behind the
rocks.

If the advanced guard had been more obser-
vant, the British captain might have been
forewarned. One of the boulders had been
set up to be rolled down upon the trail, and
the path between it and the road had been
cleared of rocks and natural elevations that
might impede the deployment of the boulder.
But the Brits gave no more than a cursory
glance ahead.

It was obvious that the soldiers were miserable in the cold rain that ran down their
shakos and dripped under the collars of their
soaked red jackets, making them miserable
and less attentive than they should have
been. Their scout ahead of the detail was
perfunctory at best; then they rode back at a
quick trot through the muddiest part of the
narrow road to report that all was well.

The captain sat on his horse for a long moment, as if trying to decide whether or not he
should trust the report.

"Come on, Brit," Elmer whispered under his
breath. "They told you it was clear. What are
you waiting for?"

Finally, the British officer gave the order to
proceed.

With a sigh of relief, Elmer waved once, and Sajadi returned to his position by the boulder that had been freed to roll easily. Elmer stood by, watching the coach and the escort detail continue ahead, waiting until all were fully committed.

Choosing the exact moment, Elmer brought his hand down. He heard two sharp reports as a sledgehammer took out the wedges that were holding the big rock back. With crunching and loud popping sounds, the boulder started down, reaching the middle of the muddy road with the crashing thunder of an artillery barrage. At the same time the boulder blocked the path of the coach, Elmer and his men moved out onto the road behind the Brits and fired several shots into the air.

"You're surrounded!" Elmer shouted, urging his horse onto the road from the boulders that were right alongside. He leveled his pistol at the soldiers. "Throw down your guns and put up your hands."

"Mercenaries!" one of the soldiers shouted, and he threw down his rifle. The other soldiers, perhaps taking their cue from him, threw their weapons down as well. Only the British captain refused the order. He brought his pistol up, pointed it at Elmer, then pulled the trigger. Elmer saw the cylinder turn and heard the hammer click, but the cartridge misfired.

Elmer aimed at the officer. "Drop your gun, Captain! Do it now! Don't make me kill you!"

The captain lowered his pistol, then let it drop into the mud.

"Good Lord! That accent. Are you a Yank?"

"Don't be callin' me a Yankee, damn you. I fought agin' them Yankee bastards for four years."

"You are! You are an American! What are you doing fighting on the side of the savages?"

"They're payin' me. You ain't," Elmer said. "Now, I want all you boys to get down off your horses."

Grumbling, the men got down. As soon as they did, a couple of Elmer's men, all of whom were Afghans, began gathering up the horses.

"You're stealing our horses?" the British officer asked.

"It ain't called stealin', Sonny," Elmer explained. "It's called confiscating enemy assets. You're the enemy of these boys, and these here horses are assets. And, speaking of assets, I'll take the money satchel."

"What makes you think we are carrying money?"

"Because you are delivering the payroll." Elmer chuckled. "But I'll bet you didn't know that you were delivering the payroll to my boys." He pointed his pistol at the captain.

56

"Now tell the pay officer inside the coach to throw out the money satchel, or I'll shoot you dead."

"Lieutenant Fitzsimmons, please, deliver the satchel," the captain called.

A canvas bag was tossed out through the coach window. Sajadi retrieved it, then, using his Khyber sword, whacked off the top part of the bag. He let out a little chortle, then reached down inside to pick up a handful of gold coins. He showed off the gold coins to a round to cheers; then he dropped them back into the bag.

"You're making a big mistake, mister," the captain said. "That money belongs to Her Majesty."

"Does it now?" Elmer asked, sarcastically. "Well, I'll just bet the old bag has a lot more where this came from."

At that moment, Elmer saw the end of a pistol poke out from the passenger window. He fired at the stagecoach, not to hit whoever was inside, but merely to get his attention.

"Get out of the coach now, friend," Elmer ordered, "or the next time I'll shoot to kill."

The coach door opened and the pay officer stepped down. He was an overweight man, wearing a red jacket with white lapels.

"You bloody bastard Yank!" the pay officer swore angrily.

"I done told this other feller, I ain't no damn Yankee," Elmer said.

By now, his men had loaded all the money into two other sacks. They tied the necks of the sacks together, then handed them to Elmer, who lay them across his saddle in such a way as to allow one bag to hang down on each side of the horse.

"Captain, would you and your boys be so kind as to shuck out of them clothes right now?" Elmer asked.

"Shuck out?" the captain replied, no understanding the term.

"Take 'em off," Elmer said. "All of you. Take off your clothes. Strip down to your long johns."

"Now, just a damn minute, sir," one of the soldiers, a sergeant said. "I have no intention of taking off my clothes."

Elmer made a signal with his pistol. "Get out of them."

Grumbling and protesting, the soldiers began undressing. A few moments later all of them, including the captain and the pay officer, were standing in the mud in their long johns. This was in accordance with the plan, since Elmer believed that a lack of clothing and horses would preclude any chase. The two men Elmer had assigned to pick up the uniforms now did so.

"Look at these here officers, men," Elmer said. "Without them fancy uniforms and all that brass and braid, they don't look all that highfalutin, do they?"

"You bloody bastard. You've no right to demean our officers like that."

Elmer recognized the man who spoke as one who, a moment earlier, had been wearing the stripes of a sergeant.

"You are a good man, Sergeant," he said with what, to the sergeant and the other British soldiers, seemed to be a surprising amount of respect. He turned to the driver. "Unhitch the team."

"What's the reason for that?" the driver asked.

"No reason," Elmer replied. "I just want to keep you folks busy for a few minutes after we're gone, that's all. It'll take you that long to get back into harness. By then we'll be gone. Oh, and you'll find your clothes in a big heap, about a mile down the road."

It was easy now to recall that day, for that was the day he had decided to quit being a mercenary. Fighting on the side of people whose language he couldn't understand, against people who spoke his same language, hadn't seemed right to him. At least during the Civil War everyone had spoken the same language.

Elmer had left Afghanistan with over two thousand dollars in cash. He'd returned to New York, where he'd spent every cent he had in less than two months.

At that moment, Duff came out onto the porch, interrupting Elmer's reverie. Although Duff wasn't particularly dressed up, he had cleaned up, shaved, and dabbed his face with a bit of bay rum.

"Looks to me like you're plannin' on doin' a little courtin'," Elmer said.

"Elmer, you know why an Englishman wears a monocle?"

"Hell, Duff, I don't even know what a monocle is."

"It's an eyepiece that you wear in one eye."

"Oh, yeah, I've seen them things," Elmer said. "The feller that's wearin' 'em has to kinda squint down on 'em to hold 'em in place."

"Aye."

"So why does an Englishman wear a monocle?"

"He wears a monocle so that he will only see half of what he can nae understand. Sure, and you remind me of that Englishman, Elmer. You see only half of what you can nae understand."

"Just 'cause I said it looks to me like you're goin' to do a little courtin'?"

Duff made a circle with his thumb and forefinger, then held to his eye as if it were a monocle. He laughed, then started toward the barn to saddle Sky.

CHAPTER SIX

Burt Kennedy was a cowboy from the Bar H Bar, a ranch that was located about three miles north of Chugwater. Kennedy had a six-foot-three-inch frame, upon which was well distributed two hundred and twenty-five pounds of mostly muscle. He was smitten with Biff Johnson's recently arrived red-haired beauty, and had put on his finest clothes to come into town this afternoon.

He brought twenty dollars with him, and intended to use as much of the money as was necessary to entice Cindy Boyce to spend all her time, just with him.

He had been waiting patiently for her to leave the table where she was sitting with Schumacher and some other man, a short, sandy-haired man whom he didn't recognize.

Finally, after waiting for at least half an hour, he walked over to the table.

"Cindy, I been here for half an hour,"

Kennedy said. "I wish you would keep me company. I got me some money to spend, and I aim to spend it on you, which you should like, 'cause I ain't seen either one of these fellers buy you so much as one drink in all the time I been here."

Cindy smiled up at Kennedy.

"I'm sorry, honey. I didn't know you were waiting for me. Of course I'll spend some time with you.

Kennedy grinned broadly, but the grin left his face when he saw the little sandy-haired man reach out and pull Cindy back down in her chair.

"You ain't goin' nowhere," he said. "You'll be stayin' right here with me."

"Mister, if you don't get your hands offen her, I'm goin' to mop up this floor with your scrawny little ass," Kennedy said angrily.

"He's right, Emile. I have been with you long enough," Cindy said. "I need to spend a little time with some of my other friends, now."

Emile smiled as well, but his smile was totally without mirth.

"Cowboy, I don't believe I know your name," Emile said.

"It's Burt Kennedy. Not that it makes any difference to you."

"Oh, that's where you're wrong. It does

make a difference to me, Kennedy. You see, me an' you are about to have us a fight."

Kennedy grinned broadly. "A fight? Yeah," he said. "But you're a little scrawny to be fightin' me all by yourself, ain't you? What about you, Schumacher? You aimin' to join in? That would make two of you and one of me. That might even the odds up a bit."

"Kennedy, I don't think you know what you are getting into here," Schumacher said.

Kennedy laughed. "Yeah, I do. Come on, I think I'm goin' to enjoy this." He made his hands into fists, then held them out in front of his face, moving his right hand in tiny circles. "Come on," he said. "I'm goin' to put the lights out for both of you."

"Huh-uh," Emile said. "That ain't the kind of fight I'm talkin' about. We're goin' to fight with guns 'cause I plan to make this permanent."

"No, I ain't goin' to get into no gunfight with you or anyone else," Kennedy said.

"I ain't in this fight," Schumacher said, getting up from the table and walking away.

"Well, that just leaves me an' you now, don't it?" Emile said.

"That's right, just me an' you," Kennedy said. He smiled. "But don't worry, I'll make it quick for you."

"How quick? This quick?" Emile replied.

64

Emile drew his pistol, pointed it at Kennedy's head, then put it back in his holster.

"Was that quick enough for you?"

The speed of Emile's draw, as well as the unexpectedness of it, caused Kennedy to react in shock. He held his hand out toward Emile.

"This here argument don't have nothin' to do with guns."

"I'll let you draw first," Emilie said.

"I told you, there ain't goin' to be no gunfight." Kennedy doubled up his fists again. "But if you'd like to come over here and take your beatin' like a man, I'd be glad to oblige you."

"I said draw," Emile repeated in a cold, flat, voice.

By now, everyone in the saloon knew Kennedy had stepped into a situation that he hadn't planned for. They began, quietly but deliberately, to get out of the way of any flying lead.

It wasn't until that moment, seeing the others move out of the way, that Kennedy began to worry that he might actually be losing control of the situation. He was still holding his fists in front of him, and he lowered them, then stared at Emile incredulously. "Are you blind, mister? Ain't you noticed that I'm not even wearin' a gun? If you're figurin' on forcin' me into a fight, you can just figure again, 'cause I ain't goin' to do it."

"I'll give you time to get yourself heeled," Emile offered.

"I told you, I ain't goin' to get into no gunfight with you."

"If you ain't goin' to fight, then get out of here. Get out of this saloon, out of this town, and out of this valley."

"No, I ain't doin' that, either," Kennedy said. "I got a right to live where I want and to say what I want. And I'll be damn if I let some sawed-off runt like you talk to me that way. Now if you ain't a complete lily-livered coward, you'll shuck out of that gun belt and face me like a man."

"Mister, the only rights you have are the rights I let you have," Emile growled. "Now, you got two choices. You either walk through that door right now, or you pull a gun. Which one is it goin' to be?"

"I told you, I'm not packin' a gun."

"Somebody give him one," Emile said coldly. He pulled his lips into a sinister smile. "This fella seems to have come to a gunfight without a gun."

"I told you, there ain't goin' to be no gunfight, and I don't want a gun."

When no one offered Kennedy a gun, Emile pointed to Schumacher. "Give him your gun," Emile ordered. "You aren't going to be using it."

"You heard the man, Emile. He don't want a gun," Schumacher said.

"Oh, I think he does."

"Emile, leave him be," Cindy said.

"You're sweet on him, are you, Cindy?" Emile asked.

"No, I'm not sweet on him. But he's a nice man, and he's always real friendly when he comes in."

"Schumacher, I said give him your gun."

"No," Schumacher said. "If I give him a gun, you'll kill him."

"That's right."

"Well, I don't want no part of it."

"There ain't no call in gettin' him into this," Kennedy said. "This is between you 'n' me. Now if you are really interested in fighting, shuck out of that gun belt and face me like a man."

Again, in a lightning move, Emile snatched his gun from his holster. This time he cocked it, the sound of the sear as it engaged and turned the cylinder making a loud double click in the now-quiet room.

"No!" Kennedy said. He held both hands out in front of him. "No, please," he begged.

Emile smiled at him, a slow, evil smile. Then he put his pistol back in his holster.

"Give him your gun, Schumacher," Emile said.

Schumacher hesitated for a moment. Then he took his gun out of the holster and lay it on the bar.

"I'll turn it so's the handle is toward you," Schumacher said. "That'll make it easier for you to pick up."

"It's — it's on my left. I'm right handed."

"No problem, go ahead and pick it up. I'll let you do it," Emile said.

Kennedy paused for a moment.

"Pick it up," Emile said again, his voice low, but demanding.

Kennedy looked at the pistol. A vein was jumping in his neck and those who were close enough to him could see his hands shaking.

"Do it," Emile said again.

"No, I ain't goin' to. You ain't goin' to get me in no gunfight."

Again, Emile jerked his pistol from his holster, and using it as a club, brought it across Kennedy's face. The blow cut Kennedy's lip, and it began to swell.

"You ready to pick up the gun?"

"No."

This time Emile slapped Kennedy in the

face, but Kennedy did nothing.

"Now, look at this. You are almost twice as big as me. But you stood there like a lily-livered coward and let me slap you in the face. I wonder, just what is it going to take to get you to fight?" Emile asked.

"Take off the gun," Kennedy said, only now it was no longer a demand — it was a plea. "Take off the gun and we will fight."

"Huh-uh. You opened this ball, that means we'll fight the way I want to fight."

Again, in a lightning draw, the pistol was in Emile's hand, and this time he brought it so hard against Kennedy's face that his knees were buckled. Now Kennedy's lip was bleeding and his left eye was swollen shut.

"Pick up the gun."

"No."

"Mister, for God's sake, that's enough!" Woodward called.

Emile drew his pistol again, and pointed it toward Woodward. "You want in on this do you, cowboy?"

"No, but . . ."

"There ain't no buts. You are either a part of it, or you keep your mouth shut."

Emile turned his attention back to Kennedy. "Pick up the gun."

"Please," Kennedy said, his voice a whimper, almost a sob. "Please."

"Cindy," Emile called. "I want you to look at your boyfriend now. He ain't so big and strong now, is he?"

"Emile, please, stop," Cindy said.

"I'm tired of playing with you," Emile said. Again, he pointed his pistol at Kennedy, and drew the hammer back.

Kennedy began to shake visibly, and he lost control of his bladder. A stain appeared on the front of his pants.

"Well, look here, folks," Emile said derisively. "This big, strong cowboy just peed in his pants."

Not one other person in the saloon said a word, shamed as they were by what they had just witnessed.

"Get out of here," Emile said, dismissively. "Get out of here and don't come back. Next time I see you, I'll shoot you on sight."

Kennedy looked around the saloon, tears of shame and humiliation in his eyes.

"I — I," he started, but he couldn't finish whatever he was going to say.

"I, I, I," Emile mimicked.

Kennedy turned and hurried out of the saloon.

"Ha! Did everyone see that?" Emile shouted.

Not one other person in the saloon responded.

"Cindy, come on back over here, girl. Come sit with us again." Even as he was speaking to Cindy, he made a motion with his hand to invite Schumacher to rejoin him at his table.

"You shouldn't have done that, Emile," Cindy scolded. "He didn't do anything to you."

"He didn't do anything to me because I had a gun. But you saw him. He is, what? Six-feet-two, six-three, maybe. He's got eight or nine inches on me in height, and at least seventy-five pounds in weight. I've seen his kind before. Muscled-up bullies who love to beat up on smaller men. If I had been unarmed, he would have beaten me to a pulp."

"I have to admit, Cindy, that Emile is right," Schumacher said. "I've known Kennedy for over two years now. He has always been quick to fight, as long as he knows he has the advantage."

"Nevertheless, I think what Emile did was wrong."

"You know, Schumacher is right," Ben said. "Kennedy always has been a bully. Maybe it was about time he got his comeuppance."

"No," Woodward said. "Nobody needs to be belittled like that. I'm ashamed of myself for backing down. I should have tried harder to stop it."

"And get yourself shot? You saw how fast this Emile person is," Walker said. "Yeah, maybe Kennedy got a little humiliated, but at least he didn't get hisself killed."

"There's the boss," Dale said, nodding toward the batwing doors just as Duff came in.

CHAPTER SEVEN

When Duff MacCallister stepped into the Fiddler's Green Saloon, he was greeted warmly by at least a dozen customers, in addition to receiving a personal greeting from Biff Johnson, the proprietor of the watering establishment.

"Duff, my boy!" Biff called. "How goes the struggle?"

"Good prevails, lad, as always," Duff replied. "I'll be for havin' a wee drop of scotch if ye nae mind. I'd like a bit of the mist of the moors on m' tongue."

"The scotch is bad stuff, but I've a new supply of bourbon that I'm sure you would like," Biff said.

"Sure 'n' away with ye now," Duff said. "Aren't you for knowin' that bourbon is the devil's own brew?"

Such banter was normal between the two, for Biff Johnson had been one of Duff's first friends when he'd come to Chugwater from his native Scotland. In addition, Biff was married to a Scotswoman, which helped to cement the bond between them.

Duff lifted his glass and gave his toast. "Here's to the heath, the hill and the heather, the bonnet, the plaid, the kilt and the feather!"

"And while goin' up the hill of fortune, may we never meet a friend comin' down," Biff replied.

"Aye, m' lad, well spoken," Duff said.

Duff took a sip of the drink, and held it on his tongue for a moment to enjoy the flavor before swallowing.

Turning, Duff saw five of his cowboys sitting at a table, and he raised his glass in greeting to them.

"Biff, won't you introduce me to your friend?" Cindy asked.

Duff took a deep breath when he saw her long red hair, her flashing blue eyes, and a figure that was well displayed by the provocative dress she was wearing. She looked so much like Skye McGregor that she could be her twin. Skye McGregor was the woman he had planned to marry. It had been Skye getting murdered by a dishonest sheriff that had caused Duff to seek revenge, then leave Scotland.

"Duff, I've hired a new girl to help squeeze

an extra coin from some of the tightwads who frequent my establishment. Cindy Boyce, meet Duff MacCallister."

"Well now, and what a foine-lookin' lass ye be. 'Tis no doubt but that you'll be able to entice the boys to buy another drink."

"If they were all as handsome as you, I'd take pleasure in my job," Cindy said.

"Handsome, you say? Now tell me, lass, how is that eyes as beautiful as the sky over Scotland could be so blind?" Duff replied.

Cindy and the others laughed.

"Would you be for doing me a favor, lass, and find out what each of the men at that table would want for a drink and provide it, on me?" He pointed to the table where his men were sitting. "They all work for me, and a more noble and loyal group of lads one is nae likely to find."

"I'll be glad to," Cindy said.

"You just missed a bit of excitement," Biff said, speaking in a quiet voice. "Although, I wouldn't exactly call it excitement. More like a bit of ignominy, I would say."

Biff told Duff about the exchange between Emile and Burt Kennedy.

"The poor man peed in his pants before he left," Biff concluded. "I doubt I'll ever see him in here again, and I don't blame him. Nobody did anything to stop it. Hell, I didn't do anything."

"What could you have done?"

"I've got a shotgun back here," Biff said.

"Aye, but from the way you were telling the story, you could nae have shot the little man without hitting Kennedy as well."

"Yes, that's probably true," Biff agreed.

The piano player finished a song, then stepped up to the bar to get a refill on his beer.

"You seem to be in good tune today, Mr. Bailey," Duff said by way of greetings.

"Well, now, I consider that a fine compliment coming from you, Mr. MacCallister," Mickey Bailey said. "Say, Biff, why don't you pick up the pipes and have our friend give us a tune?"

"Would you be willing to do that, Duff?" Biff asked.

"Aye, 'n' what kind of Scotsman would I be now, if I refused a request to play the pipes?"

Although Duff had his own pipes, Biff's wife, Rose, had inherited a set of pipes from her father and after Duff and Biff had become friends, Biff had begun keeping them under the bar just for such an occasion as this.

Cindy had not returned to Emile Taylor's

table since the incident with Burt Kennedy several minutes earlier. No one else in the saloon had shown any interest in joining Emile and Schumacher either, so the two men sat at their table talking quietly. Because they were engaged in their own private conversation, neither of them noticed as Duff took the pipes, filled the bag with air, and began playing "Scotland the Brave."

The music filled the saloon, and Emile Taylor looked around in irritation.

"Who the hell is that? And what is that contraption he is blowing into?"

"His name is Duff MacCallister," Schumacher said. "He owns a big ranch north of here. He's from Scotland and that thing he is blowing into is a musical instrument that's called bagpipes. That's somethin' they play over there."

"I ain't never heard nothin' so loud."

"First time I heard it, I thought it was kind of strange too," Schumacher said. "But truth is, I kind of like it now."

"How can anyone like that? If you ask me, it sounds just like a train blowin' its whistle or somethin'. Someone needs to teach that son of a bitch some manners," Emile said. "Ain't he got better sense than to start makin' noise like that when folks is talkin'?"

Schumacher chuckled. "Well, there's the problem, my new friend. Duff MacCallister is not the kind of man you can teach anything to."

"Really? It has been my experience that if you use the right tools, you can teach anybody, anything." Emile loosened his pistol in his holster. "If you know what I mean."

"Yeah," Schumacher responded. "Well, I said you couldn't teach MacCallister anything, but seeing the way you gave Burt Kennedy his comeuppance, I might just change my mind. It could be that you might just be the one who could talk to MacCallister." He chuckled. "MacCallister is such an arrogant son of a bitch, I wouldn't mind seeing him drag his ass out of here the same way Kennedy did."

"Mayhaps I'll just do that for you," Emile suggested.

When Duff finished, he handed the pipes back to Biff. There was a polite applause from most of the people present, as well as several comments as to how good it had sounded. The comments for the most part were from people who now understood and appreciated the music of the bagpipes. But there was one dissenter.

"What do you call that?" he shouted.

Duff knew that this was Emile Taylor, because Biff had pointed the diminutive man out to him. And from the tone of Emile's voice, Duff realized that the question wasn't actually being asked for information. However, he purposely ignored the animosity and answered as if the question had been friendly.

"Ah, 'tis called 'Scotland the Brave,' " Duff said. "A song that is dear to every Scotsman's heart."

"I wasn't talkin' about the name of the song, I was talkin' about that caterwaulin' sound you was makin'. It sounded like cow bellowin' for its calf."

"There's some that say you have to develop an ear for the pipes, I'll admit," Duff said. "But to me, the sound of the pipes is like m' own mither's voice."

"Then you mother must've had a voice like a screechin' tomcat," the man said.

The smile left Duff's face. "Sure now, friend, and I'd take it kindly if you wouldn't be for talkin' about my mither in such a tone."

"Is that a fact? Well, mister, I don't really give a damn what you take kindly," the man said. Getting up from the table, he walked to within a few feet of Duff and let his hand hang loosely near the handle of his pistol. "Of course, you are a big man so it could be that you would like to do something about it."

"Would I be talking to Emile Taylor, now?" Duff asked.

Emile smiled. "Yeah, you are. I reckon you've heard of me."

"I'm afraid I have nae heard of you. Mr. Taylor, I am Duff MacCallister, and I tell you my name, because I have found that when two civilized gentlemen learn each other's names, then there is apt to be less hostility and more comity between the two. I was rather hoping that would be the case here."

"What is comity?"

"It just means a more harmonious relationship."

"You mean like as if we was friends?"

"Something like that, yes."

"I tell you what. You apologize to me for hurtin' my ears like you done with that screechin' contraption you was makin' noise on, and maybe I won't shoot you."

"Oh, I have nae intention of apologizing to you for that, or for anything else," Duff said. "I gather, from your demeanor, that you consider yourself quite skilled in the art of quickly extracting your pistol from its holster."

It took Emile a moment to comprehend what Duff was talking about; then he laughed.

"You do have a strange way of asking me if I'm fast with a gun, mister, but yeah, you might say that." By way of demonstration, as he had done with Kennedy, Emile snatched his pistol from his holster, brought it up to Duff's face, and glared at him for a moment. Then, with a self-satisfied and arrogant laugh, he put the pistol back in the holster.

"If you had been here a little earlier, why, you would have seen me in action. Right, fellas?" he called aloud to the others in the saloon.

Not one person responded. Everyone in the saloon knew Duff, and knew he could not be buffaloed as Kennedy had been. They watched the drama unfold with increasing interest.

"And tell me, lad, is it your skill with the pistol that gives you license to be so unpleasant? Or is it that you are just naturally such an arse?"

Everyone in the saloon laughed at Duff's remark.

"You can't talk to me like that," Emile said.

"Mr. Taylor, it would seem that he already has," Biff said. "I should have said something to you earlier when you were tormenting poor Mr. Kennedy, but I wasn't sure how far you were going with it. But I'll not let you do something like that a second time. So now, I'll be asking you to leave."

"And if I'm not ready to leave?" Emile challenged.

"Then I'll just have to have you thrown out."

"Oh?" Emile turned toward Biff and lifted his right hand to shake his finger in the man's face. "And just who do you think you can get that can throw me out?"

Taking advantage of the fact that Emile's attention was diverted, and his right hand was no longer close to his pistol, Duff quickly closed the distance between them.

"Sure now, lad, 'n' that would be me," Duff said.

With his left hand he grabbed the back of Emile's collar. With his right hand, moving so quickly that Emile didn't even realize it had happened, Duff pulled Emile's pistol from its holster and stuck it down in his own waistband. Then he grabbed Emile by his collar and the seat of his pants and, picking him up, hurried toward the batwing doors, where he threw Emile bodily into the street.

Duff's action was met with a loud cheer and applause.

"You son of a bitch! You're going to die for . . ." That was as far as Emile got with his challenge, because when his hand went to the holster, he discovered that the pistol wasn't there.

"What the hell?" he shouted. "Where's my gun?"

"Would you be lookin' for this now?" Duff asked, throwing Emile's pistol into the street.

Emile ran to pick it up and, swinging it toward Duff, pulled the trigger. The hammer made a clicking sound, and that was when Emile noticed for the first time that the cylinder was missing.

"Oh," Duff said. "And you'll be needing this."

Duff was holding the cylinder in his hand and he threw it out into the street as well. But when Emile started to reach for it, Duff shot at it and the bullet sent the cylinder farther down the street. Emile ran after it, and Duff shot again, sending it even farther down the street.

"Hey, Taylor, turns out maybe you ain't the only one can shoot a gun around here!"

shouted one of the many saloon patrons who had come out front to stand on the porch.

Duff stood in the doorway with the pistol in his hand watching Emile Taylor, who, hesitantly, reached for the cylinder. Duff let him pick it up this time and watched as Emile put the cylinder back in his gun. Once his pistol was reassembled though, Emile made no further demonstrations toward Duff. Instead, he just put it back in his holster, then turned and walked away.

CHAPTER EIGHT

"Bravo!" Biff said when Duff came back in to the bar. Everyone in the bar cheered, and Cindy sidled up to him again.

"That was the bravest thing I've ever seen," she said.

"Let me get you a fresh drink," Biff offered.

"No need," Duff said. He held up the half-empty glass of scotch. "Sure 'n' you know that it only gets better with age. But I'll be for buying a glass of tea for the little lady."

"Tea?" Cindy asked.

"Lass, I know 'tis tea the ladies drink in establishments such as this," Duff said. "For sure 'n' if you drank whiskey every time a man bought a drink for you, you'd be a sot."

Cindy laughed, leaned against him, and put her hand up on his neck.

Gently, Duff took her hand and moved it.

"Don't be for wastin' your time on a Scotsman like me," he said. "I know there are many others in here that would welcome the attentions of a lass as winsome as yourself."

"Yeah, Cindy, how come you ain't never tried to put your arm around my neck?" one of the customers asked in a good-natured complaint.

"Because you've never thrown a bully out in the street," Cindy said, and her reply drew laughter.

Cindy left Duff and began mingling with the others.

"Honey, I could have told you you wouldn't get anywhere with him," Nell said. "There's already a woman in this town who has him staked out, and she doesn't work in a saloon. Her name is Meagan Parker, and she owns the dress emporium that's right next door."

"She might have him staked out. But there have been claims jumped before, so my advice to Miss Meagan is to hang on tight if she doesn't want to lose him."

"Duff MacCallister is a good and honest man. You are makin' a big mistake if you think you can get him away from Meagan Parker."

"We'll see," Cindy said.

"What do you think about the new girl?"

Biff asked, speaking so quietly that only Duff could hear him. "She's a pretty thing, isn't she?"

"Aye, that she is," Duff agreed. "She reminds me of a lass I once knew."

Duff grew quiet then, and Biff, knowing that Duff was having a moment of recall, moved down the bar to attend to someone else, leaving Duff with his thoughts.

Duff was remembering another young woman, one who, like Cindy, had had long red hair and flashing blue eyes.

"Skye, would you step outside with me for a moment?" Duff asked.

"Ian, best you keep an eye on them," one of the other customers said. " 'Else they'll be outside sparking."

Skye blushed prettily as the others laughed at the jibe. Duff took her hand in his and walked outside with her.

"Only four more weeks until we are wed," Skye said when they were outside. "I can hardly wait."

"No need to wait. We can go into Glasgow and be married on the morrow," Duff suggested.

"Duff MacCallister, sure and m' mother has waited my whole life to give me a fine church wedding now, and you would deny that to her?"

87

Duff chuckled. "Don't worry, Skye. There is no way in the world I would start my married life by getting on the bad side of my mother-in-law. If you want to wait, then I will wait with you."

"What do you mean you will wait with me?" Skye asked. "And what else would you be doing, Duff MacCallister? Would you be finding a willing young lass to wait with you?"

"I don't know such a willing lass," Duff replied. "Do you? For truly, it would be an interesting experiment."

"Oh, you!" Skye said, hitting Duff on the shoulder.

"Oh!" she said. "I'm sorry. You just made me mad talking about a willing lass."

Duff laughed, then pulled Skye to him. "You are the only willing lass I want," he said.

"I should hope so."

Duff bent down to kiss her waiting lips.

"I told you, Ian! Here they are, sparking in the dark!" a customer shouted and, with a good-natured laugh, Duff and Skye parted. With a final wave to those who had come outside to "see the sparking," Duff started home.[1]

That had been four years ago. Skye had been killed shortly after that, and Duff had

1. *MacCallister, The Eagles Legacy.*

killed the man who had killed Skye. It was for that reason he'd left Scotland.

The piano player returned, and the music brought Duff out of his reverie.

After he finished his drink, Duff stepped next door into Meagan's dress emporium. She was sitting at a sewing machine, working the treadle briskly.

"Duff," she said with a bright smile. "How nice to see you."

"You look busy," Duff said.

"Yes, I'm making a dress for Juanita Guthrie."

"Well then, I'll nae be bothering you."

"It's no bother, Duff, you know that. By the way, what was the shooting earlier? I heard two shots, but by the time I looked out there was nothing to see but a bunch of men who seemed to find it amusing."

"Meagan, sure 'n' have I nae told you, when you hear shooting outside, do nae go toward the windows. You should go away from them."

"I was curious."

"Curiosity killed the cat. It could also kill you."

"Are you goin' to tell me? Or will I have to walk next door and ask Biff what happened?"

"There is nae need for that," Duff replied.

He told Meagan about his run-in with Emile Taylor, downplaying his own role to one of, "a lucky break," and "he wasn't expecting it," and other explanations that made it seem as if his rousting Emile had been nothing more than a bit of luck.

"One thing I've noticed about you, Duff MacCallister, is that you seem to have a way of making your own luck," Meagan said.

"Aye, there are those that say that is the best kind of luck. Meagan, 'tis wondering, I am, if we might be able to have dinner together tonight?"

"Oh, Duff, I would love to," Meagan said. "But I've scheduled some fittings with Mrs. Guthrie and I'm afraid it's going to take up most of my evening. I'm so sorry."

"That's all right. 'Tis your job, and I understand. Perhaps you could find time tomorrow to have lunch?"

"Yes, I would love to."

"Good, I've some business with the bank tomorrow, so I'll be for coming back into town."

"That's the only reason you will be coming back into town?"

"Aye, so 'twould be no trouble to be seeing you for lunch."

Meagan chuckled. "You are such the romantic, Duff MacCallister."

"Beg your pardon, lass?"

"Nothing. I'll see you at lunch."

Duff touched his fingers to the brim of his hat, then withdrew.

Down at the Wild Hog, as the afternoon progressed into evening, more and more people came in until, eventually, the saloon was noisy and crowded with its evening customers. Three of the most recent arrivals were the same people Reid had done business with earlier in the day: Kid Dingo, Creech, and Phelps. Half drunk even before they arrived, they were louder and more boisterous than anyone else in the entire establishment.

Reid had not yet made his presence known to them, but sat alone at a table in the farthest corner of the saloon, watching as they made a place for themselves at the bar. They did this by the simple expedient of elbowing others out of the way. Occasionally one of them would get off a joke at someone else's expense, and he and the other two would laugh uproariously at his cleverness, unaware, or unconcerned, that the rest of the people in the saloon were not laughing with them, but were instead taking it all in, in embarrassed silence.

"Who are the funny boys?" someone asked

Nippy Jones.

"The one with blond hair and the loudest mouth calls hisself Kid Dingo," Jones said. "He's the youngest. The one with the red hair is a man named Creech. Don't know if that's his first or second name. The one with the dark hair and moustache is Phelps. I think they rode for Matt Heckemeyer for a while until he got rid of them. Since then, they've rode for first one rancher, then another, 'til, one by one ever'one got sick of 'em. I guess they been fired by near 'bout ever' spread within fifty miles of here."

"They ain't never rode for MacCallister," one of the customers said.

"No, now that you mention it, I don't think they have," Nippy Jones replied. "Now they mostly drift about, rounding up a few strays here and there for whatever money they can make."

"Yeah, and sometimes the strays ain't even strayed yet," one of the others at the bar said. "What gets me is why the ranchers ain't figured that out."

"They got it figured out, all right," Nippy Jones said. "They just ain't caught anyone red-handed yet. But the moment they do, you can believe, there will be a necktie party."

"That's a party I want to attend."

92

"I wonder if the marshal knows they're in town?" Marcus asked.

The three men who were the subject of the table conversation, perhaps sensing that they were the subject, left the bar and wandered over to the card game.

"Well, now, this here looks like a friendly game," Creech said. "Any of you 'bout ready to give up your seats?"

No one answered.

"Hey, you," Creech said to one of the players. "I'm talkin' to you, harelip."

Kid Dingo and Phelps laughed.

"Why don't about three of you boys get up and take a rest for a while and let us sit in the game?"

"Hey, Creech, you want to play, you go right ahead," Phelps said. "I didn't come into town to play no cards. Hell, we can do that anywhere. I come for somethin' else."

"Yeah, Phelps, we know what you come for," Kid Dingo said. "You come to dip your wick."

"Hey, look over there," Creech said, pointing toward Reid. "Come on, let's go join our old friend Simon Reid. You boys go ahead and play without us."

Though none of those playing cards said anything, it was obvious that they were glad to see the three men direct their attention somewhere else.

"What are you doing here?" Creech asked as they joined Reid at his table. "How come you ain't out at the ranch?"

"How come I ain't out at the ranch? 'Cause I quit, that's how come," Reid said. "What are you doin' here? What happened to the cows?"

"You don't be worryin' none about them cows. We done got 'em all took care of."

"Not anybody local, I hope. They could track them cows back to MacCallister."

"We didn't get rid of 'em here," Creech said. "What are you goin' to do now?"

"Right now I'm going to spend some of that money." Reid smiled, then pointed upstairs. "Betty's upstairs with somebody now. I'm next in line."

"Yeah, but I mean after that. I mean since you ain't workin' out at Sky Meadow no more, what are you goin' to do for a job?"

"I don't know. I ain't thought about it yet."

"You could come on up to Bordeaux and throw in with us," Creech invited.

"Yeah," Phelps said. "If they was four of us, we could likely get somethin' goin'."

The man who had gone upstairs with Betty came back down the stairs. His immediate need taken care of, he was aware now that he was the object of attention of

94

everyone else in the saloon, and he had a self-conscious, rather sheepish expression on his face. Keeping his eyes down so as not to meet the gaze of anyone, he hurried on down to the bottom of the stairs, then out of the saloon.

"Ahh," Reid said, getting up from the table and starting toward the stairs. "Betty is finished."

"Hadn't you ought to wait 'til she comes back down?" Creech asked.

"What for?"

"What about Bordeaux?" Kid Dingo asked. "You goin' to come up and join us?"

"Might as well," Reid tossed back over his shoulder as he started up the stairs, taking the steps two at a time.

"How was your trip into town?" Elmer asked when Duff returned with a bag of his purchases hanging from his saddle.

"It was good trip," Duff said. "And I got some coffee." He pulled a sack of coffee beans from the bag and handed it to Elmer.

"Good. I'll take this out to the cook so he can grind us some up," Elmer said, holding the bag up. "By the way, how is Miss Parker doing?"

"I dinnae get to spend much time with her. She is very busy. She is making a dress for Mrs. Guthrie."

"That doesn't mean anything. Don't you know that women just say things like that so they can test you?" Gleason asked.

"Sure now, an' what would she be testing me for, I ask?"

"To see whether or not you are serious about her," Gleason answered with the ease of one who considered himself an expert in such matters. "If you listen to her and stay away like she's askin' you to, then that's exactly what she don't want. What she does want is for you to do what she said she didn't want you to do. Do you understand?"

Duff smiled and shook his head. "I'm not sure that I do understand."

"Well, there ain't no real need for you to understand, 'cause the more I try to explain it to you, the harder it's goin' to be for you, you not knowin' women quite as much as I do. I guess what I'm tryin' to say is, when she told you she was just real busy, you didn't let her get away with it, did you?"

"I have to go back into town tomorrow anyway, for 'tis some business I have with the bank. So I asked her to have lunch with me."

"When you asked her, did you say it was because you had to be in town tomorrow, anyway?"

"Aye, for that is the truth of it," Duff replied.

Gleason shook his head in exasperation. "See now, Duff, that's exactly what you don't want to say. It makes it look like your main purpose for coming to town is so you can do some business with the bank. But a woman likes to think that you're comin' into town just to see her."

Duff thought about Meagan's comment about him being "such a romantic" and realized then that this was what Elmer was talking about. He chuckled. "What can I say, Elmer? 'Tis a way you have with women that I don't have."

"I know, but I'm tryin' to bring you on, iffen you'd just listen to me."

"Now, Elmer, sure 'n' if you know all there is to know about women, would you be for tellin' me why I've any need to know? I've but to ask you when confronted with a problem too big for m' wee brain to wrap around."

Gleason smiled broadly. "That's what I'm here for."

At that moment, five miles outside of the town of Chugwater, six men were sitting around a fire, over which two rabbits were cooking.

"While you was in town, we rounded up the horses we're goin' to need," Johnny said. "But we got to keep 'em tied up good tonight, 'cause if they was to get loose, like as not they'd go on back to where we took 'em from."

"I ain't never been to Chugwater," Al Short said.

"Ain't none of us been there," Johnny said, "which is why I chose it to rob. Won't nobody know anything about us. Except now Emile has been there."

"What's the town like?" Calhoun asked.

"They got a good restaurant in town," Emile Taylor said. "It's called the City Cafe. They got a good hotel too, called the Antlers Hotel. We could be eatin' a meal of steak and taters, fresh-baked bread, maybe some apple pie, then spend the night in a bed. Instead, we're out here fixin' to eat rabbit, then go to sleep on the ground. How come that is?"

"I told you why," Johnny said. "I don't want us to be seen in town."

"Why not? We ain't done nothin' yet."

"Not yet. But tomorrow we are going to hold up a bank. If we was to go in there now and folks get a good chance to look at all of us, then tomorrow, once we hit the bank, ever'one is goin' to remember seein' us. That's why I told you not to do anythin' that would get you noticed while you were in town."

"Yeah, I know."

"Nobody noticed you, did they?" Johnny asked.

"No, I kept to myself. Didn't do nothin' but have a drink and case the bank like you said."

"Where is the bank?"

"It's the Chugwater Bank and Trust on Clay Avenue, halfway between First and Second Street."

"Did you check for an alley?"

"Yeah, there's an alley right behind the bank. All we have to do is follow it north, and we'll be out of town within a minute."

"And you're sure nobody noticed you? I mean, you didn't start drinking and do something dumb, did you?"

"Why? What have you heard?" Emile asked, nervously.

"I haven't heard anything," Johnny replied. "Is there somethin' I should have heard?"

Emile thought of his run-ins with Kennedy and the Scotsman.

"No, nothin' happened," he said. "I was just wonderin' why you was askin' is all."

"Looks like the rabbits is done," Johnny said. "Let's eat."

CHAPTER NINE

In Chugwater, Meagan Parker had a light supper then took a cup of coffee out onto the balcony and stood there for a moment, enjoying the coolness of the evening. She lived in a small, but very nice apartment over her place of business. In her shop downstairs, a nearly finished blue dress was fitted to a dress form. Meagan was making the dress based on a woodcut Mrs. Guthrie had brought to her.

"I cut this picture out of the *San Francisco Chronicle*," Mrs. Guthrie had said when she'd approached Meagan about the dress. "And I think it is the prettiest thing I've ever seen. Do you think you could make me one that looks just like it?"

"I'm sure I can, Juanita. What color do you want?"

"Oh, I don't know. What do you think would be nice?"

"I have some blue velvet that I think

would work perfectly. And it would bring out the blue of your eyes, beautifully," Meagan had said.

Mrs. Guthrie had beamed, and touched her hair. "Then by all means, make it blue."

That had been four days ago, and Meagan was nearly finished with the dress. She had promised it by tomorrow, and she intended to have it done by then, even if it took her all night. Besides, she had other plans for tomorrow. Tomorrow she was having lunch with Duff MacCallister.

She smiled as she recalled what Vi had told her Elmer had said to Duff about her.

"She's all sass and spirit, with a face as brown as all outdoors, and yeller hair as bright as the sun. She's as pretty as a newborn colt and as trustin' as a loyal hound dog. Why, she could capture your heart in a minute if you would but give her the chance."

Meagan was giving Duff every chance she could. She was a pretty girl, and there had been men in her life, men who had shown interest in her. But not until she'd met Duff MacCallister had she found the man who she really wanted to show interest.

When Meagan Parker was twelve years old, both of her parents had been killed in a riverboat accident. She could still remember the pain and sorrow of their loss. And the fear, the absolute, mind-numbing fear of being alone.

What would happen to her?

She needn't have worried, because even though her grandmother had already been very old, she'd stepped in and raised Meagan as if she were her own. Meagan and her grandmother had had a wonderful relationship, and when her grandmother had died, three days after Meagan's nineteenth birthday, the pain and sorrow had been as great as it had been when her own parents had died.

Meagan had been in college at the time, and although losing her grandmother had been a terrible emotional blow to her, it hadn't been a financial blow because she still had the money that had been left to her by her parents, over which her grandmother had been a good steward. And by selling her grandmother's house, she had added to her coffer. As a result, she'd been able to finish her education without experiencing any financial burden at all.

She had gone to college to be a schoolteacher, but her grandmother, who had been a seamstress, had taught Meagan how to design, cut cloth, and sew women's clothes. It was a skill that Meagan had picked up easily, and one she enjoyed.

"I know you are studying to be a teacher and teaching is a good thing, but it is also good to have something to fall back on," her grandmother had told her. "That's why I think you should learn how to sew. Folks are always going to need clothes."

What Meagan especially enjoyed was creating original dresses and gowns. She had a great talent for it, and as it turned out, that advice may have been the most valuable thing Meagan Parker's grandmother had left her. She had come to Chugwater to be a schoolteacher only to learn when she arrived that another woman had already been hired. She'd been about to return to St. Louis when she had been given the opportunity to buy a dress emporium, and she'd had just enough money left over to do that. Contrary to the popular belief that women had no head for business, Meagan had an acute business sense and the Ladies' Emporium was one of the most profitable business establishments in Chugwater. Her business acumen was not only manifested by the success of her shop, but also by the fact that she was valued and respected member of the Chugwater Association of Business Owners. It had been, before Meagan became a member, the

Chugwater Association of Businessmen.

And now Meagan was extending her business holdings by investing in the cattle Duff was raising. It, too, had proven to be a very good investment, but she hadn't done it for the economic return. She had done it because it ensured a physical connection between them.

She was looking forward to the luncheon engagement with Duff tomorrow, and wondered if she was doing the right thing by not pressing him into more of a commitment.

"Meagan, you need a better understanding of men," Vi had told her. "They are cowards when it comes to women. I know, I know — I would be the last person to call Duff a coward about anything, Lord knows he has proven his bravery enough times. But all men have a weakness when it comes to advancing their relationship with women. They have to be led into it."

She thought of Duff, and wondered what he was doing and what he was thinking about at that very moment.

Duff was in bed at that very moment, but Meagan would not be happy if she knew what he was thinking. Because he was thinking about the young woman he had met at

Fiddler's Green today. She had looked so much like Skye McGregor that it had nearly taken his breath away. He knew that looks weren't everything — there had been much more to Skye than her flaming red hair, bright blue eyes, and slender curves. Skye had been intelligent, with a well-developed sense of humor, but most of all, she'd had a good heart. He had never met another woman like her.

Until he'd met Meagan.

That's funny, he thought. Although Meagan looked nothing like Skye, anytime he thought of another woman who most reminded him of Skye, he didn't think of the girl he had met in the saloon today, even though she looked so much like Skye that they could be sisters.

No. He thought of Meagan.

The next morning, Johnny and Emile Taylor, Clay Calhoun, Bart Evans, Julius Jackson, and Al Short were going over their final plans.

"When we go in, we'll ride down the alley until we get to the back of the bank. Al, you stay outside with the horses, and remember, these is all stole horses, so we don't have any idea how they are going to act, so you damn well better hang on to 'em tight, so that they don't get away. The rest of us will go around the bank so that we come in through the front door. After we do our business, we'll leave the bank by going out through the back door."

"Why don't we go in through the back door too?" Evans asked.

"More 'n likely the back door will be bolted shut from the inside. We can go out through it, but can't go in through it," Johnny explained.

"Say, Johnny, how much money do you reckon there is in that bank, anyhow?" Jackson asked.

"I figure there's at least thirty thousand," Johnny said. "That means you boys can split up fifteen thousand between you. 'Course, it might be more."

"What do you mean, we can split up fifteen thousand between us? If there's thirty thousand, why ain't we splittin' it all up?" Short asked.

"We done been over that," Johnny replied. "Me 'n' Emile are the ones that got the idea to rob this bank. And we're the ones that put ever'one together. You know'd that, comin' into this job."

"Johnny's right, Al," Evans said. "This was what we all agreed to when we come into the job."

"All right, all right," Short said, waving his hand. "I don't think it's none at all fair, but iffen ever'one else is willin' to go along with it like this, I am too."

"What's one fourth of fifteen thousand dollars?" Jackson asked.

"Three thousand, seven hunnert, and fifty dollars," Evans said. I done figured it all out."

"Three thousand dollars? That ain't bad," Jackson said. "Truth is, it's more money 'n I've ever had before."

"More money 'n I've ever had, too," Evans said.

"If you boys stick with Johnny 'n' me, you'll have lots of money," Emile said. "This here bank is just the first one we got planned out. We got lots of 'em planned out after this."

"Let's get into town," Johnny said. "I want to get there right soon after the bank opens."

Mrs. Guthrie was checking on her dress when Duff walked in through the front door of the Ladies' Emporium.

"Mr. MacCallister," Mrs. Guthrie said. "What do you think of the new dress Meagan is making for me?"

"Sure now 'n' I've never seen a more beautiful dress, Mrs. Guthrie," Duff said.

"And 'twill look even better worn by a beautiful woman such as yourself."

Mrs. Guthrie laughed. "I'm not so old that I can't tell when a man is spreading it on thick. I'll be wearing the dress and if Mr. Guthrie himself recognizes it as new and gives me a compliment, then I'll be satisfied. Meagan, if you don't mind, I'll just pay for the dress now so that when you finish it all I have to do is pick it up."

Meagan smiled. "I never turn down an early payment," she said.

Mrs. Guthrie gave Meagan a bank draft as payment, and when she left the store, Meagan laughed.

"My, my, Duff, you may be a Scotsman, but it's the Irish blarney you are spreading."

"Aye, but 'tis no harm to make a lady feel good about herself."

"I see. And you know all about women, do you?"

"I make no such claim, lass, but 'tis no need for me to know everything because Elmer does," Duff replied with a chuckle, recalling the conversation with his foreman yesterday.

"And just what makes you think Elmer knows all about women?" Meagan asked.

"He told me he knows. And he wouldn't

be for lying to me about such a thing now, would he?"

Meagan laughed with him.

"Now, that's funny. Vi told me that if I needed to know anything about men, all I have to do is ask her."

Vi Winslow was a widow who owned Vi's Pies. She and Elmer Gleason had been "keeping company," as Vi described it.

"Sounds as if they are perfect for each other," Duff said.

"Didn't you say you were going to the bank this morning?" Meagan said.

"Aye, I'm going to have to move some money from my business account into my personal account."

"Good, then we can walk down to the bank together. This is a pretty large draft. I'll just deposit it."

Down at Fiddler's Green at that moment, Cindy Boyce was counting out the money she had received in tips from the male customers the night before.

"Mr. Johnson, if it's all right with you, I'm going to walk down to the bank and make a deposit," she said.

"That's fine by me," Biff replied. "I think that is very smart of you."

"You had better watch out for Cindy,

110

Biff," Nell said. "As many tips as she gets, and saving money the way she does, she might just wind up buying you out."

Duff and Meagan were the only other customers in the bank when Cindy arrived, and she smiled broadly at Duff.

"Hello, Duff," she said, brightly.

"Hello, Cindy," Duff said. Then, seeing the questioning look on Meagan's face, he introduced them.

"Meagan, this young lass is Cindy. I do nae know her last name, but 'tis a new girl for Biff, she is."

"It is nice to meet you," Meagan said. She looked at the rather revealing dress Cindy was wearing, then added, "And if you find yourself in need of a new dress, I own the Ladies' Emporium."

"Yes, I know your place," Cindy said. "It is right next door to Fiddler's Green, isn't it?"

"Yes, it is. And speaking of the emporium, I need to get back to it," Meagan said.

"I can nae leave just yet," Duff said. "Mr. Welch isn't finished with the transfer."

"That's all right. Just don't forget that we are having lunch together."

"Not to worry, lass. As soon as I'm finished here, I'll be callin' for you with bells on m' toes," Duff said.

"Good-bye, Mr. Welch," Meagan called to the teller who had handled her transaction.

"Good-bye, Miss Parker," Welch called back.

"She is your lady friend, is she?" Cindy asked after Meagan left.

"You might say that," Duff replied.

"She is a very pretty woman."

"As fair as the Scottish thistle, she is."

"Thistle? You mean, like a sand spur?"

"Nae like a sand spur. The thistle is the national flower of Scotland, a purple bloom."

"Oh."

Suddenly the front door of the bank was pushed open and five masked men wearing long, tan-colored dusters, barged in. All five were brandishing pistols.

"Here, what is this?" Welch shouted, and bending down, he came back up with a shotgun in his hand.

The shortest of the six robbers shot him, and Welch fell back with a bullet hole in his forehead.

"Don't shoot! Don't shoot!" Bernie Caldwell, the other bank teller, shouted. He stuck his hands into the air.

"You!" the short one said to Duff. "Take your gun out and drop it into the spittoon."

Duff hesitated, and the robber grabbed Cindy and pulled her to him, putting his gun to her head.

"Do it now, or I kill the woman!" he shouted. "Use two fingers."

Obeying the instructions, Duff pulled his pistol from the holster and dropped it into the brass container of expectorated tobacco juice.

One of the other robbers took out a cloth bag and handed it to Caldwell. "All right, Mr. Bank Teller," he said. "I want ever' dollar this bank has to be put in this sack." He cocked the pistol and pointed it at Caldwell. "And if you hold back as much as one dollar, I'll blow your head off."

"I won't hold anything back!" Caldwell said, taking the bag with shaking hands. He moved quickly to the safe, opened it, then began taking out packets of bills and dropping them in the bag.

"Whooee, look at that money, Johnny! Did you ever think we would get so much?"

"Clay Calhoun, you ignorant son of a bitch! Don't use my name!"

When the bag was filled, Caldwell handed it to the man Clay Calhoun had identified as Johnny.

"All right, boys, let's get out of here," Johnny said.

The robber who was holding Cindy gave her a shove as the five men started toward the back door of the bank. Duff watched until all were outside. Then he stuck his hand down in the spittoon and came up with his pistol, now dripping with brown slime. Ignoring the odorous goo, he started toward the back door.

"No!" Cindy said, running in front of him. "Don't go out there! They'll kill you!"

"Let me by, lass!" Duff said.

"No!" Cindy grabbed him and tried to hold him back. "Don't you understand? They will kill you!"

Gently, but firmly, Duff pushed Cindy away, then stepped out into the alley. Mounted now, the six bank robbers were galloping down the back alley, shouting and shooting their pistols into the air to keep everyone back.

CHAPTER TEN

Outside in the alley behind the bank, Duff took careful aim and squeezed off a shot, and one of the riders fell from his horse. He fired a second time, and another rider fell. But before he could shoot a third time, the remaining four riders went around a corner. Duff ran back through the bank, where he saw Cindy standing by the front window looking out onto the street, while Caldwell bent over Welch's body. Duff ran out of the front door to see if he could get a shot, and he saw the bank robbers at the far end of the block, where they had come back out from the alley. He raised his pistol to take aim, but there were too many townspeople drawn into the street by the commotion. Curious men and women were standing in the street between Duff and the fleeing robbers, preventing him from getting a clear shot.

By now, Marshal Jerry Ferrell, as well as

Deputies Willie Pierce and Frank Mullins, showed up, their own pistols drawn. "What's going on?"

"The bank's been robbed, Marshal!" someone shouted.

Seeing Duff with pistol in hand, standing in front of the bank, Ferrell hurried down to him.

"Did you get a shot at them?" Ferrell asked.

"Aye, two of them," Duff said. "One I think I killed, and one I but wounded. They are out back in the alley."

"Ha!" Ferrell said. "When I took this job over from Marshal Craig, he told me you were like an unpaid deputy. Willie, Frank, you keep an eye on things out here. Duff, what do you say you and I go back there and take a look at them?"

Ferrell and Duff moved quickly back into the alley. There they saw two men on the ground, one lying, and one sitting up. The two robbers were behind Guthrie's Building and Lumber Supply, and R.W. Guthrie and Fred Matthews were standing over them, holding pistols on the one who was sitting up. The masks had been pulled away from both of them.

"I thought I recognized you. Marshal, this gentleman is Emile Taylor," Duff said. "Or at least, that is what he said his name was when I met him in Fiddler's Green."

Ferrell chuckled. "Yes, I heard about that meeting." Ferrell looked at Emile. "And I heard about your little episode with Burt Kennedy too. Not so much now, are you, Taylor?"

"I'm hurt," Emile said.

"Are you now?" Ferrell replied, though there was absolutely no compassion in his voice. "Have you checked him over, Fred? How bad is he shot up?"

"He's got a crease in his shoulder is all. He was hurt worse when he fell off his horse than he was by the bullet," Matthews said.

"You're slipping, Duff. I would have thought you would have killed both of them."

"I thought you might want to speak with one of them," Duff said.

"That's a fact," Ferrell said.

Deputies Pierce and Mullins arrived then.

"Ain't nothin' more happenin' out front," Pierce said.

"Folks still standing around in the street?" Ferrell asked.

"Yeah, they're doin' that, all right."

"I'd better get back out there. Come on, Taylor, you're going to jail. You two, keep him covered."

"I heard what you done to Burt Kennedy," Mullins said. "So I would really love it if you would try and run."

"I ain't runnin' nowhere," Emile mumbled.

Duff and Marshal Ferrell walked back out into the street, where the crowd of curious onlookers had grown even larger.

"Folks, the show's over," Marshal Ferrell shouted. "You may as well get out of the street so horses and wagons can pass."

"I heard Mr. Welch was killed," someone said. "Is that right?"

"Aye, I'm afraid it is," Duff said.

"He is the one who shot Danny," Caldwell said, pointing to the prisoner that Pierce and Mullins had in tow.

"Let's string the son of a bitch up!" another shouted. "Get a rope! I'll put it around his neck myself!"

Marshal Ferrell saw who had shouted, and he pointed at him. "Prentiss Montgomery, if you so much as open your mouth again, I will throw you in jail. And if anyone else makes such a comment I will throw him and you in jail! There will be no more such talk in this town. Do you hear me? I'm talking to all of you."

"Marshal, Danny Welch was a good man,"

someone said. "We can't let this son of a bitch get away with killin' him."

"Welch was a good man, that is a fact," Ferrell said. "And if Mr. Taylor here is the one who shot him, there is no doubt in my mind but that he will hang. But if he, or anyone else, is hanged in this town, it's going to be legal. Or else there will be two hangings. The one that is illegal, followed by the legal hanging of the son of a bitch who did it."

"Duff! Oh, Duff!" Meagan shouted, running up from her place of business. There was an expression of fear and worry on her face, but when she saw Duff standing uninjured in the street with the marshal, the expression of fear and worry was replaced by one of relief and joy.

"Oh," she said. "I heard — I was afraid — I'm so glad to see that you are all right." Without hesitation or embarrassment that they were standing in front of the entire town, Meagan went to him and embraced him.

She looked up at him, her eyes shining with tears of relief; then she saw his hand, still soiled with the expectorated tobacco offal. She stepped back with an expression of repulsion.

"Oooh!" she said. "What *is* that?"

"Och . . . 'tis naught but tobacco juice," Duff said with a wry grin. "They made me drop my pistol into a wee pot o' the stuff."

"And you stuck your hand down into it?"

"Aye, for 'twas the only way I could retrieve my gun," Duff said.

"Which, I may say, Miss Parker, he put to excellent use," Marshal Ferrell said. "He put two of the varmints down."

"But the others got away with the money," Duff said.

"How much money did they get?" one of those standing in the street asked.

"I don't know yet," Marshal Ferrell replied. "We'll have to go through the records and find out."

"Damn! I had money in that bank!"

"We all had money in that bank, Snellgrove," Guthrie said.

Johnny Taylor and the others galloped for two miles before they slowed their horses to a trot. There, the riders dismounted, unsaddled their horses, then gave the animals a swat on their flanks and sent them galloping off.

"Where's Emile?" Johnny asked.

"Him 'n' Julius didn't make it," Calhoun said. "They was both shot."

"My brother was shot?" Johnny said

distressed by the news.

"Emile wasn't kilt though," Short said.

"He wasn't kilt? How do you know?" Johnny asked anxiously.

"He was right beside me, and I seen where it was that he got hit. He just got hit in the shoulder is all."

"Julius is dead though," Calhoun said. "Hell, I seen blood and brain comin' out of his head where the bullet hit."

"Did anybody see who it was that shot 'em?" Johnny asked.

"Yeah, I seen 'im," Calhoun said. "It was the one we made drop his gun into the spittoon. He must've fished it out."

Carrying their saddles, the four men walked almost a mile into a closed canyon where six horses were hobbled.

"When are we goin' to divide up the money?" Short asked.

"We'll divide it up now," Johnny answered

"Good," Calhoun said. "And now with two of 'em gone, that just gives us that much more money to divide up."

"Not quite. Emile and I still get half of the money," Johnny said. "But you three can divide up the money that would have gone to Jackson."

"What do you mean, Emile and you get half the money? Emile ain't even here,"

Short said.

"He ain't dead, either. So that means I'm goin' to keep his money for him."

The four men sat down then and counted the money. It came to forty-five thousand dollars.

"All right," Johnny said. "Half of forty-five thousand is twenty-two thousand five hundred, which I'll keep for Emile and me. That leaves seven thousand five hundred dollars for each of you."

"That don't seem no way right," Short said.

"Is that, or is that not, what you agreed to?" Johnny asked.

"Johnny is right, Al," Evans said. "We did agree to that, and if you think about it, what with Julius gettin' hisself kilt an' all, why, we're gettin' a lot more 'n we bargained for."

"Plus, we come up with more money that we thought we would," Calhoun added.

"Yeah, and if you boys just stick with me, there will be a lot more where this come from," Johnny said as he continued to count the money. "I've got at least two other jobs in mind."

"All right. All right, I like the sound of that," Short said.

"Now, that you've seen it, I want you keep some of it back, but wrap the rest of your share up in your spare shirt, and we'll bury it here."

"What do you mean, bury it here?" Calhoun asked. "Why the hell would we want to do that?"

"You want to be wandering around carryin' that much money with you?" Johnny asked. "Nobody walks around with that much money."

"But bury it?" Evans asked.

"You don't have to bury it. You could go into town somewhere and open yourself a bank account. Of course, they might ask where you got twenty years' worth of salary. On the other hand you could probably take it back and open up an account in the bank we just robbed, then they wouldn't have to ask, because they would know."

Short chuckled. "Yeah, I see what you mean."

"How do we know one of us won't come back here and take all the money?" Calhoun asked.

"Who's going to do that, Calhoun? You?" Johnny asked.

"Well, no, I won't but . . ."

"There's a real easy way to handle this," Johnny said. "We won't none of us separate until we're ready to move on to somewhere else. Then we'll all come here together, dig up our money, and go on to the next job."

"All right, I'll bury my money if the rest of you do," Short said. "But I ain't goin' to bury all of it. I plan to keep some with me."

"I suggest you men back no more'n a couple hunnert dollars apiece," Johnny said. "That's enough money to last you for a while. I'm going to keep back about two thousand."

"Why are you keeping so much back?"

"We are going to have some operating expenses, and I'll need enough money to cover that."

"All right, sounds good to me," Evans agreed.

After the money was buried, Johnny saddled his horse. "I don't know about you boys, but I'm goin' into town," he said.

"What? Why are you goin' to do a dumb thing like that?" Short asked. "In case you forgot, we just robbed a bank in that town."

"I need to know if my brother is still alive, and see what I can do about gettin' him out of there."

"You're goin' to get yourself caught," Calhoun said.

"No, I ain't. They didn't nobody see us without we was masked. And we was ridin' different horses then."

"Hell, Johnny's right. We could all go back

124

into town," Evans said.

"Are you crazy?" Short asked.

Evans smiled. "Yeah, like a fox," he said. "Think of it. We was all wearing these here long coats, so they didn't nobody see what we wearin' underneath. And like Johnny says, we was all masked and we was ridin' different horses. Ha! More'n likely they've got a posse out lookin' for us right now all over hell's half acre, and all the time they're a-lookin' for us out here, why, there we'll be right there in town, right under their noses. They won't never think we'll be there."

"Damn if I don't think Evans is right," Calhoun said with a broad smile. "And we sure as hell can't spend none of the money out here, but if we're in town, why, we could have us a good supper at that restaurant Emile told us about."

"And maybe get us a few drinks, and play some cards," Evans said.

"What do you say about it, Johnny?" Short asked.

Johnny smiled. "I'd like to have me a steak and some taters."

"And maybe a woman to warm my bed," Evans added. "Lord, with this much money we can get any woman we want."

"All right," Johnny said. "We'll go back into town. We'll have us a good meal, and do some drinkin' and whorin'. But don't none of you get drunk."

"What do you mean, don't none of us get drunk?" Evans asked. "Hell, what's the purpose of drinkin', if you can't get drunk?"

"Johnny's right. Sometimes when you get drunk you say things you don't mean to be sayin'," Short said. "The last thing we need is for somebody to get drunk and start talkin' about the job we just pulled."

"It's not only the talkin'," Johnny warned. "Drunk, or sober, if you start spendin' money like it's water, you'll give us away."

"Don't worry, I ain't goin' to spend all my money in some place like Chugwater," Calhoun said. "I'm goin' to save it, and maybe after another job or two like Johnny was saying, why, I'll go to Denver, or maybe San Francisco or some such place where I can live like a king and nobody will ever suspect a thing."

"I tell you what I'm goin' to do," Short said. "I'm goin' to buy me a saloon some-place. And have me some whores workin' there. Then I can have all the beer and whiskey I want to drink anytime I get thirsty, and all the whores I want, anytime I get to wantin' me a woman."

"Not me," Evans said. "I'm goin' back to Scott County, Missouri, and buy a farm and be one of the bigwigs in the county."

"All right," Johnny said. "But there ain't none of them plans goin' to come true if anyone does something stupid in town that will get us found out."

"Can we drink some, and whore some?" Short asked.

Johnny smiled. "I don't know about you boys, but I sure plan to," he said.

"Ha! Now you're talkin'!" Calhoun said.

"Hey, what about our hats?" Evans asked.

"What about 'em?" Short asked.

"We was all wearin' these same hats when we was in town last. Someone might recognize 'em."

"Leave the hats here," Johnny said.

"I ain't goin' to go around without no hat to wear," Short said.

"What the hell you worryin' about, Al?" Johnny asked. "You got money. Buy yourself a new hat."

"Yeah," Short said, as if just realizing that. "Yeah, I'm goin' to get me a new hat."

"We'll all get new hats," Evans said.

"And new shirts, seein' as I just buried the only other shirt I got," Calhoun said.

CHAPTER ELEVEN

Down at the mortuary, Tom Nunnelee had just finished preparing Danny Welch's body. Mrs. Welch was too distraught to come to the mortuary, so Mrs. Adams, a neighbor, had brought Welch's finest suit. Welch was well known and much liked around town, so Nunnelee took his time with him. Not until he was finished with Welch, and the cleaned-up and embalmed body was lying in a red, felt-lined, black lacquer coffin, did Nunnelee turn his attention to the robber who had been killed.

"Well now, Mr. Jackson," Tom Nunnelee said. "What do you think about robbing our bank now? Still think it was a good idea, do you?"

Nunnelee washed away the blood from the entry wound at the back of Jackson's head, and from the exit wound just under his left eye. He did not embalm the body, because it would be buried by tomorrow.

Once he had Jackson cleaned up, he strapped the body to a board and stood him up in front of his establishment. Jackson's arms were crossed over his chest, and his pistol was placed in his right hand. That done, he printed a sign to post above the body.

JULIUS JACKSON
KILLED WHILE ROBBING
THE BANK OF CHUGWATER

Shortly after Nunnelee stood Jackson's body up in front of his funeral parlor, citizens of the town began to gather around in morbid curiosity. Ken Dysart, who owned a photography studio, saw an economic opportunity, and he set up his tripod and camera, then posted a sign.

Pictures Taken WITH BODY–25 cents.
HOLDING GUN *in picture*–35 cents.
GUN FURNISHED *for*–15 cents.

Moe Kitteridge, a cowboy from a nearby ranch, stood there looking at the body for a moment, and Nunnelee called out to him, "Mister, would you like to have your picture taken standing beside this outlaw? It's just a quarter."

Kitteridge smiled, then nodded. "Yeah,"

he said. "Why not?"

"For ten cents more, you can hold your gun while you are standing alongside him."

"Why would I want to do that?" Kitteridge asked. "Hell, ever'body knows it was Duff MacCallister what shot him."

"Yes, everyone in this town knows that now," Dysart said. "But think about this. You can pass this photo down to your grandson, and he can pass it down to his grandson, and a hundred years or so from now, your great-great-grandchildren will be showing this picture to their friends, and telling the story of how you were the one that killed this notorious outlaw."

"Yeah," Kitteridge said, a broad smile spreading across his face. "Yeah, that's true, ain't it? A hunnert years from now, there ain't nobody goin' to know no better as to who kilt him, and all my kin will think it was me."

"Do you need a pistol?" Dysart asked, offering his.

"Nah, I got my own," Kitteridge said, drawing his pistol from the holster. The pistol was of dull gray steel, with wooden pistol grips. One of the pistol grips was only half there, the other half broken off.

"That gun?" Dysart asked. "You really want your great-great-grandchildren to think that was the best you could do? I mean, if you are posing for a picture, you need something like this."

Dysart picked up a silver-coated pistol with mother-of-pearl handles. "This is what you want," he said.

"Yeah," Kitteridge agreed, taking the gun in hand. "Yeah, this looks good."

Kitteridge stood beside the body, but Dysart, ever the director of his little drama tableau, posed him so that his left hand was held across his heart, while his right hand was crooked at the elbow, pistol pointing up.

"Don't be smiling," Dysart said. "This is no joke, you have just killed, in a deadly shoot-out, one of the most desperate criminals in the West. Give me a grimace."

Kitteridge reacted as told, and when Dysart thought the pose was just right, he took the picture.

As the commotion continued around Julius Jackson's body, Dr. Urban was down at the jail treating the flesh wound Emile Taylor had received.

"Unfortunately, he'll live," Dr. Urban said when he finished examining Emile Taylor.

"Unfortunately?" Emile said. "I'll live and you say unfortunately? What kind of doctor are you?"

"The kind of doctor who just lost his life savings in the bank holdup you pulled," Dr. Urban said.

"Yeah, he'll live. But only until we hang him," Marshal Ferrell said. "Thanks, Doc, for comin' to see him."

"I'd rather see him the way I saw the other man," Dr. Urban said. "Dead."

"I expect you'll see him that way soon enough," Marshal Ferrell said. "According to Duff and Mr. Caldwell, Emile here is the one who killed Mr. Welch. Which means that once we have this fella's trial, I don't reckon it'll be too long before we hang him."

"You'll need someone to sign the death certificate," Dr. Urban said. He looked over toward Emile. "And, Mr. Taylor, that is a task I am looking forward to."

Six miles out of town, at the farm of Clyde Barnes, twelve-year-old Jimmy Barnes was out at the pump, drawing a bucket of water, when he saw a horse come trotting in. With a broad smile and a shout, he dropped the bucket and ran into the house.

"Pa! Ma! Harry has come back!"

"What?" Mr. Barnes said.

"It's Harry. He's come back. Come look!"

Clyde and Ruby Barnes and their daughter, Helen, followed Jimmy back outside. They saw their horse, Harry, drinking thirstily from the water trough.

"It is Harry," Mrs. Barnes said. "Where in the world do you think he's been?"

"I don't know," Mr. Barnes said. He walked up to Harry and began rubbing the animal behind the ear. The horse nodded his head in appreciation.

"I thought you said he was stole," Jimmy said.

"I thought he was. I can't imagine him just running off. But here he is, come back home. I'd better get him in the barn. Jimmy, get him a bag of oats. There's no tellin' where he's been, but like as not he's hungry."

Half an hour later, Jimmy and his father were in the barn. Harry was back in his stall, and Mr. Barnes was looking him over to make certain he hadn't been injured in any way during his absence.

Suddenly the barn door was kicked open and three armed men came running in.

"Get your hands up!" one of the men shouted.

"What is this? Are you robbing me? I don't have any cash money," Mr. Barnes said.

"Oh? What did you do with the money

133

you stole from the bank this mornin'?" the leader of the three armed men said.

"What are you talking about? I didn't steal any money from the bank. I ain't left the house this livelong day!"

"Don't lie to us, mister. We tracked your horse here from the bank."

Barnes and his son looked at each other for a moment; then the confused expression left Barnes's face.

"I'll be damn," he said. "That's where Harry was."

By midafternoon the four horses that had taken part in the bank robbery had all been tracked to neighboring ranches and farms. And because all four owners of the horses had substantially the same story, Marshal Ferrell was predisposed to believe them.

"I still got two horses missing," Sam Dumey said. "One is a paint gelding, the other is a bay."

"Mr. Dumey, we have two horses out back that sound like that," Marshal Ferrell said. "The two robbers who didn't get away were riding them. Maybe you'd like to take a look."

Dumey followed Marshal Ferrell out back to the lean-to that served as a temporary shelter anytime someone who owned a horse was in jail.

"Damn!" Dumey said. "That's them, all right! Vick and Dandy!"

"Can we have our horses back now?" Dumey asked.

Marshal Ferrell nodded, then went back into his office, where his deputies, Willie Pierce and Frank Mullins, were drinking coffee.

"Seems like we got us a smart bunch this time," Marshal Ferrell said as he poured himself a cup. "These boys stole horses for the robbery, then set 'em loose after they got away. That sent us trackin' down the horses while they got away clean."

"That's smart, all right," Pierce said.

Marshal Ferrell heard voices coming from the back, and he looked at his two deputies in confusion. "Who's that talking back there?" he asked. "I thought we let everyone go but Taylor."

"We did," Mullins said. "Schumacher is back there talking to Taylor."

"Schumacher? What's he doing back there?"

"Turns out they are friends. Schumacher says he met Taylor a couple of days ago, and he thought he might be able to get something out of him."

Marshal Ferrell put his cup down, then

stepped through the door that separated the office area from the two jail cells.

"Schumacher?" he called. "What are you doin' back there?"

"Just havin' a conversation with the prisoner is all," Schumacher replied. "It ain't nothin' I've never done before."

"That's when you were a deputy. You aren't a deputy anymore and you got no business bein' back there."

"Let's just say I'm having a friendly visit."

"You were here long enough. You know the rules. You want to have a visit, you come between two and three in the afternoon."

"I hear you found out about us stealin' horses to pull off the bank robbery," Emile said. "That was pretty smart, don't you think?"

"You think it was smart, do you?" Ferrell asked.

"Yeah, I think it was smart. I mean, you wasn't able to track us down now, were you?"

"Taylor, has it dawned on you that we don't have to track you down? Here you are, in our jail, and here you will stay until we hang you."

The smile left Emile's face as he realized the truth of what Ferrell was saying.

"Come on, Schumacher, let's go," Ferrell said.

"Francis, come back and see me at two this afternoon," Emile called to Schumacher as he and the marshal were leaving. "And bring me some tobacco."

When Marshal Ferrell and Schumacher returned to the front office where the deputies were still drinking coffee, none of them paid any attention to the four horsemen who were riding by at that moment. The lawmen had no way of knowing that the men they were looking for were no more than one hundred feet away from him at that very moment.

Johnny Taylor, Clay Calhoun, Bart Evans, and Al Short rode slowly, quietly, looking straight ahead so as not to draw any attention to themselves. As they continued on down the street, they passed by the undertaker's establishment where the crowd had gathered around Julius Jackson's body. All four men glanced toward the gruesome display, but they continued to ride by until they reached the Chugwater Mercantile. Here, they dismounted.

"That ain't right, them havin' Julius standin' up there like that for ever'one to gawk at," Short said.

"It ain't botherin' Julius none," Calhoun said.

Evans laughed. "Yeah, I guess you got that right," he said.

"Johnny, you reckon they got hats and shirts in this store?" Short asked.

"Look at the sign," Johnny said, pointing to the painted sign in the window. "It says goods for all mankind. What kind of goods would that be, if he didn't have hats and shirts?"

Fred Matthews had three store clerks, but all three were busy when the four men came in so, putting on his best "salesman's smile," he walked over to greet them himself.

"Yes, gentlemen, what can I do for you?" he asked.

"We just rode into town," Johnny said. "And we noticed there was a body propped up back in front of one of the stores. Who is it?"

"That is the late but unlamented Julius Jackson. There were six men who held up our bank this morning. Four of them got away. He is one of the two who didn't get away."

"You said two of 'em didn't get away. Where is the other one at?" Johnny asked.

138

"Is he dead too?"

"No, not yet. Emile Taylor is his name. We've got him in jail, now, and he's the one who gave us the Julius Jackson name."

"What do you mean, he ain't dead yet?"

"Turns out that the very one we got is the same one who has already been identified as the one who killed the bank teller. So, like I said, he isn't dead yet, but I expect he will be before long, because soon as we get him tried and found guilty, we will hang him."

"Has he told you any of the other names?" Evans asked.

"He didn't tell us any more names, but we know two of them." Matthews chuckled. "That's because they were so dumb as to call each other by name. Or at least, two of them did. We know that one is Clay Calhoun, and we believe the other one is Johnny Taylor. I say believe, because we only heard the first name, Johnny, being used, but seeing as how we have Emile Taylor, and Johnny is his brother, we're pretty sure that's who it is."

"How bad hurt is this fella that you've got?" Johnny asked. "Is he shot real bad?"

"How did you know he was shot?"

"Well, if two of 'em didn't get away, and one of 'em was kilt, seems only normal that you wouldn't have caught the other one unless he was shot too."

"Yes, I guess that makes sense. Well, he isn't bad hurt at all. Now," Matthews said, ever the businessman. "I'm pretty sure you gentlemen didn't come in here just to get the latest news. So, what can I do for you?"

"We come to buy hats," Johnny said.

"And shirts," Calhoun added.

"My," Matthews said. "All four of you have come in to buy hats and shirts at the same time? This is most unusual."

"What's unusual about it?" Evans asked. "If nobody ever come in here to buy a hat, you wouldn't have any to sell, now, would you?"

Matthews chuckled. "I guess you've got me there, partner," he said. "Now, what kind of hat can I show you?"

"The best you got," Short said.

"Yeah, me too," Evans said.

Johnny and Calhoun added their own requests for "the best he had," and for the next few minutes the men tried on hats until each of them found the one he wanted. Once they had their hats, they picked out shirts. While Johnny, Short, and Evans made their choices quickly from a pile of gray shirts, Calhoun took a while longer because he wanted a red shirt. He finally settled for one that was wine colored. All four men took off the shirts they were wearing, and put on the new ones.

"About the bank robbery this morning," Johnny said as he was buttoning up his shirt. "Whole town turned out shootin' did they?"

"Oh, no, it was just one man. I reckon they hadn't figured on Duff MacCallister being in the bank."

"Duff MacCallister?" Johnny asked. "Who is Duff MacCallister?"

"He's a Scotsman who hasn't been in this country all that long, but since he arrived he has really made himself welcome. This isn't the first time he's made some outlaws rue the day they ever decided to try and come into Chugwater. I mean, he may be a Scotsman instead of your typical Western man, but I swear if he ain't about the best shot I've ever seen in my life, and I've seen some good ones in my day."

"Fast on the draw, is he?" Calhoun asked.

"No. At least I don't think so," Matthews said. "I've never seen him draw, and I'm not sure that anyone has. But once he gets that gun in his hand, it's 'Katy, bar the door.' Well, now, it looks as if you gentleman have chosen your shirts and hats. Is there anything else I can get for you?

"No, this is all," Johnny said.

"You fellows have excellent taste. Those hats are a dollar fifty each, and the shirts are fifty cents each."

Each of the four men presented him with a twenty-dollar bill.

"Oh," Matthews said. "Because of the bank robbery, I'm rather short on change. I'm afraid I don't have enough to handle this. Do you not have anything smaller?"

"No, we ain't."

"This is most unusual," Matthews said. "I mean to think that there are four of you, and not one of you has anything smaller than a twenty-dollar bill. But then you all asked for the most expensive hats I had. Perhaps you gentlemen are wealthy?"

"Nah, that ain't it," Johnny said. "It's just that we, uh, was ridin' for a ranch some north of here, and all of us just got paid off with a couple of twenty-dollar bills. So you see, that's how come we ain't got nothin' any smaller."

"All right, I have a suggestion if you are amenable to it. You four men came in together, so I assume you are friends. Could I suggest that just one of you pay for all four hats and shirts, then later, when you get change, you can settle with each other?"

"Yeah," Johnny said. "We can do that. I'll

pay for 'em now."

"Very good, sir. I see that you all put on your shirts. What about your hats? Do you want them in boxes?"

"Nah, we'll wear them out of here, too," Johnny said.

Matthews made change for the twenty, then watched as the four men, wearing their new hats and shirts, went back out onto the street. He walked to the front to look through the window at them as they mounted their horses, then followed them with his gaze as they rode on down the street.

"Something wrong, Mr. Matthews?" one of his clerks asked.

"No," Matthews said. "Not really. It's just that — well, I have a strange feeling about those four men. There is something about them that doesn't seem right."

"There were four bank robbers who got away. Do you reckon these men might be those four?"

"I don't know," Matthews said. Then he shook his head. "I mean, I gave it some thought, but it seems unlikely that they would show up here again, so I don't think so. Besides the robbers were all wearing masks and dusters, so nobody has any idea what they looked like."

"Then what makes you feel funny about them?"

"I don't know," Matthews said. "Probably nothing. Did Mr. Sikes find the tool he was looking for?"

"Yes, sir."

"Good, good. He is one of my best customers. I always like to see him leave satisfied when I can."

CHAPTER TWELVE

After they left the Chugwater Mercantile, Johnny Taylor and what was left of his gang went down the street to Fiddler's Green. There, they found that everyone in the saloon was talking about the bank robbery. One man at the next table had obviously gone out with the posse in pursuit, because he was now telling some of the others about it.

"I was with the posse that went after 'em. We tracked 'em to where they all split up, so we split up to follow 'em. Well, sir, the horse that me and Simmons and Clark was trackin' led us right to Clyde Barnes's place. Turns out his horse was stolen and used by the bank robbers, then it was turned loose to lead us back."

"Yeah, same thing with the group I was with," one of the others said. "It was a wild goose chase all right."

"I had over five hundred dollars in the

bank," one of the men was saying, angrily. "That's damn near all the money I had in the world and them sons of bitches stole it."

"Well, hell, Randy, if you had so much money in the bank, why didn't you go out with the posse?" one of the others asked.

" 'Cause I didn't know nothin' about the posse, that's why. I didn't even know nothin' about the bank bein' robbed 'til late this afternoon, when I come back into town."

"Besides which, the posse didn't do no good, anyhow," still another customer said. "They come back in with not even a sign as to what happened to them bank robbers. It was like they just disappeared into thin air."

Johnny, Evans, Calhoun, and Short were sitting at a table near the piano, listening to the conversation.

"Disappeared into thin air," Short said, smiling. "I've got to hand it to you, Johnny, changin' horses like we done was one smart move."

"Yeah? Well, it ain't all that smart to talk about it, though, is it?" Johnny asked, chastising Short.

"Hello, boys, my name is Mattie," one of the bar girls said as she stepped up to their table. "Can I get you something?"

"What are those men talking about?" Johnny asked. "Was your bank robbed?"

"Oh, yes, it was. And one of the girls who works here was in the bank when it was robbed."

"Was she? Where is she now?"

"Mr. Johnson gave her the rest of the day off. It was quite a frightening experience for her."

"Was it?"

"Yes, sir. The bank robbers killed poor Mr. Welch. Then one of them grabbed Cindy and held a gun to her head." The bar girl shivered. "I just don't know what I would do if someone did something like that to me."

"I guess that would have been pretty frightenin'," Johnny said.

"Now, what can I get you boys?" Mattie asked, her smile returning. "Beer? Whiskey?"

"How 'bout goin' upstairs with us?" Short asked.

"I don't do that," Mattie replied.

"What do you mean you don't do that? You're workin' here, ain't you?"

"I, like the other girls who work here, am a hostess only," Mattie said. "We'll serve you drinks, and if you buy us a drink we'll even sit down and spend some time with you. But we don't go upstairs with the customers. If you want that, you'll have to go down to the Wild Hog."

"The women there are whores, are they?" Evans asked.

"The women there will go upstairs with the customers," Mattie said without commenting on the word "whores."

"Let's go down to the Wild Hog," Calhoun suggested.

"Maybe later," Johnny replied. "For now, let's stay here for a while. This seems like a nice place to have a drink."

"Oh, it is," Mattie said, smiling again. "Believe me, it is. I'll be right back with the beers."

"Mattie, was you tellin' 'em about the bank robbery?" Curly Lathom called over to her. Lathom was the town barber, an occupation that was belied by the fact that there was not so much as one hair on his head.

"Yes," Mattie replied. As she left for the beers, Curly Lathom came over to talk to four men.

"I don't know if Mattie told you, but they killed Danny Welch, who was as fine a man as you'll ever meet. Had a wife and two kids. They are an evil bunch of bastards, that's for sure," Curly said.

"I heard some of the talk," Johnny said. "Sounds like most of 'em got away."

"Yeah, they did, but I don't reckon they'll

be free for too long."

"Why do you say that?" Johnny asked. "I just heard someone say that the posse lost all track of 'em."

"That's true, but we got one of 'em over in the jail," the customer said. "And I figure it's just a matter of time before he tells us ever'thing we want to know. I mean, once we start buildin' the gallows and he sees it goin' up just outside the jail window, he'll get that itch in his neck, if you know what I mean, and next thing you know he'll be singing like a bird."

"Hey, Curly! You was wantin' in the card game, wasn't you? Well, we got us a seat open, now," someone called from the other side of the room.

After Curly walked away, Johnny drummed his fingers on the table for a moment. "We need to get us some more men," he said.

"What do we need more men, for?" Short asked.

"To get Emile out of jail."

"You're goin' to take a chance on gettin' him out, are you?" Calhoun asked.

"Yeah," Johnny said. "You got somethin' against that, do you?" he challenged.

"Here's the thing, Johnny. Emile knew the risk just like the rest of us did. Only problem is, him and Julius got themselves caught. Well, Emile got hisself caught. Julius didn't exactly get caught 'cause what he done was get hisself kilt."

"I say he's your brother. If you want to take a chance on gettin' him out, then it's your problem, not ours," Short added.

"Unless Emile starts talking," Johnny said. "Then he becomes ever'body's problem."

"You know Emile better'n any of us. You think he is liable to start talkin' do you?" Short asked.

"You heard what the man said. Once they build the gallows, who knows what Emile will do?"

"All right, maybe you got a point there. You got 'ny ideas on how to do it?"

"Like I said, we need about three, maybe four, more men."

"I can get Jim and Leroy Blunt," Short said.

"Who are they?"

"Just a couple of men I know, is all. They're good men too, but they ain't goin' to do it for free, and I sure don't feel like dividin' up any more of my money."

"Do you think you could get them for two hundred fifty dollars?"

"Is that two hundred fifty together, or apiece? If it is two hundred fifty for the both of 'em, I'm not sure I could. But if it's two hundred fifty dollars for each one of 'em, why then, I reckon I could get 'em. But where we goin' to come up with the money? Like I said, I ain't givin' up any of mine."

"Two hundred fifty apiece, and I'll take the money out of Emil's share," Johnny said.

"Do you think you could come up with another two hundred fifty dollars? Because if you can, I'm pretty sure I can get my cousin, Ike Thomas, to come in with us," Evans suggested.

"All right, good. Al, you get them two you was talkin' about, and Bart, you get your cousin. Like I said, I'll come up with the extra money from Emile's share. After all, he's the one we're tryin' to save, here."

"So, after we get the extra men, what are we going to do? I mean, if you're plannin' on stormin' the jailhouse, well, you can just do it without me, even if we do have more men with us," Calhoun said.

"No, I don't have anything like that in mind," Johnny said.

"So, what do you have in mind?"

"I don't know yet. Let me think about it for a while."

"We goin' to get us some whores while you're thinkin' about it?" Short asked.

"Hell yes, we are. That's one of the reasons

we come into town, ain't it?" Evans asked.

"What do you mean one of the reasons?" Calhoun quipped. "Hell, that's the only reason I come to town."

The others laughed.

"Then it looks to me like we're goin' to have to move down to the Wild Hog," Short said.

"I agree," Johnny said. "But I've always found that I enjoy women better when I'm doin' it with a full stomach. And right now, I'm thinkin' I'd like to get myself a steak and some taters."

"Yeah, me too," Calhoun said. "Them women ain't goin' nowhere. And a steak and taters sounds mighty damn good."

"Seein' as you are the richest one of us, maybe you'll be buyin' our supper," Evans suggested.

"We all came into town with the same amount of money in our pockets," Johnny said. "And I done bought you all a drink."

"He's right, Bart. Don't be so damn cheap," Calhoun said.

After having drinks at Fiddler's Green, and generally enjoying themselves, in large part because of the satisfaction of knowing they were in plain sight of the very people who were looking for them, Johnny Taylor, Clay

Calhoun, Bart Evans, and Al Short were now gathered at the City Cafe to have dinner. They were finalizing their plans for the rest of the evening, those plans being that after their meal they would go down to the Wild Hog and get women for the entire night.

"I don't think I've ever spent a whole night with a whore before," Short said. "What's it like?"

"What do you mean, what's it like? You've been with a whore before, ain't you?" Calhoun asked.

"Yeah, but after you — uh — do it, what then? I mean, onliest time I've ever been with a whore before after I do it, well, I can't do it no second time."

"Sure you can," Calhoun said. "All you have to do is rest for a while, then the next thing you know, why, you're ready all over again."

"Ha!" Short said. "Ha! Yeah, that's prob'ly right, ain't it."

"Hell yes, it's right. I've done it lots of times," Calhoun said.

"Johnny," Evans said. "Johnny, look over there at the door. Look who's a-comin' in."

"Damn, that's the fella we saw in the bank, remember?" Calhoun said.

"Yeah, and from what I've heard today,

153

he's also the one that kilt Julius and shot Emile," Evans said.

"And here the son of a bitch is, walkin' around just as bold as you please," Short said.

"He ain't goin' to be walkin' around long, if I have my way about it," Short said.

"Look at 'im, Johnny. You ain't even looked," Evans said.

"I seen 'im," Johnny said as he continued to stare at the food on his plate. "Don't nobody be starin' at him now. The whole trick about hidin' out is not drawin' attention to yourself."

"Yeah, well, we shoulda kilt the son of a bitch when we had the chance, if you ask me," Short said.

"We'll be gettin' the chance soon enough," Johnny promised.

Because of the bank robbery this morning, as well as all the commotion that had come immediately afterward, Duff and Meagan had had to postpone their luncheon date, but they were making up for it by having dinner together tonight at the City Café.

"Hello, Mr. MacCallister, Miss Parker," the maître d' said effusively. Quinton Collier had been a maitre d' at Delmonico's in New York and when Norman Lambert, who owned the City Café, had visited New York, he'd been so impressed by the maître d' that he'd hired him on the spot. It had done wonders for his business, for Collier was always dressed in a suit, and he brought just the right degree of snobbery to the restaurant to make it appear upper class.

"What's good tonight, Mr. Collier?" Duff asked.

"That's a trick question, Mr. MacCallister," Collier said. "Everything here is good, you know that."

Duff chuckled. "Aye, I'll nae be arguing with that, now."

"I was in the kitchen and the cook just brought out a nice buffalo hump roast. You might want to try that."

"Buffalo hump roast, is it? Well, that sounds good. I'll try that."

"I will, as well," Meagan said. She laughed.

"And would you be for tellin' me, lass, what it is that you find funny?"

"Sure 'n' 'tis the thought of a Scotsman like yourself eating buffalo," Meagan said, perfectly imitating his brogue.

"Mocking me 'tis a cruel thing," Duff said.

"But you are so easy to mock," Meagan said, and she was rewarded with a broad smile.

"And as for eating buffalo hump, I've nae spent m' entire life in Scotland, now. I've eaten things that would turn the stomach of a buzzard."

"You're not putting buffalo hump in that category, are you?"

"I'll wait and see how it tastes."

"It's quite good, actually," Meagan said.

"So, tell me, lass, did you finish the dress for Mrs. Guthrie?" Duff asked.

"I did. It's beautiful," Meagan said.

"Sure now 'n' I hope the dress is beautiful, because you can nae say the same thing for Mrs. Guthrie."

"Duff!" Meagan said, slapping his hand across the table, though she ameliorated the slap by laughing as she did so. "You are awful! Juanita Guthrie is a very attractive woman."

Duff joined her in laughter. "Attractive, is she? Lass, you are choosing kindness over honesty. Sure 'n' if you were to tell the truth, you' be for admitting that Mrs. Guthrie is not what one would call a winsome lass."

"But Cindy is," Meagan said.

"Cindy?" The smile on Duff's face was replaced by an expression of surprise. "And why would you be for bringing up her name, I'm asking you."

Meagan chuckled. "Don't play coy with me, Mr. Duff MacCallister. You know full well that you find her to be a most attractive woman."

"Aye, that I do," Duff confessed. "And how can I not be thinkin' Cindy is pretty, when 'tis like my own dear Skye, she looks. But, lass, that is as far as it goes."

Meagan reached across the table again, but this time it wasn't to slap Duff's hand. This time it was to lay her hand on his.

"Yes, from the way you have described Skye, I thought Cindy might look like her," Meagan said.

"Meagan, 'tis nae need for you to be jealous, now," Duff said.

"I'm not in the least jealous, Duff MacCallister. I know why you may feel attracted to her."

"I am nae attracted to her. I was drawn to her looks only, lass. 'Tis as if she is a living likeness, but that is all."

"I understand, Duff MacCallister. And I like to think that our relationship is secure enough that no explanation is necessary."

"And 'tis probably wrong of me to so often bring up Skye's name in front of you."

"Don't be silly, it isn't wrong at all. You loved Skye, dearly. Can't you see that that is one of the things I find most endearing

157

about you? When a man commits himself heart and soul to a woman, it is only natural that the love doesn't go away just because the woman has died."

"You're a good woman for knowin' that, Meagan."

As Duff sat at the table with Meagan, his attention was drawn to another table in the restaurant, one that was occupied by four men.

"Meagan, don't look directly, but there are four men at that table in the corner. Would you be for knowing any of them?"

Meagan dropped her napkin, and as she bent down to retrieve it, she looked at the four men Duff had mentioned.

"I don't think I have ever seen any of them before," she said. "Why do you ask?"

"I don't know," Duff replied. "There's just something about them that seems a mite curious. But I can nae put m' finger on the why of it."

CHAPTER THIRTEEN

After finishing their meal the bank robbers had gone to the Wild Hog Saloon, where at the moment the four men, Johnny, Evans, Calhoun, and Short, were occupying a table with three women: Kathy, Annie, and Betty. Short was the one who was without a female companion.

"We need us another whore," Short said.

Kathy, one of the three girls who was sitting at the table, frowned. "If you want a whore, you might try one of the cribs outside," she said.

"Wait a minute. Ain't you done said that you women was goin' to spend the night with us?" Short said. "Why do you think we come here instead of Fiddler's Green if it wasn't for that here you can take the women up to their rooms?"

"Not if you use that kind of language, you can't."

"What kind of language is that?"

"You said you needed another whore. We aren't whores."

"Well, dammit, if you ain't whores, just what is you would call yourself? What kind of language is it that you're a-wantin' me to use?"

"We are ladies of the evening. Hostesses, who allow gentlemen to engage our services," she said.

"You tell 'em, Kathy," Betty said.

"All right, well, we need another one of them ladies of the evenin' who will let us engage her services," Short said.

"That's more like it," Kathy said, allowing the smile to return to her face. "Suzie will be here soon."

"That's what you said a while ago, only she ain't here yet," Short said. "What's takin' her so long?"

"Relax, cowboy," Annie said. "You've got all night."

"Yeah," Short said with a ribald smile. "Yeah, that's true, ain't it? I got all night."

"Only it ain't goin' to take me all night," Evans said.

"Me neither," Short added. "I'll bet you I'll be about the quickest you ever seen."

The three women exchanged smiles.

"How long has it been since you have been with a woman?" Betty asked.

"A long time," Short said. "It's been so long since I had me a woman that I don't hardly even remember."

"Well," Kathy said. "That doesn't speak well of the woman you were with. We promise you, you will remember tonight. Right, ladies?"

"Right," the other two said.

"Son of a bitch, if you don't quit talkin' about it, I ain't likely to even make it up to the bed," Short said.

The women laughed again.

Duff walked Meagan home from the restaurant.

"I have a bottle of Scotch in my apartment, if you would like a drink before your long ride out to your ranch," Meagan invited.

"Scotch, is it? 'Tis good to see that you have learned to appreciate the drink."

Meagan chuckled. "I have no appreciation for it whatsoever," she said. "But I know you have a taste for it, so I keep some for you. I'll have a glass of wine."

Meagan led the way up the outside stairs, then unlocked the door to her apartment. Just inside the door was a lantern, and she lit it, filling the room with a golden bubble of light.

"How are my cattle doing?" Meagan asked. She had recently invested some money in the ranch, so she was now half owner of the outstanding herd of Black Angus cattle that populated the fields of Sky Meadow.

"My cattle are growing fat, while yours are growing thin," Duff replied.

"How do you know which cattle are mine and which are yours?"

"Because yours are thin," Duff said, laughing.

"You may be Scot instead of Irish, but you do have a bit of the blarney in you," Meagan said.

Meagan put two fingers of Scotch into a tumbler, then poured wine for herself. Carrying the drinks over to the settee, she handed Duff his drink, then sat beside him. The amber fluid in Duff's glass caught the light from the lantern and glowed as if lit from within.

"Is it true that the robbers got all the money?" Meagan asked.

"Aye. Over forty thousand dollars."

"Thankfully, I keep half of my money in a bank down in Cheyenne," Meagan said. "I've always believed the old adage, you shouldn't put all your eggs in one basket."

"Aye, 'tis a good policy to follow," Duff

said. "I've not lost as much as some of the others in town . . . Mr. Matthews, Mr. Guthrie. Even Biff was hurt by the robbery."

They talked a while longer, speaking of cattle and business, sharing stories from their past and talking of mutual friends, such as Elmer and Vi. But there were always, just beneath their conversation, words that were not spoken, words that Meagan so wanted to say and wanted to hear even more.

But if he didn't speak how he felt about her, he did let it be known by the way he looked at her, the way he treated her, and his occasional touches, intimate without being compromising. And for now, Meagan was satisfied to take what she could from him.

Duff finished his drink, then put the glass down and stood up. She stood as well.

"I'd best get back to the ranch," he said, starting toward the door. She went with him, and just before he left, he put his finger to her chin, then turned her face toward his so that they were but a breath apart. "Take care, Meagan, that you not put yourself in danger. I don't know what I would do if something should happen to you."

"I am always careful," she said.

Still holding his finger under her chin,

Duff leaned forward, closing the distance between them. He kissed her, not hard and demanding, but as soft as the brush of a butterfly's wing.

When the kiss ended, Meagan reached up to touch her own lips, and she held her fingers there for a long moment. She knew that the kiss had sealed no bargain, nor, by it, had he made any promise to her. It was what it was, a light, meaningless kiss.

No, it wasn't meaningless. She had very strong feelings for Duff, and she knew that he had strong feelings for her. She knew, too, that it wasn't because his heart was too full of Skye. He had told her that he had accepted her death, was ready to get on with his life, and Meagan believed him. But what he wasn't ready to do was love another woman, then lose her as he had lost Skye. Meagan knew that was what he meant when he said, *"Take care, Meagan, that you not put yourself in danger. I don't know what I would do if something should happen to you."*

With a smile and a nod, Duff walked down the steps, mounted his horse, and rode away. She stayed on her balcony, watching him until he disappeared in the dark. Overhead, a meteor streaked through the night sky.

■ ■ ■ ■

Three blocks away, upstairs in the Wild Hog Saloon, Johnny Taylor lay in bed staring at the moon shadows on the ceiling. Finally, he sat up and looked back at the whore who was sleeping beside him. She was snoring loudly as she inhaled, and her lips were flapping as she exhaled.

Provocative clothing, the artful use of makeup, subdued lighting, and the effect of a generous consumption of liquor had made Kathy sexually appealing downstairs in the saloon. But now, a little line of spittle hung from her lips, and the cover was down, exposing a large, pillow-like breast that was lined with blue veins, and much of her sexual appeal was gone.

Johnny got up in the middle of the night and, leaving the whore in bed behind him, went downstairs and let himself out into the dark. He wasn't sure exactly what time it was, but he knew that it was after midnight. The town was exceptionally quiet, too late even for late-night revelry from any of the saloons. He walked down the street, staying on the boardwalk close against the buildings, lost in the shadows.

Locating the marshal's office, he walked

across the street, then went between two buildings into the alley behind the jail. He could smell the pungent odor of the several outhouses that lined the alley. He was startled when the door of a nearby outhouse slammed shut and, looking toward it, he saw a man, wearing a sleeping gown, scurrying back into his house.

Johnny stood quietly in the shadows for a moment longer until he was calm again, and then he picked up a rock and tossed it in through the barred window. When he got no response, he tossed another one through, then another one.

"Stop throwin' them rocks in through the winder!" Emile shouted angrily from inside.

"Keep it down, Emile," Johnny called out in a harsh whisper.

A moment later Emile's face appeared in the window. "Johnny? Was that you throwin' them rocks?"

"Yes, that was me — who'd you think it was? Now keep it quiet," Johnny said again.

"I know'd all along that you was goin' to be a-comin' for me," Emile said. "How are you goin' to do it?"

"I ain't quite come up with a way, yet. But I'll get you out of here."

"You better get me out. They're talkin' about hangin' me, Johnny. I heard the deputy say they was goin' to start in a-buildin' the gallows in the next day or so."

"You ain't had no trial yet, have you?"

"No, there ain't been no trial."

"Well, they ain't goin' to hang you 'til they have a trial and find you guilty, so that gives me some time to come up with some idea about gettin' you out."

"You're goin' to do it, ain't you, Johnny? Get me out, I mean. 'Cause I tell you the truth, I'll do whatever I have to, to stop from hangin'."

"Don't you go talkin' to nobody about anything, you hear me."

"Well, you just get me out, is all I got to say."

"If I can't get you out before the trial, I'll get you a real good lawyer. We've got lots of money now. I hung on to your share for you. The others wanted to go ahead and divide it up, but I wouldn't let 'em do it."

"You're a good brother, Johnny. Just don't let me hang."

"Who you talkin' to back there, Emile?" Johnny heard a voice call from the front of the building.

"I ain't talkin' to nobody, 'ceptin' myself," Emile replied as Johnny darted quickly down the alley, then up between the hardware store and the apothecary.

CHAPTER FOURTEEN

When Johnny returned to the room, he saw, in the moonlight, several sheets of stationery on the chest of drawers and that gave him an idea. Lighting a candle, he wrote a note, then folded it double and blew out the candle.

The whore was still sleeping, so he slipped out for one more errand. Moving stealthily through the dark, he found the office of the *Chugwater Defender,* the town's only newspaper. Looking around to make certain he wasn't seen, he slipped the note under the front door.

When he came back in this time, he woke up Kathy.

"Where you been, honey?" she asked. "I thought you'd done run out on me."

"I went out back to take a piss," Johnny said.

"Well, my goodness, you didn't have to do that. I've got a chamber pot, right here in the room."

"I don't like to piss in front of a woman."

Kathy laughed. "Honey, after last night, I've done seen ever'thing you've got, and you've seen ever'thing I've got, so why get so bashful all of a sudden?"

"It's just the way I am," Johnny said.

"We still got a couple of hours 'til daylight," she said. "You comin' back to bed?"

"Yeah, I might as well."

"You got 'nything left for me?" she asked. "You did pay for all night, you know."

Johnny smiled. "Yeah," he said. "Yeah, I reckon I got somethin' left for you."

The next morning Johnny was awakened by a knock on the door.

"Go away!" Johnny called, sleepily. Angrily, groggily, he threw one of his shoes, and it hit the door with a loud thump, then slid to the floor.

"Damn, Johnny," Al Short called through the door. "You still a-goin' at it in there? Whooee, if you are, you got to be some kind of a man."

Short's calls awakened Johnny, and he got out of bed to go relieve himself. Remembering that the whore had said she had a chamber pot, he pulled it out from under the bed, then began to pee, actually manag-

169

ing to get some of it into the pot.

"Hold on, hold on, I'm takin' a piss in here!" he said. "Quit makin' such a racket."

"Can we come in?"

Johnny padded over to the door barefoot, and in his long johns. By now Kathy was awake as well, and when she saw four men coming in to her bedroom, she suddenly got shy and jerked the quilt up to cover her naked breasts.

"Damn!" Evans said. "Your'n sure has got bigger tits than mine did."

Johnny started putting on his pants.

"What are you doin' in here so early?" he asked.

"It ain't all that early, Johnny," Calhoun said. "It's damn near nine o'clock, and we was gettin' hungry for breakfast."

"All right," Johnny said, pulling on his boots. He put on his shirt and tucked it down into his trousers, then strapped on his gun. "Let's go get somethin' to eat."

"Will I see you again, Johnny?" the whore asked.

Quickly, and unexpectedly, Johnny turned and swung a wicked backhand slap at her. The slap popped loudly, and Kathy cried out and put her hand to her lip, which began to bleed.

"Who give you permission to call me

that?" he asked. "That ain't my name, any-how."

"I — I didn't mean nothin' by it," she said, her voice quaking with fear. "I just heard them callin' you that, so I figured that was your name. I was just tryin' to be friendly, is all."

"Well, you heard it wrong. What they called me was Donnie. That's my name, ain't it boys?"

"Yeah, Donnie," Calhoun said. "That's what I called him. I called him Donnie, I didn't call him Johnny."

"So you just forget that name, you hear me?" Johnny challenged.

"Yes, sure, Donnie, of course I will. I'm sorry I made a mistake callin' you the wrong thing. I didn't know it would make you so mad."

Johnny looked at her for a moment, and then he took out his wallet and pulled out a twenty-dollar bill and gave it to her.

"What's this for?" she asked. "It only cost three dollars for the whole night and you done give that to me."

"This is just my way of tellin' you I'm sorry I hit you," Johnny said. "I didn't have no call to do that."

A broad smile spread across her face. "That's all right, Donnie," she said. "I

171

shouldn't have made you mad. It was all my fault."

"Come on, boys. Let's get some breakfast," Johnny said. As they left, Kathy held the twenty-dollar bill out, staring at it as if unable to believe her luck.

The four men did not return to the City Café, but took their breakfast of biscuits, bacon, and coffee downstairs in the Wild Hog Saloon.

"You know what? We shoulda maybe et our breakfast over to the City Café," Short suggested. "I bet you we could get us a pile of pancakes over there, and I can't hardly remember the last time I had me a pile of pancakes."

"We don't have time," Johnny said. "We've got to be out of town before the newspaper comes out."

"Before the newspaper comes out? What for?" Evans asked.

"On account of 'cause they's goin' to be a letter in the newspaper that's goin' to set this town on its ear. Only, for it to work good, we're goin' to have to be clean out of town."

"What does the letter say?" Evans asked.

Looking up, Johnny saw a boy of about

twelve come into the saloon, carrying a stack of newspapers. The boy put a few of the new papers down, then picked up the remainder of the older papers. That done, he took money out of a can, then went on to the next stop on his route.

"The paper's out," Johnny said, getting up from the table. "We'd best be getting on our way."

"I ain't finished my breakfast yet," Short protested.

"Take your biscuit and bacon with you," Johnny said.

"I ain't drunk my coffee yet."

Johnny picked up Short's cup of coffee, then carried it over and poured the rest of it into a spittoon.

"What coffee?" he asked

On the way out, Johnny grabbed a newspaper, and left a coin in the can. Not until they were a good distance out of town, did they stop long enough for the others to read the paper.

TO THE EDITOR:

To the marshal and them what live in Chugwater, this here is a warning. Let my brother Emile go. If you don't let him go, you will be sorry because I will

173

do anything I have to do until you set him free.

JOHNNY TAYLOR

"Damn, Johnny, what for did you write that? I mean you done told 'em your name and ever'thing," Calhoun said.

"They already knew my name. And I done this to make 'em scared about what might happen if they don't let Emile go."

"What will happen?" Evans asked.

"I don't know, I ain't figured it out yet," Johnny admitted.

Less than one hour after the letter appeared, Marshal Ferrell showed up at the office of the *Chugwater Defender* with the paper in his hand, folded in such a way as to highlight the letter.

"Charley, let me ask you something. Why in the Sam Hill did you print this?" Ferrell demanded.

"It's news," Blanton replied. "And my job is to print the news."

"Yeah, well, your job isn't to print demands from outlaws, is it?"

"It is, if it is news," Blanton argued.

"This here isn't news," Ferrell said, emphasizing his comment by shaking the newspaper.

"It might not be good news, and as you said, it might even be a demand from outlaws, but it is news," Blanton insisted. "And as long as I'm editor of the *Defender,* and unless you have taken it upon yourself to overthrow my right of freedom of the press, then I intend to print anything I find newsworthy."

"Get down off your high horse, Charley," Marshal Ferrell said. "I'm not challenging your right to freedom of the press."

"I didn't think you would," Blanton said.

"I would like to find out about this letter to the editor though. Where was it mailed from? Can I see the postmark?"

Blanton shook his head. "You can't see the postmark because there isn't any."

"What do you mean, there isn't any? Where did you get that letter then if it wasn't mailed to you?"

"When I came to work this morning, I found a piece of paper folded over and shoved under the front door. I unfolded it, and there was the letter."

"May I see the letter, please?" Ferrell asked.

"Yeah, I don't see why not," Blanton replied. "I left it back in the composing room."

Blanton went back to the composing

room, where he found the little piece of paper lying alongside the drawers of type.

"Here it is," he said, coming back to the front with the paper in his hand. He held it out toward the marshal, who took it from him.

"Hmm," Ferrell said, pointing to something at the top of the page. "I wonder what this is."

"What?"

"This little curve mark here, at the top of the page. It looks like there was a picture of something there that got torn off."

Blanton examined the paper more closely, then he chuckled. "I'll be damned," he said. "I don't know why I didn't notice it before, but I know exactly what that is."

"You do?"

"I do indeed."

"Then what is it?

"It is the bottom part of a pig's foot. The Wild Hog Saloon has stationery with the symbol of a Wild Hog on the top," Blanton said. "The reason I know this is because I'm the one that printed up the stationery for Mr. Jones."

"You're sure?"

"Damn right, I'm sure. I told you, I'm the one printed it up in the first place. And look here, you see this tiny skip here in the bottom part of the pig's foot? That's 'cause it was that way in the woodcut."

"Interesting," Marshal Ferrell said.

"More than interesting, I would say. I think it means that whoever sent this letter is more than likely over at the Wild Hog," Blanton said.

"Not necessarily," Ferrell said. "But seein' as this paper for sure came from there, then it is a lead."

Chapter Fifteen

"The bank takes our money, then uses it to make loans and such, and that's how they make money. So I say if a bank is robbed, they ought to pay us whatever it is we lost," a baldheaded man with a white shirt and red suspenders said. This was Nippy Jones, owner of the saloon, and he was talking to his bartender.

"But where are they goin' to get the money, Mr. Jones?" the bartender asked. "I mean, if they got all the money took away from 'em, then they don't have no money to pay none of the rest of us back."

"That's their problem, where they get the money," Jones said. Looking around, he saw Marshal Ferrell and Charley Blanton coming into his establishment.

"Well, well, the press and the law," he said, smiling. "What can I do for you gentlemen?"

"Did you read the letter to editor in my

paper this morning?" Blanton asked.

"You mean the one from the brother of the bank robber?" Jones asked. "Yeah, I seen it."

"It was written on a piece of your stationery," Marshal Ferrell said.

"What? Wait a minute, you aren't tryin' to say I wrote it, are you?" Jones asked.

"No, but someone you gave the stationery to, did."

"I ain't give no stationery to nobody," Nippy Jones said.

"You agree with me that this piece of stationery came from here, don't you?" Ferrell asked, showing Jones the letter.

"Not so's I can tell" Jones replied. "What makes you think it came from here?"

"Nippy," Ferrell said, speaking less forcefully than he had been before. "I'm not accusing you of anything, and you aren't in any kind of trouble. I'm just trying to get to the bottom of this is all. I want you to look at the paper again and tell me if you recognize it."

"I told you, that I don't think it came from here. All my stationery has a Wild Hog on top. Hell, you know that, Charley. You're the one who printed 'em up for me."

"May I see that?" the bartender asked.

Ferrell showed the piece of paper to the

179

bartender, and he looked at for a moment. "It's from here, all right," he said. "I cut the tops off of the stationery when I give some of 'em to her, so's she wouldn't be writin' nothin' that might embarrass the saloon."

"Who are you talkin' about? Who did you give the stationery to?" Ferrell asked.

"I give some to Kathy. I'm sorry, Mr. Jones, I never said nothin' to you about it, but I didn't think it would matter none. I mean you got a whole lot more 'n you'll prob'ly ever use."

"That's all right, Jack. You shoulda told me about it, but it's all right."

"Have you had any strangers come in here, lately?" Marshal Ferrell asked.

"No, not that I can recall. 'Cept maybe them fellas with the new hats and shirts."

"New hats and shirts? What are you talking about?"

"It's the damndest thing. Four of 'em there was, and they was all four of 'em wearin' brand-new hats and brand-new shirts. They was here yesterday. Good customers, too. They bought drinks all day, played cards, then all four of 'em took a girl upstairs for the night."

"All four of them with one girl?" Ferrell asked, surprised by the comment.

Jones laughed. "Now, that truly would be

somethin', wouldn't it? I mean one girl with four men, all at the same time? No, sir, I didn't mean it the way it sounds. They each one had 'em a girl."

"Was Kathy one of them?"

"Yes, why?"

"I was just wondering. I mean, Jack said he gave some of the stationery to Kathy."

"Yes, sir, that's what I done, all right," Jack said.

"Is Kathy here today? I'd like to speak to her," Ferrell said.

"Yeah, sure, that's her back there," Jones said. "Kathy?"

The young woman was bending over a table talking to a couple of customers, and she looked up when Jones called.

"Would you come here, please?"

"What ya need?"

"The marshal wants to talk to you."

Kathy looked at the marshal quizzically.

"Kathy, Nippy tells me you took a man to your room last night."

"I ain't done nothin' wrong," Kathy said, defensively. "The city says we can whore long as we do our whorin' in the same place of business."

"That's not what I want to talk about," Marshal Ferrell said. "Nippy tells me that the man you took upstairs with you was a stranger in town."

"Yeah, he was one of the men with a new hat and shirt," Kathy said.

"Tell me about him."

"Nothin' to tell," Kathy said. "We just — uh — did it, then we went to sleep."

"Did you notice anything unusual about him?" Ferrell asked.

Kathy smiled. "No, he was pretty much like ever' other man I've slept with," she said. "Him an' his friends left this mornin'. After he peed all over my floor."

"Peed on your floor?" Ferrell asked, confused by the remark.

"Yeah, he was aimin' for the chamber pot. Which I guess *is* strange when you think about it, 'cause last night in the middle of the night he went out in the alley to pee 'cause he said he didn't want to pee in front me. But last night it was dark and I couldn't even have seen him. This mornin' it was broad daylight, and it didn't seem to bother him none."

"How long was he gone when he left in the middle of the night?" Ferrell asked.

"I don't know, 'cause I was asleep when he left. He woke me up when he come back in."

"Did he say anything?"

"A few things now and then, yeah," Kathy

said. "But we didn't talk a whole lot. I mean he wasn't payin' me to talk, if you know what I mean."

Ferrell noticed that Kathy's lip was swollen and bore the scar of a recent cut. He put his finger on her lip and she winced as he touched it.

"That hurt?" Ferrell asked.

"Yes."

"When did it happen?"

"I — I don't know," Kathy said.

"How can you have a cut lip all swollen like that, still hurting, and you don't know when it happened?"

Kathy didn't answer.

"He hit you, didn't he?"

"Yeah," Kathy said. "But he didn't mean nothin' by it, and he apologized. Besides which, he give me twenty dollars to make up for it."

"Hold it!" Ferrell said. "He gave you twenty dollars?"

"He sure did."

"Gold, or paper money?"

"It was paper money, but that spends just as good."

"Why did he hit you?"

"Because of somethin' I said. Like I told you, it was my fault."

"What did you say to him?"

"Well, it ain't so much what I said, as to what I called him."

Ferrell smiled. "You called him a son of a bitch, did you?"

"No, I called him Johnny."

The smile left Ferrell's face. "He hit you because you called him Johnny?"

"Yeah. I thought sure one of the others called him Johnny, so that's what I called him, and it made him mad, so he hit me. He said his name was Donnie."

"Donnie?"

"That's what he said. But . . ."

"But what?"

"I'm sure the other man called him Johnny. I just don't know why he got so upset about it."

"Kathy, do you have any of Wild Hog stationery in your room?" Ferrell asked.

"Yeah, I do." She looked at Jones. "I didn't steal it, Nippy. Jack, he give it to me. Anyhow, it wasn't some of the good stationery. The picture of the Wild Hog couldn't be seen."

"That's all right, Kathy. I know about it, and I don't mind."

"I didn't think you would mind, or I wouldn't 'a took it."

"Where do you keep it?" Ferrell asked.

"I've got ten sheets of it left up on my

184

dresser."

"Ten sheets? You mean you know exactly the number of sheets you have?"

"Yes. I've been keepin' a count of it."

"Would you mind if I went up with you and counted it?"

Kathy laughed. "Now, Marshal, what's Mrs. Ferrell goin' to say when folks tell her they seen you 'n' me goin' up the stairs together?"

Marshal Ferrell chuckled as well. "You've got a point," he said. "All right, would you do me a favor? Go up and count the number of pieces of the stationery you have left, then come back down and tell me."

"All right," Kathy said.

"Marshal, what's this all about?" Jones asked after Kathy left to respond to Marshal Ferrell's request.

"There were six men took part in the bank robbery yesterday," Marshal Ferrell said. "Four of them got away. I'm sure one of them was Emile Taylor's brother, Johnny. And I think he, and they, came back to town to have a look around."

"That's kind of bold of 'em, ain't it? I mean to come back into town right after they held up the bank?"

"Not when you stop to think about it. They were all wearing masks so nobody could see their faces, and they were all wearing long dusters, so nobody could see what kind of clothes they actually had on. They could have come back to town and nobody would have been the wiser."

At that moment Kathy came back down with an expression of surprise on her face.

"You only had nine sheets of stationery left, didn't you?" Marshal Ferrell asked.

"Yeah," Kathy said. "But I don't understand. I was sure I had ten. How did you know there would only be nine?"

"Because I've got one of them," Ferrell said, showing the letter to Kathy.

"Yes," Kathy said. "That's one of them all right. All ten were torn at the top so that only the bottom part of the pig's foot shows."

"Damn," Jones said. "You think Johnny Taylor is still in town?"

"I doubt it," Marshal Ferrell said. "I think he came back to check on his brother, and to see if there was any way he could break him out of jail."

"There ain't, is there?"

"Have you ever heard the saying, forewarned is forearmed?" Blanton asked.

"No, I don't think I have," Jones said. "What does that mean?"

"It means there's not a chance Johnny

Taylor is going to break his brother out of jail," Marshal Ferrell said.

CHAPTER SIXTEEN

He was called Harper, and though his first name was Vernon, nobody ever used it. He was tall, rawhide thin, with a handlebar moustache and hair that hung to his shoulders. He was sitting in a saloon in Cheyenne, drinking coffee and playing a game of solitaire, when someone at the bar yelled at him.

"Harper!"

The man who yelled was young, with blond hair and blue eyes.

Harper didn't respond to the summons.

"Harper! I'm callin' you out, you son of a bitch!" the young man said.

Harper made one more play, then put the cards facedown on the table and looked back at the man.

"Are you speaking to me?" he asked. His voice was soft and sibilant, barely loud enough to be heard, but as frightening as the hiss of a rattlesnake.

"Yes, I'm speaking to you," the young man said. "My name is Blake Toomey. Does that mean anything to you?"

"I can't say that it does."

"I don't expect you to remember me," Toomey said. "I was only twelve years old the last time we met. That is, if you could call it meeting. I watched you kill my pa and I swore then that some fine day I would find you, and I would kill you." He patted the handle of his gun. "I've been practicing for six years, and this is that day."

"Boy, you need to learn not to get involved in other people's fights unless you're getting paid for it," Harper said.

"Like you were paid to kill my pa?"

"I'm sure I must have been paid for it," Harper said. "I don't kill for free."

"You son of a bitch! You don't even remember him, do you?" Toomey said, shouting so loud that spittle was flying from his mouth.

"I'm not sure that I do."

"Have you killed so many men that you can't even keep track of it?"

"Something like that," Harper said.

"Well, it ends today," Toomey said.

Until this moment, Harper had been sitting down, but now he stood up and stepped away from the table. Because he was so thin,

189

the gun hanging low from his right side seemed almost big enough to tip him off balance.

"So now you are planning to kill me?"

"I'm not just planning on doin' it, I'm goin' to do it," Toomey said.

"Go away, Toomey. I don't kill boys, not even for money. And I especially don't want to kill one for free."

"You think I'm not good enough for you, don't you? You think I don't know how to handle a gun? Well, watch this, you son of a bitch!"

Toomey stepped up to the bar, empty now because the patrons who had been standing at the bar, like the others who had been sitting at the tables, had all moved to the sides of the saloon to be out of the line of fire, should the gun battle actually break out.

Toomey picked up a shot glass.

"I'm going to throw this glass into the air, and shoot it before it falls," he said.

The expression on Harper's face was unchanged.

"I know what you are thinking," Toomey said. "Lots of people can toss a glass into the air and shoot it. But how about this?"

Toomey picked up a second glass. "It's more than one glass," he said.

He picked up a third glass, and smiled,

broadly. "It's three glasses."

"Nobody can shoot three glasses before they come down," said one of the saloon patrons who had moved up against the wall.

Toomey tossed all three glasses into the air, then drew his pistol and fired three times, fanning the pistol so rapidly that they sounded as if they were one, sustained shot.

All three glasses were shattered before they came down, and the feat was greeted by several gasps of surprise, and exclamations of admiration.

Toomey put his pistol back in the holster, then looked at Harper with a triumphant smile. "What do you think about that?" he asked.

"I noticed none of the glasses were shooting back," Harper said.

"Still think I'm no more than a boy, Harper? Still think I'm not good enough for you?"

"Well now, you see, son, that's the problem," Harper said. "Goodness has nothing to do with it. In fact, it is that very goodness that is going to get you killed today."

"What are you talking about?" Toomey asked.

"Have you ever killed anyone?"

"Not yet, but I'm about to."

"Now me, I've killed so many men that,

like you said, I can't even remember all of them. I can kill a man like stepping on a bug. It means absolutely nothing to me," Harper said. "But now, take someone like you, a good man who has never killed anyone, when the time comes you are going to have just a slight hesitation. You see, it's an awesome thing to take another man's life. And it isn't always the fastest on the draw that wins. People like me, boy, we aren't good because we are fast. We are good because it doesn't bother us to kill, and we don't really care if we get killed. Now, do you still want to do this?"

"Yeah, I want to do it. I told you, I've waited six years to . . ."

That was as far as Toomey got before Harper drew his pistol and fired. His bullet hit Toomey in the chest and knocked him back against the bar. He got a surprised look on his face.

"You — you didn't even — that wasn't . . ." Toomey slid down to the floor, then sat there for a moment with his arms hanging limp and useless by his side.

"What were you going to say?" Harper asked. "That I didn't play fair? Killin's not a game, boy. Killin' is killin'. And it don't matter how fast you are if you never get around to pulling your gun."

Toomey fell to one side, then gave a last, life-surrendering sigh.

"Is there anyone here who didn't hear this boy threaten me?"

"We heard it, Mr. Harper," someone said. "We all heard it."

"We sure did," another patron said. "What you done was self-defense, pure and simple."

Harper leaned down and pulled the pistol out of Toomey's holster. Turning the cylinder, he ejected one bullet, then put it in his pocket. He stood there for a moment, then walked back over to his table to resume his card game. He started to take a sip of his coffee, then made a face and held the cup up.

"I need a fresh cup," he said.

"Yes, sir, Mr. Harper. Comin' right up," the bartender said.

Two city policemen came into the saloon then, both with guns drawn.

"What happened here?" one of them asked.

"This boy here challenged Harper," one of the patrons asked.

"That right, Harper?"

Harper studied his board, then put a red jack on a black queen before he answered.

"That's right," he said.

"This is the second killing you've been in this month," the other policeman pointed out.

"A man has a right to defend himself," Harper said.

"You seem to have an unusual number of people that you have to defend yourself against."

"I've made a few enemies in my day," Harper said.

"A few enemies? Mister, I've never known anyone with as many enemies as you have. If I were you, I'd go somewhere and change my name. One of these days the other man is going to win."

"That's the chance you take in our line of work," Harper replied.

"Our line of work?" the policeman challenged. "What do you mean, our line of work?"

"We're alike, you and I," Harper said. "You put people away that society has found undesirable. I do the same thing, but when I put someone away, it's permanent."

"All right," one of the two policemen said. "We're goin' to need some statements. We'll be sitting over there at that table, and would appreciate it if anyone who actually saw what happened would come talk to us."

As the rest of the patrons of the saloon

rushed over to the table to be certain that their stories got told, one man came over to speak with Harper.

"I saw you take a bullet from the boy's pistol," he said. "Why did you do that?"

"Because that bullet was meant for me," Harper said. "I collect bullets that were meant for me."

The man who asked the question was Johnny Taylor. His arrival at the saloon, no more than three minutes before it had all begun, had been most fortuitous, because it answered both questions Johnny had about Harper. Was he good? Well, he had proven that. And could he be hired? In his own words, he had stated that he would kill for money.

Johnny dropped a stack of money on the table in front of Harper.

Harper looked at the pile of money, but he didn't look up at Johnny.

"What is this?"

"It is two hundred and fifty dollars," Johnny said.

"Two hundred and fifty dollars for what?"

"Two hundred fifty dollars for a job I want you to do for me. And there will be another two hundred and fifty dollars when the job is done."

"What is the job?"

"It's the kind of job you specialize in," Johnny said.

Out at Sky Meadow, Duff was standing on the porch of his house, talking with Elmer Gleason.

"I'm sending some of the boys out tomorrow to bring in the unbranded calves," Elmer said. "We pulled two of them out of a bog today." He laughed. "They had mud from tailbone to nose hole. Took a while to clean 'em up."

"And 'tis betting, I am, that when they were finished, the calves were clean and the cowboys had mud from tailbone to nose hole," Duff said.

Elmer laughed again. "You got that right," he said. "Tell me, Duff, is it true that the bank robbers got more 'n forty thousand dollars?"

"Aye, including the three thousand I had just transferred."

"I had more'n a thousand dollars in there my ownself." He chuckled. "But I got me near ten thousand hid out in a sock. I'm glad I ain't never trusted banks all that much. I always figured out they was too easy to rob. 'Course, ever' now 'n' then it don't work out quite like you planned. I mind the time that Jesse James decided to hold up the bank up in Northfield, Minnesota.

"It was Bill Chadwell who suggested the idea, seein' as he was from Minnesota. He convinced Jesse that we could get in and out of the state real easy. Me 'n' Cole Younger and Frank James tried to talk Jesse out of it, but he was convinced we could pull it off.

"On the day of the robbery, we met outside of town to make our plans. We was supposed to break up into three groups, one to go inside the bank, one to stand guard outside of the bank, and one to cover the bridge, which was the way we was goin' to get out of town. Frank, Jesse, and Bob Younger went inside. Cole Younger and Clell Miller stayed just outside the bank, while me, Jim Younger, Charlie Pitts, and Bill Chadwell was to guard the bridge. We also decided that no citizen was to be killed, no matter what. If we was shot at by anyone, we was supposed to just shoot back to keep their heads down. We wasn't supposed to kill nobody."

Elmer was quiet for a moment.

"I've read about the Northfield bank robbery," Duff said. "It dinnae work out that way, did it?"

"No. The whole damn town got guns and started shootin' at us. We was butchered like hogs, Charlie Pitts, Clell Miller, and Bill Chadwell was all killed. Frank and the Younger brothers was bad shot up. Only ones not hit a'tall was me 'n' Jesse."

"And if what I read is correct, 'twas nae successful, for they dinnae get away with any money at all."

"Twenty-seven dollars," Elmer said. "The bank teller and one of the townspeople was kilt, and we lost three kilt, and all for twenty-seven dollars."

Elmer saw a grasshopper clinging to a weed and he spit, the wad of tobacco taking the grasshopper off. "That was the last time I ever done anythin' against the law," he said. "I never was much of a God-fearin' man until then, but I figured that was a message, and I'd better listen to it."

Duff smiled, and put his hand on his foreman's shoulder. " 'Tis glad I am that you've reformed," he said.

CHAPTER SEVENTEEN

Harper dismounted in front of Fiddler's Green, tied his horse off, then automatically lifted his pistol from the holster about an inch before dropping it back down. That kept the gun loose in the holster, making for a quicker, smoother draw.

Harper had been born in New York City. He had no idea who his father was, his mother was a prostitute who had died of puerperal fever three days after giving birth to her second illegitimate child. The child had died as well, and Harper, who was twelve years old at the time, had been on his own.

He'd earned a living by running errands for the criminal element of the Lower East Side of Manhattan, and he'd killed his first man when he was fourteen, taking the job for one hundred dollars. It had been exceptionally easy. Because he'd been only fourteen his target, Guido Costaconti, who had been himself an assassin, had taken no notice of the young towheaded and barefoot boy who'd been coming toward him, carrying a bag.

"What you got in that sack, boy?" Costaconti had asked. "It wouldn't be a piece of pie, would it? Yeah, I'll bet that's it. It's a piece of pie that your mama made for you, ain't it? I tell you what. You just give that pie to me, and that way I won't have to box your ears." Costaconti had laughed out loud.

Harper had walked up to within two feet of him, then reached his hand down into the bag.

"That's a good boy," Costaconti had said, holding his hand out. "Give it to me."

Harper had pulled a pistol from the bag, pointed it at Costaconti, and pulled the trigger. Costaconti had been dead before he'd even realized he was in danger.

Harper had gotten such a thrill from that killing that he would have done it for nothing, and over the next four years he'd become one of the most successful assassins in the city. He'd had to leave when the city got too hot for him.

He'd gone west and learned the art of the fast draw. Now he was very skilled at it, but, as he'd told young Toomey, being fast isn't the most important thing about being a gunfighter. The most important thing was to have a willingness, almost an eagerness, to kill. And that, Harper did have.

Now he was in Chugwater to kill Duff MacCallister. He had never seen Duff MacCallister, so he wouldn't be able to recognize him on sight. But he was told that MacCallister was a good friend to the owner of Fiddler's Green, so his plan was a simple one. He would wait here until MacCallister showed up.

His strange, brooding appearance was off-putting to all the bar girls except for one. He had bought drinks for Cindy Boyce at least three times during the day, though he'd had drunk nothing but coffee. Now he was sitting with Francis Schumacher.

"So, you know who I am," Harper said.

"I know. I used to be a lawman."

"That don't mean anything. I don't have any dodgers out on me."

Schumacher chuckled. "No, you don't," he said. "And I've always wondered how someone like you could avoid it."

"Someone like me?" Harper replied with a challenge to his voice.

"Yeah," Schumacher said, not backing down. "Someone like you. Someone who has the reputation you have, but has managed to stay off wanted posters."

"Because I've been careful," Harper said. "Very careful."

Schumacher glanced up at the clock, and saw that it was nearly two.

"I've got to go," he said. "I have a friend in jail, and the only time I can visit with him is between two and three in the afternoon."

"You used to be a lawman, and you have friend in jail?"

"Yeah," Schumacher answered. "Funny, ain't it?"

"How can you stand to sit at the same table with him?" Nell asked.

"He's no bother," Cindy said. "All he does is drink coffee and talk."

"There is something about him that frightens me," Nell said.

"And I don't trust a man who doesn't drink anything but coffee," Mattie said. "There's something mighty strange about that."

"Well, at least you don't have to worry about him getting drunk and angry," Cindy suggested with a smile.

"I don't know," Nell said. "I agree with Mattie. I'm not sure I trust someone who doesn't drink either."

"What does he talk about?" Mattie asked.

"He doesn't talk much at all," Cindy said. "I think he must be a friend of Mr. MacCallister's."

"Wait a minute," Nell said. "Are you saying he is a friend of Duff MacCallister?"

"I guess he is. He has asked about him a few times."

"I can't see someone like that being a friend of Duff MacCallister," Nell said.

"Me either," Mattie added.

"Well, all I know is he is looking for Duff MacCallister," Cindy said.

Out at Sky Meadow, the day's work was done, supper was over, and while several of the cowboys had ridden into town, there were three who stayed behind. One was lying on his bunk, while the other two were sitting across a small table playing cards. Dale and Ben were playing poker with Poke and Vaughan, two of the other cowboys who worked at the ranch. They were playing for pebbles, not for money, but that didn't lessen the intensity of their game. When one of them took the pot with a pair of aces, the other one complained.

"What the hell, Poke? How did you come up with that ace?" Dale asked.

"That was easy," Poke answered. "I just took it from Meacham's boot when he wasn't lookin'." Meacham was the one lying in the bunk.

"What do you mean? Are you saying Meacham keeps an ace in his boot?"

"Oh yeah," Poke said. "Meacham always has an ace in his boot. I ain't never know'd him to do anythin' honest when he could cheat. Ain't that right, Meacham?"

"That's right," Meacham answered without protest or embarrassment. "But don't let Poke fool you none, Dale. He's just as bad."

"Hell, Dale cheats as much as I do," Poke said.

Dale laughed. "I reckon we all cheat," he admitted. "It don't matter much if I get caught cheatin' for pebbles. But if I ever get real good at it, I'm goin' to go into one of them big gamblin' tables down in Cheyenne 'n' win my fortune."

"I wouldn't advise that," Poke replied. "Cheatin' among us, when we ain't playin' for nothing more 'n pebbles, is one thing. But cheatin' in a real game is liable to get a fella killed."

The cards were raked in, the deck shuffled, then dealt again.

"You think Mr. MacCallister will be able

to make our payroll this month?" Dale asked as he was dealing.

"Sure, why not?" Poke asked.

"Well, from what I heard, he had a lot of money in the bank that got stoled."

"Mr. MacCallister is a smart man," Meacham said. "It wouldn't surprise me none if he didn't have money in half a dozen banks."

"Lord, wouldn't it be good to have that much money?" Dale asked.

"No. When you got money, you got responsibility," Meacham said.

"What does that mean?" Dale asked.

"It means you got more 'n yourself to look out for. Now you take us. Only worry we got is where are we goin' to get our next meal. Well, that ain't no worry. Come mealtime we just walk over to the cook shack and eat. Where are we goin' to sleep? Well, this bunkhouse is here. We've each got a bunk, blankets, a pillow. We don't even have to furnish our own horse. And we get forty dollars ever' month.

"But where do all those things come from? They come from Mr. MacCallister. He had to build the cook shack, he has to keep it supplied with food, and he has to pay the cook.

"He had to build the bunkhouses, he had

to buy the beds, and in the wintertime he has to make sure we have enough wood to burn. He furnishes the horses we ride, and the tools we use. That's responsibility."

"Damn," Dale said when Meacham finished his lecture on responsibility. "I guess if you put it that way, I'm glad I don't have a lot of money."

"Where is Mr. MacCallister, tonight?" Poke asked.

"I don't know. I saw him ride out a while ago. He's goin' into town, I reckon," Dale said. He chuckled. "I've heard that he is sweet on that lady that owns the dress emporium."

"Yeah, well, have you ever seen her?" Meacham asked. "She is one pretty woman."

"Yeah, she is," Poke said. "I wish he would go ahead and marry her and bring her out here, so I'd have me a pretty woman to look at."

"What are you talkin' about?" Dale asked. "If he was to marry her, you wouldn't have no right to be a-lookin' at her."

"Hell, Dale, what are you sayin'? That I ain't got the right even to look at a pretty woman?" Poke asked.

"Oh," Dale said. "Well, I reckon if you put it that way, well, yeah, sure, you got the right to look at her. I mean as long as you know she ain't for you."

"She's a rich woman that owns her own business, and, from what Elmer says, has an interest in the cattle that's out here on the ranch. I make forty dollars a month and found. Do you think I don't know she ain't for me? Show me your hand."

Dale put down three nines, and, with a smile, Poke put down three queens.

"Damn," Dale said as he watched Poke rake in the pile of pebbles.

When Duff dismounted in front of Fiddler's Green, Biff met him on the front porch.

"Duff, before you go in, I think you should know that there's a man in there who has been asking about you," Biff said.

"Do you know him?"

"I don't know him, but someone told me that his name is Harper."

"Harper? And could you be for telling me if that his surname, or his Christian name?"

"I've never heard his first name, but I have heard of him, Duff. They say he is a hired killer. I don't like it that he is asking for you."

"And where would this gentlemen be sitting?"

"He's in the table nearest the stove. That way he can see the front and the rear door, and he is studying everyone who comes in."

"What about the stairs? If he is watching both doorways, he can nae also be watching the stairs."

"No, he can't see the stairs," Biff agreed. Biff smiled. "And there's a ladder lying on the ground behind the saloon. Climb up to the last window on the left. I know it isn't locked, and it opens onto the end of the upstairs landing."

Moving around to the back of the saloon, Duff saw the ladder Biff had told him about. It was lying in the weeds up against the back wall of the establishment. Duff leaned it up against the last window on the left, then climbed up.

Testing the window, he discovered that it wasn't locked, so he slid it up, then climbed in.

Walking toward the front, he stepped up to the banister that provided a safety rail between the upstairs landing, and the main floor below. Looking out over the room, he saw the man Biff was talking about. He studied him for a moment and saw the way he was sitting so as to provide quick access to his pistol. The man was staring intently at the only two entrances to the saloon.

Or, at least, he was watching the only two entrances he knew about. Harper had no idea that the man he was searching for so diligently had come into the saloon through a back window.

Duff started down the stairs, moving slowly, deliberately, and quietly. Within a moment, he was standing less than three feet behind Harper. That was when he noticed that Harper was drinking coffee only. He waited until Harper lifted the cup to his lips. That effectively occupied his gun hand.

"My name is Duff MacCallister," Duff said. "I am told that you are looking for me.

"What the hell?" Harper shouted. Standing up quickly and spinning around, Harper's hand dipped toward his pistol, but he never reached it. Duff was so close to him that he laid Harper out with one powerful punch. With Harper lying unconscious on the floor, Duff picked up his pistol, then searched him quickly for a second weapon.

Biff came over to look down at Harper.

"Have you ever seen him before?" Biff asked.

"No."

"Then, if you've never run into him before, whatever he has against you isn't personal — and that makes it worse. From what I've heard of him, he's a hired killer. That means someone may have hired him to kill you."

Duff picked up Harper's pistol, removed all the bullets, then put it back in Harper's holster.

"Tell me, Biff, would you be havin' an idea as to what we do with him now?"

"I don't know. I'd say have the marshal throw him in jail, but I don't know as he can do that. Harper hasn't done anything yet."

"You son of a bitch!" Harper shouted. Jumping up, he jerked his pistol from his holster and pulled the trigger. The hammer fell on an empty chamber.

"What the hell?" he said. Raising the pistol as a club he came toward Duff, and, once again, Duff laid him out on the floor, this time knocking out a couple of teeth in the process. Harper went down again.

"Have you come up with any idea of what to do with him?" Duff asked.

"I suppose you could just keep knocking him out," Biff said with a chuckle.

"I think I'll just tie his carcass belly down across his saddle, take him about five miles out of town, and drop him off," Duff suggested.

He picked Harper up, threw him over his shoulder and took him outside, followed by everyone who was in the saloon at the time.

Those who were on the street soon joined the saloon patrons.

"Who's the fella that Duff just laid across the saddle like that?" one of the street people asked.

"That's Harper," Schumacher said.

"Harper what? Only Harper I know is a gunfighter."

"This is that Harper."

"What happened to him? Is he dead?"

"No, he ain't dead, but he's goin' to be some pissed with he comes to. What happened is Duff MacCallister come up behind him and dropped him like a poleaxed steer," Schumacher said.

"Why did he do that?"

You'll have to ask MacCallister that."

Harper began to regain consciousness as Duff was tying him across the saddle.

"Here! What the hell is going on?" Harper demanded.

"We're going to take a ride," Duff said, mounting Sky, then taking the reins to Harper's horse and leading him out of town.

Most of the townspeople followed the two men down the street, laughing and calling out to Harper.

"Harper, I thought you were a gunfighter!"

"Ha, Harper, tell me, how does the belly

of your horse look?"

"You'll regret this, MacCallister! I'm going to kill you, first chance I get!"

Marshal Ferrell stepped out into the street in front of Duff then, and held up his hand.

"Hold up, Duff," he called. "Didn't I just hear him say he was going to kill you?"

"You damn right I'm goin' to kill this son of a bitch!" Harper shouted angrily.

"Well now, Mr. Harper, you have just talked yourself into jail for threatening murder. Bring him over to the jail, if you would, Duff."

"Aye, the jail is as good a place as any for him," Duff replied.

CHAPTER EIGHTEEN

The little town of Bordeaux, Wyoming, was on the Chugwater Creek in Laramie County, about fifteen miles north of the town of Chugwater. The land immediately around Bordeaux was arid and too poor for farming or ranching. Many tried though, and a few even managed to eke out a meager existence. There were some who searched for gold or silver, and though little of those commodities were found, enough nuggets turned up to hold out tantalizing prospects, thus the hunt continued.

Despite the bleakness of its agricultural and mining prospects, Bordeaux was, nevertheless, a bustling town. It saw a surprising amount of money flow through its half a dozen saloons, whorehouses, gaming establishments, and cafés.

Bordeaux supported a most unusual enterprise. Outlaws who were on the run often wound up in Bordeaux. And since many of those same outlaws were fleeing from bank robberies or other sources of ill-gotten gains, money was in abundance. Bordeaux existed to provide a safe haven from those on the run, and it found the rather unique venture to be most profitable.

Bordeaux had a town marshal and a deputy. The marshal was C.F. Cline, a man of average size, but with a face that was scarred from the pox he had as a child. His unattractiveness was exacerbated by a scar that caused his upper lip to be misshapen. One wall in the marshal's office was decorated with wanted posters, but they were all for show. Neither Marshal Cline nor his deputy had ever made any attempt to apprehend any of the men on the wanted posters, nor did they intend to. The way that Cline explained it, he had been hired by the people of Bordeaux to keep the peace in Bordeaux.

Whatever happened outside Bordeaux was none of his business. If a man who had a price on his head in Colorado, or the Dakota territories, or even anywhere in Wyoming, happened to pass through Bordeaux, he was just as welcome as any other traveler, so long as he didn't disturb the peace in Bordeaux. In addition, Cline had a very loose definition of disturbing the peace.

The outlaws were very aware of Marshal Cline's policy toward wanted men, so they tended to behave while in his town and around him. In fact, some of them even became friends with him and the Marshal's "Rogues' Gallery" became somewhat well known throughout the West for a most unique reason. Almost three-quarters of the wanted posters on the wall in the sheriff's office were autographed by the very outlaw whose face graced the dodger.

Johnny, Short, Evans, and Calhoun were in Bordeaux, having come there from Chugwater. They'd come for several reasons: one, because it was a place of refuge for them; two, because here they could spend some of the money stolen from the bank; and finally, because here they would meet up with Jim and Leroy Blunt. Ike Thomas had already joined them.

"I've taken one more man into our group," Johnny said as the five men gathered around a table in the back of Red Eye Saloon. "He'll be here soon as he takes care of a little job I've give him to do."

"Who is that?" Ike asked.

"Harper."

"Are you talking about the gunfighter?" Ike Thomas asked.

"Yeah."

"He ain't comin'."

"What do you mean, he ain't comin'?"

"He's in jail down in Chugwater."

Johnny smiled. "He killed MacCallister, did he? Well, he knew the chance he was takin'."

"No, he didn't kill 'im. He threatened to kill him, and the marshal throw'd him in jail."

"He threatened to kill him? Why would he do a dumb thing like that?

Ike shrugged. "Beats the hell out of me. But what I heard was that MacCallister had Harper tied, belly down, on his saddle, leading him out of town. Ever'one in town was laughin' at Harper and he got mad and yelled out that he was goin' to kill MacCallister. The marshal heard him, and, like I said, throw'd him in jail."

"I thought Harper was supposed to be good," Short said. "How did MacCallister get him belly down on the saddle?"

"I don't know," Ike said. "I never heard the tellin' o' that part of the story.

"Hell, if he's that dumb, we're probably just as well off without him," Calhoun suggested.

Al Short smiled then, and stood up. "Here comes my two friends, Jim and Leroy." He waved them over, then introduced them all around.

Leroy was short and wide, with powerful shoulders, no neck and no hair so that he somewhat resembled a cannon ball. Jim, on the other hand, was tall and thin. They bore little resemblance to each other, for all that they were brothers.

"Al said to come join you folks. What you got in mind?" Jim asked.

"Money," Johnny answered. "I've got money in mind."

"How much money?" Jim asked. "The reason I ask is, Al said somethin' about two hundred fifty dollars."

"Apiece," Leroy added.

"To start with. But once we finish this job, if you boys want to stay on, there will be other jobs that make lots more money."

"He's tellin' the truth, boys. I can testify to that," Short said.

"Are you boys interested?"

Leroy smiled. "Hell yes, I'm interested."

"Me too," Jim added. "But I'm wonderin' what this first job is that you have planned."

"There's a couple of men in jail down in Chugwater. I want to get them out."

"Why?"

"Because they were working for me," Johnny said. "And I like to take care of them

217

that works for me. If you two was workin'
for me and you got caught and put in jail,
wouldn't you like for me to get you out?"

"Besides which, one of 'em is his brother,"
Short said.

"You got a plan? 'Cause I ain't exactly too
keen on attackin' a jail head on," Leroy said.

"Don't worry, that ain't nothin' near what
I got in mind."

"Look here," Jim said. "This two hundred
and fifty dollars you was talkin' about. We
ain't goin' to have to wait 'til you brother is
out of jail afore you pay that, are we?"

Johnny smiled, then reached down into
his pocket and pulled out two little packets
of bills, each packet bound by a piece of
twine. He handed a packet to each of the
two men.

"Here is the two hundred fifty dollars,
right now," he said. "And like I said, after
this, there will be more money. A lot more
money."

Jim and Leroy smiled broadly upon receipt
of the money. "We ain't goin' to get started
right away, are we?" Leroy asked. "The
reason I ask is, I ain't had me this much
money in two or three years maybe. I'd like
a little time to enjoy it."

"You'll have a little time to enjoy it,"
Johnny said. "I'm goin' to send Ike back

down to Chugwater to take a look around for us."

"What are you sendin' Ike for?" Evans asked. "Hell, why don't you send me?"

"We've already spent too much time there now. Someone might see you and start putting things together."

Back at Sky Meadow, Duff and Elmer were engaged in conversation when Elmer squinted as he noticed a man on horseback on the road from Chugwater. "That's Willie Pierce, ain't it?" he asked, pointing toward the rider.

"Aye," Duff replied. "I saw him when he crossed the stream."

"What do you think the deputy wants out here?"

"Wouldn't it be nice now, if he was coming for to tell us that they've recovered the money?"

"Yeah, but somehow I got the idea that he ain't comin' for that," Elmer said. " 'Cause if he was, I figure he'd be comin' at a gallop, all a-whoopin' and a-hollerin' and takin' on, so."

"Aye, I think you are right," Duff said.

The two men watched as the deputy approached, never moving faster than a rather quick lope until he reached the gate that led into the compound. There, he urged his horse into a trot.

"Good morning, Deputy Pierce," Duff said. "Would you be for steppin' down and havin' a wee bit of tea, with us now? Or coffee if you prefer?"

"I wish I could, Mr. MacCallister, but the marshal told me to be gettin' on back. That's what he told me. 'Deliver the message to Mr. MacCallister, then come on back here,' he told me."

"All right," Duff said. "What is the message?"

"Justice of the Peace Norton is goin' to have the preliminary hearin' first thing tomorrow mornin', and Marshal Ferrell wants all the witnesses to stay at the Antlers Hotel tonight, just so's he can sort of keep an eye on things."

"Oh? And would the good marshal be havin' any special reason for such a request?" Duff asked.

"No, sir, nothin' particular, and he didn't tell me to bring you in neither, so I reckon if you say you don't want to come in then I'll just go back and tell him, you said no."

"There's no need for that. I'll come in if that's what the marshal wants."

"Yes, sir. He said it would only be 'til after the preliminary hearing. Of course, Justice of the Peace Norton, he ain't really a judge," Pierce said. "Not so's he can actual hold a trial 'n' all. He is a justice of the peace, so 'bout the only thing he can do is hold a hearin' to see if a fella needs to go to a higher court, and that's what he's fixin' to do."

"All right," Duff said, taking the last swallow of his tea. "Let me get my horse saddled, and I'll go back with you."

"Yes, sir, that's pretty much what the marshal was hopin' you'd do."

"Don't worry none about the ranch," Elmer said. "I'll look after things while you're in town."

"I'll nae be worryin' with you here," Duff called back over his shoulder as he started toward the stable.

When Duff and Deputy Pierce reached town, they went straight to the Antlers Hotel. Cindy Boyce and Bernie Caldwell were waiting with Deputy Mullins in the lobby.

"Go ahead 'n' get signed in, Mr. MacCallister," Deputy Pierce said. "Don't worry, the court will pay for your hotel room."

"And the court is taking us out to dinner tonight too," Cindy said enthusiastically. "Isn't it exciting?"

"No," Caldwell answered. "I would much prefer to be home with my wife and children. Besides, I don't consider being a possible target of those murderers exciting in the least."

Duff signed the guest register, then came back to the lobby to join the others. Cindy made a point to move so that she was as close to him as she could get.

"Here, I just met you, and already you are taking me out to dinner," she said, smiling flirtatiously at Duff.

"No, ma'am. The city of Chugwater is taking you out to dinner," Duff corrected.

"It's almost the same thing though, isn't it?" Cindy said. "I mean, we will be eating together."

When Marshal Ferrell arrived a few minutes later, he greeted Duff and the others. "Folks, I'm sorry about this, but I just think it is prudent to take precautions. So if you're all ready, we'll go have our dinner now, the city's treat."

Ike Thomas was enjoying his two-hundred-and-fifty-dollar windfall. He spent the entire afternoon with one of the girls at the Wild Hog. He played cards for a while, and now he was at the City Café, enjoying a dinner of fried chicken, mashed potatoes, gravy, and biscuits. He was just about finished with his dinner when he saw Marshal Ferrell, his deputy, and two men and a woman come in.

"Mr. Lambert," he heard the marshal say to the owner. "Give these good people anything they ask for. The city will be paying for it."

"The city?" Lambert replied, curious by the statement.

"Yes, indeed. These are our witnesses to the bank holdup. The city is feeding them tonight, and putting them up in the hotel so they will be handy for the preliminary hearing tomorrow."

Norman Lambert smiled at the potential size of the meal order. "Mr. Collier," he said, summoning his maître d'.

"Yes, sir?" Collier replied, responding to the summons.

"Take these nice folks back to our New York room and seat them at the banquet table."

"Yes, sir," Collier replied.

Lambert looked at Duff and the others. "I am sure you will find something on our menu that you will enjoy."

The banquet table was in the New York room, which wasn't really a completely separate room, but rather an alcove from the main dining room. Here, the banquet table was always preset with china, silver, and crystal, and a gleaming chandelier hung over the middle . . . the dangling crystals acting as prisms to glisten in many colors.

"I'll have a Caesar salad, shrimp cocktail, steak, potatoes, and champagne," Cindy said after perusing the menu.

"Yes, ma'am," Collier replied.

"Marshal, are you sure the city is goin' to pay for all this?" Deputy Pierce asked. "She just ordered the most expensive things on the menu."

"The mayor assured me that the city would," Marshal Ferrell replied.

The orders given by Duff and Caldwell were considerably more modest. Even though the mayor had told Marshal Ferrell that the city would pay for everything, Ferrell breathed a sigh of relief that the orders of the two men had not been as extravagant as Cindy's.

Ferrell and Pierce joined them, also at the city's expense. This was a treat for Pierce, who rarely got to eat at a place this fancy.

"He is at the City Café right now," Vi told Meagan.

"I wonder why he came to town without

224

telling me?"

"I don't think this is a social call. He's having dinner with Marshal Ferrell, Deputy Pierce, Mr. Caldwell, and that saloon girl from Fiddler's Green."

"What?"

"You didn't let me finish. He's having dinner with all of them, and the city is paying for it. Seems they are witnesses, and the marshal wanted them all together until after the preliminary hearing tomorrow."

"And you say they are in the café now?"

"Yes."

"Well, if the mountain won't come to Mohammed, then Mohammed will go to the mountain."

"What?" Vi asked, confused by the strange comment.

"I'm going to the café."

"Good evening, Miss Parker," Collier said when Meagan stepped into the café.

"Mr. Collier, I'm told that Mr. MacCallister is dining here."

"Indeed he is, miss. He is with Marshal Ferrell and the others, back in the New York room."

"If you don't mind, I think I shall join them."

"I don't mind at all," Collier said. "I

reckon the marshal will have to decide about that, though."

"You leave the marshal to me," Meagan replied with a pretty smile.

CHAPTER NINETEEN

Duff stood when he saw Meagan step into the opening between the New York room and the main dining room.

"Are you going somewhere?" Marshal Ferrell asked.

"I'm going to invite Miss Parker to dine with us," Duff said.

"I don't know about that," Deputy Pierce said. "I don't think the city will pay for her."

"The city won't pay for her, I'm sure," Cindy asked. "Miss Parker was in the bank, yes, but she left before the robbery."

"I'll nae be askin' the city to pay for her," Duff said. "I'll be for payin' for her meal myself."

Duff moved to a part of the table where there was an empty chair adjacent to him, and as Meagan approached the table, Marshal Ferrell, Deputy Pierce, and Mr. Caldwell stood.

"Thank you, gentlemen, and Miss Boyce,"

Meagan said as she sat in the chair that Duff pulled out for her. "I do hope I'm not intruding."

"Nonsense, you are not intruding at all, Miss Parker," Marshal Ferrell said.

"Although, I suppose with an outsider among us, we must be careful about what we say," Cindy said. "I mean, us being witnesses, and all."

"The only problem that could cause would be if a potential juror was tainted by listening to evidence before the trial," Marshal Ferrell said. "And while there have been a few women serving on juries here in Wyoming, the practice has almost been discontinued. And I know for a fact that if it actually goes to trial, Judge Pendarrow will not allow a woman to serve on one of his juries. So I see no problem with Miss Parker being here."

"How lovely you look tonight, Miss Boyce," Meagan said with a disarming smile.

The frown that had started on Cindy's face was replaced by a self-conscious smile.

"You understand, I don't have nothin' against you bein' here an' all," she said. "I was just wantin' to do what is proper, is all."

"I quite understand, and you are wise to be concerned. Being a witness in a case like this carries quite a responsibility."

"Tell me, Miss Boyce, do you know the defendant?" Marshal Ferrell asked.

"What?" Cindy gasped. "Why would you ask that?"

"I told the marshal that I seen you with him back in Fiddler's Green," Deputy Pierce said.

"You probably saw me with a lot of men," Cindy said. "That's my job. I'm supposed to be friendly to the men who come so's they will buy drinks. That's what Mr. Johnson pays me for."

"It just seems that you were a little more than normal friendly with him is all," Deputy Pierce said.

Marshal Ferrell smiled. "Now, Willie, that sounds to me like you might be just a little jealous that a pretty girl was spendin' too much time with someone other than you."

The others around the table laughed, and Deputy Pierce blushed.

"No, it ain't nothin' like that it's just that, well, I . . ."

Cindy reached out to put her hand on Deputy Pierce's arm. "Honey, don't you worry. We're spendin' time together now. And after this is over, why don't you just come on into Fiddler's Green and I'll spend as much time with you as you want — that is, as long as you keep buyin' the drinks."

Again, everyone at the table laughed, including even Deputy Pierce.

After dinner, Marshal Ferrell signed the ticket for the communal dinner, while Duff paid for Meagan's meal.

"All right, folks, it's back to the hotel with you," the marshal said.

"I'll be along later, Marshal," Duff said. "For now, 'tis my intention to escort Miss Parker back to her own place."

The expression on Marshal Ferrell's face indicated that he was against that idea, but as he considered it further, he relented, then smiled.

"Duff MacCallister, I've drawn everyone together for mutual protection. But I know you well enough by now, my friend, to know that if there is anyone who needs no protection, it is you. By all means, escort the lady home at your pleasure."

"I hope you weren't upset that I imposed myself on you tonight," Meagan said as they strolled from the City Café back toward her dress emporium. They turned off First Street and walked up Clay Avenue, passing under street lamps at the corners of First, Second, and Third streets, moving in and out of the bubbles of light that spilled out onto the boardwalk. They could hear the piano from Fiddler's Green. Meagan's dress emporium was right next door to Fiddler's Green.

"Of course you dinnae impose. Now, why would you be for saying such a thing?" Duff replied.

"I don't know. I thought perhaps I might have come across as a bit too pushy."

"Lass, you can nae be too pushy with me," Duff said. They reached the emporium, then stepped under the awning that extended over the front porch. Here they were in shadows, shielded from view by anyone who might be passing by in the street at the moment. From the saloon next door, they could hear the piano player. Then he began playing a song that several of the cowboys knew, and they started singing along, the music raucous and off-key.

"There is a fair young lady who lives in this
     town,
She welcomes the cowboys when they
     come around,
Buy her whiskey and beer if you want a
     little squeeze,
Then give her a quarter and she'll show
     you her knees."

The cowboys laughed at the ribald lyrics and continued to sing, each verse getting more ribald than the one before.

Duff and Meagan looked at each other for a long, wordless moment. Then he kissed her, at first gently, showing both his affection and his respect for her. But the kiss continued, and as Duff felt this soft, beautiful woman press herself against him, he was powerless to hold onto his own sense of propriety. Her lips parted under his, and her tongue darted into his mouth. His blood turned to molten steel and he knew there would be no turning back. The kiss lasted for a long, drawn-out moment — a moment that neither of them wanted to end.

Then a strange thing happened. As if planned, the music from the saloon next door changed. No longer was it the loud and raucous caterwauling of many. Now the music was soft and melodious, being sung by only four voices, which blended in perfect harmony.

"I'll never forget you, my sweet Darlene,
    With roses in your hair so fine.
When I come home again, my Darlene,
    Now and forever you'll be mine."

"Duff, must you return to the hotel right

away?" Meagan asked in a quiet voice that was husky with desire. "Couldn't you come up and stay with me for a while?"

"Lass, if I come up, I fear I can nae trust myself to be the gentleman you think I am."

Meagan tugged gently at his hand.

"Come," she said.

"Meagan, do you know what you are asking?"

Meagan smiled at him, and even though they were standing in the shadow under the awning, he could see her eyes gleaming with the light of a distant street lamp.

"Aye, Duff," she answered, smiling as she mocked his accent. She reached up to trace the tip of her finger across his lips. "I know exactly what I am asking." She leaned into him and they kissed again.

Next door, the music continued, as if the quartet were now singing just for Duff and Meagan.

"Darlene, I'll never, ever let you go;
No other love will I ever know."

Tugging him gently by the hand, Meagan started up the stairs with Duff right behind her. She unlocked the door to her apartment, then led him into her bedroom. There she lit a candle, the single taper lighting the distance between them. Then, without once looking away in shame or embarrassment, Meagan began to undress.

Downstairs, the music continued. Outside, on the street, a horse passed by, the hollow clump of its hoofbeats echoing back from the buildings that flanked Clay Avenue. A clock chimed in Meagan's bedroom, and in the distance a coyote howled.

Duff and Meagan were oblivious to all sounds and intrusions. They had built a cocoon around them, constructing a world in which only they existed.

Johnny Taylor and the others left Bordeaux at dawn the next morning, then stopped for a little palaver when they were less than two miles from Chugwater.

"You are sure the witnesses are all in the hotel?" Johnny asked.

"Yeah," Ike said. "Like I told you, I was in the café last night when they all come in and had supper. It was the marshal and the deputy, some real big feller, the banker, and some woman."

"The big man is Duff MacCallister, the other fella's name is Caldwell. He was the bank teller," Johnny said. "And the woman's name is Cindy Boyce."

"You know all their names?" Leroy asked.

"Yeah, I do. It's always good to know who you are dealin' with," Johnny said. "Most especially if I'm goin' to get my brother out of jail."

"If Emile hadn't shot that other bank clerk, like as not we wouldn't be in this trouble right now," Short said.

"Are you saying that if we just stole the money they'd let it go and nothing would ever come of it?" Johnny asked.

"No, I ain't a-sayin' that. But what I am a-sayin' is, if Emile hadn't shot him, we'd be off plannin' our next job right now. Instead, we're hangin' around tryin' to rescue Emile, who got his ownself into trouble in the first place. I mean, we said before we ever even started on this that we wasn't supposed to shoot nobody."

"That ain't quite the right tellin' of it, Al," Bart Evans said. "You was out back with the horses, so you didn't see what happened. The fella that Emile shot reached down under the counter and brung up a scattergun. Like as not, if Emile hadn't 'a shot him, that banker woulda took the head off one of us."

"Which one?" Short asked.

"I don't know. Coulda been mine for all I know. But the thing is, he didn't kill none of us, 'cause Emile kilt him first. Seems to me like we, all of us, owe it to Emile to get him out . . . seein' as he saved our lives 'n' all."

"He didn't save my life," Short said.

"Well, he saved mine, and that's good enough," Evans said.

"We're goin' to rescue him from the jail, and that's all there is to it," Johnny said.

"How are we goin' to do that? Have you got 'ny plans?" Ike asked.

"Not exactly."

"If I was you, I think 'bout the first thing I would want to do is take care of the witnesses," Ike said. "I mean, all three of 'em bein' together like they are, it shouldn't be that hard. And if they got no witnesses, even if your brother goes to trial, they won't be able to find nothin' on him."

"Yeah," Johnny said. "And if we do that, we can kill two birds with one stone, so to speak. MacCallister is with them, and I want that son of a bitch dead."

CHAPTER TWENTY

It was just after eight o'clock in the morning when Deputy Pierce came down to the hotel to escort the three witnesses to the city courthouse where the preliminary hearing was to be held. Duff was waiting in the lobby when he arrived.

"Good morning, Mr. MacCallister. You're up early this morning," he said.

"Aye, ready to take care of my civic duty," Duff replied.

"Have you seen the others?"

"Nae."

"I'll get the clerk to roust them up," Pierce said. He walked over to the front desk.

"I wonder if you could send someone up to fetch Miss Boyce and Mr. Caldwell for me?"

"Yes, sir, I'd be glad to," the clerk replied. He wrote a couple of room numbers on a piece of paper, then called the bellboy, a youngster of about sixteen. "Tommy, please go knock on the doors to these two rooms," he said.

"Yes, sir, Mr. Helms."

"Deputy, can I speak to you for a moment?" Helms asked after Tommy left.

"Sure, what is it?"

"It's about the room for Mr. MacCallister."

"What about his room?"

"Well, sir, I'm not sure if it would be right for me to charge the city for it."

"Why not?"

"He didn't sleep in his room last night, Deputy. He never even picked up the key."

Pierce looked over at Duff and, remembering that he had escorted Meagan Parker home last night, smiled.

"I'll be damned," he said.

"But here is the problem," Helms continued. "He did sign the registration book, you see. And Mr. Calhoun . . . he owns the hotel as you know . . . well, he keeps track of the money by the names in the registration book. And seein' as Mr. MacCallister's name is there, I don't see how I can't charge him. Not without paying for the room myself."

"Don't worry about it, Mr. Helms. The city agreed to pay for the room. We didn't make any provision that he had to sleep there. Go ahead and charge for it."

"Yes, sir, Deputy, if you say so. That will make it a mite easier on me — I mean, dealin' with Mr. Calhoun and all."

"I hope it doesn't take them a long time to get ready. I should have come over earlier to fetch them," Pierce said, looking nervously toward the clock.

Bernie Caldwell was the first one to come downstairs. They had to wait a little longer for Cindy Boyce to make her appearance.

"You'll nae be needing us after this hearing, will you, Deputy?" Duff asked.

"The marshal didn't say one way or the other, but I don't think so," Pierce replied. "Leastwise, not until the regular trial. Then, of course, we'll be needin' you again." He looked up at the clock. "The hearing starts in fifteen more minutes. What do you think is holding up Miss Boyce?"

"You aren't married, are you, Deputy?" Caldwell asked.

"No, why?"

"Because if you were married, you would know better than to even ask such a thing. I'll tell you what holding her up. What's holding her up is that she is a woman. That's all there is to it."

Duff and Caldwell laughed at the deputy's

239

expense. A moment later, Cindy came down the staircase, then walked into the lobby flashing a big smile to the three men who were waiting for her. Duff stopped in mid laughter. Never had Cindy looked more like Skye than she did this morning. She was even wearing her hair exactly like Skye, as if someone had told her how Skye wore her hair. A few errant strands of hair fell across her forehead and she reached up to push them back, using just her index and middle fingers, exactly as Skye had.

For just a moment, Duff felt a twinge of guilt over the night he'd just spent with Meagan, as if, somehow, he had cheated on Skye. He forced the thought out of his mind.

"Why, Mr. MacCallister. You look as if you have seen a ghost," she said.

"I beg your pardon, lass. 'Twas nae my intention to stare, so."

"I waited up for you to come in last night, but you must have slipped past me without my noticing."

A frown of curiosity spread across Duff's face. "And would you be for tellin' me, lass, why it is you were waiting on me?"

"No reason," Cindy said. "I just wanted to tell you good night."

"Well then, 'tis sorry I am that I missed

it," Duff replied without any further explanation.

"We've only got about six or seven minutes to make it to the hearing," Deputy Pierce said. "We'd best be goin'."

Deputy Pierce led them out onto the front porch of the hotel.

Meagan Parker had awakened that morning to an empty bed. She had no idea how long it had been since Duff left, but the aroma of him lingered in the sheets . . . the spice, wood, and lavender scent of his soap, a hint of leather, bay rum, and his own musk. She had mixed feelings about him having left without awakening her. On the one hand, she would have welcomed the intimacy of his being in her bedroom this morning; on the other hand, she knew it might also have been an awkward moment for both of them. She was sure that he had thought that as well.

Getting dressed, Meagan went downstairs to the emporium, but instead of opening her shop, left the CLOSED sign hanging in the window of the front door.

Johnny Taylor and the other riders had pulled hoods down over their faces, and were riding into town at the very moment

Deputy Pierce and the others were coming out of the hotel.

"Look!" Ike shouted, pointing. "There they are!"

"We can end this right now. Let's gun 'em down!" Johnny said, slapping his legs against the sides of his horse.

The riders all broke into a gallop. Johnny pulled his gun as a signal to the others, and they rode hard down the middle of the street.

Seven masked men, riding galloping horses, raised quite a commotion, and those who were crossing the street had to move quickly to get out of the way.

Meagan had planned to attend the preliminary hearing, and had just stepped out onto the porch in front of her shop when the gang of riders came galloping down the street, firing their pistols. At first she thought the firing was indiscriminate, but then she saw that they were all wearing hoods, and they were shooting toward Duff and the others who had just stepped out from the hotel. She saw Deputy Pierce go down.

Duff MacCallister made no effort to get out of the line of fire, but seemed to expose himself even more. Her heart was in her throat with fear that he might get shot, but she had to admit that she had never seen anything quite as magnificent as the sight of him standing there, totally unconcerned for his own welfare while he engaged the group of outlaws.

"Get back in the hotel!" Duff shouted, pulling his pistol to return fire. Cindy and Caldwell darted back inside, but Deputy Pierce was sitting on the boardwalk, leaning back against the front wall of the hotel, bleeding from a leg wound.

Duff returned fire. He had the disadvantage of standing in the open, but the advantage of having a stable platform from which to fire. The riders had the advantage of being fast-moving targets, though that was counteracted by the disadvantage of having to fire from the saddles of galloping horses.

For a moment, the shooting sounded like a battlefield as the guns popped loudly, the echoes rolling back from the lines of buildings that flanked both sides of the street. By now, everyone had gotten themselves out of the line of fire as Duff continued to engage the galloping horsemen. Two of the riders were shot from their saddles as the horses galloped out through the other end of town.

Moving quickly toward the two downed men, Duff approached them cautiously, and with his pistol at the ready. Reaching down carefully, he pulled the hoods off their heads. As it turned out, caution wasn't necessary. Both men were dead.

Although everyone had run for cover when the gunfire erupted, they began to drift back out onto the street now. Because of that, the street was crowded with people who had gathered around to stare at the bodies of the two outlaws.

"I'll be damn! I know that feller," someone said, pointing to one of the bodies. "That's Al Short. He was playin' cards with a bunch of us just the other day."

"The other one is Jim Blunt," Schumacher said.

"A friend of yours, Francis?" Marshal Ferrell asked.

Schumacher shook his head. "Only reason I know him is that I've seen him in the Wild Hog a time or two."

"Make way, folks, make way!" Nunnelee called as he brought his wagon down the street, parting those gathered around the bodies like Moses parting the Red Sea.

"Hey, Tom, are you giving Mr. MacCallister some of the money you're makin' from the city on these folks he's kilt? This makes three, don't it?"

"It'll be four once we hang the one we got in jail," another added.

There was a spattering of laughter at the comment.

"It isn't as if I were getting rich off this. The city gives me five dollars apiece for burying them," Nunnelee said.

"Plus two dollars for the coffins, don't forget," another said. "I told the others in the city council, why bother with a casket? We could just wrap 'em up in burlap and bury 'em."

"That's just real Christian of you, R.D.," Curly Lathom said. Curly was the town barber, and his current client was standing beside him, still wearing the barber cover, and with half his face lathered. R.D. Clayton, the man Curly had spoken to, was a mule trader, and a member of the Chugwater City Council.

"Why pay for a coffin for an indigent? There ain't nobody around that's goin' to be offended, 'cause if they was, they would be paying for the funeral. And it sure as hell don't make no difference to the folks we are buryin'."

As the discussion was going on, Nunnelee got help from a couple of the others, and the two bodies were loaded into the back of his wagon. Climbing back into the seat, he clucked at his mule, turned it around, and started back toward the mortuary.

"All right, folks, nothin' left to see out here now," Marshal Ferrell said. "Get on back out of the street so traffic can get through. The stagecoach will be arrivin' here soon, and you know how Don Pratt likes to whip up his team to make a show of it when he comes into town. I wouldn't want to see any of you get run over."

"Hey, Nunnelee!" the man who was getting a shave called out to the undertaker. "You goin' to put these two boys up on display like you done the other one?"

Nunnelee neither replied nor looked around. But he did hold his hand up and wave a finger.

"What do you think that means?" the half-shaved man asked. "You think that's a yes or a no?"

As soon as the shooting was over, Meagan hurried down to the hotel to be with Duff, but he had gone out to check on the two downed men. She saw the deputy sitting on the porch, leaning back against the wall. He had taken off his hat and was holding it over a wound in his leg.

"Deputy Pierce, you are hurt!" she said, squatting beside him.

"I don't think it's too bad," Pierce said,

though his voice was strained with pain.

"Let me see the wound," Meagan said as, gently, she lifted his hat to see the dark red, nearly black hole of the bullet entry wound. "It's not bleeding badly. That's a good sign," she said.

By now a couple of other men had arrived.

"We'll look after him, ma'am," one of the said. "No need for you to get all bloody."

"Thank you, Miss Parker," Deputy Pierce said.

"I didn't do anything," Meagan said.

"You come to check on me," Pierce said. "And for that, I thank you."

Meagan smiled at him, then moved to the edge of the porch to wait as the crowd in the street began to disperse and Duff came back to the hotel. He frowned when he saw her.

"Were you outside when the shooting started?" he asked, concern for her showing in his voice.

"I was in no danger," she replied. "What about you? Are you all right? Were you hit or anything?"

"I've nae a scratch," Duff replied. "And it does nae look as if Deputy Pierce is bleeding all that much, so I do nae think the bullet hit an artery. Soon as we get him to the doctor I think he'll fare all right."

"If you fellas will help me up, I'll walk down to the doc's office," Deputy Pierce said.

"Nonsense, Willie, my buckboard is right here," one of the two men answered. "We'll ride down."

After the bodies in the middle of the street were removed, the crowd dispersed, and Deputy Pierce taken down to the doctor's office, Marshal Ferrell came over to the hotel. He touched the brim of his hat toward Meagan.

"Good morning, Miss Parker."

"It appears to have been a busy morning, Marshal," Meagan replied.

"Yes, ma'am, you've got that right," Marshal Ferrell replied. He looked around. "Where are my other two witnesses?" he asked.

"They stepped inside," Duff replied.

Marshal Ferrell chuckled. "Stepped inside, did they? Well, I'll just get them out here and we'll go on down to the city court to do what we started out to do."

Marshal Ferrell went into the hotel, but the lobby appeared to be empty.

"Hello? Anyone here? Where is everyone?"

Mr. Helms, the desk clerk, stuck his head up from behind the desk.

"Has the shooting stopped?"

"Yes. Where are my witnesses?"

"We're back here, Marshal," Caldwell said, stepping around from behind a big, potbellied stove. "The bullets were coming in here."

"Really?"

"Indeed they were," Mr. Helms said. "Look at this, will you? A bullet hit the ink well and got ink all over the hotel register book. Mr. Calhoun is very particular about his register books. He's not going to like this. He's not going to like this one little bit. I'm afraid he is going to be very angry with me."

"Don't worry about it," Marshal Ferrell said. "I'll tell him what happened." He looked back at Caldwell and Cindy, neither of whom had fully presented themselves from behind the stove.

"Come on, you two. We have a hearing to attend."

"Is it safe to come out now?" Caldwell asked.

"It's safe," Marshal Ferrell said. "The outlaws are gone, and thanks to Mr. Mac-Callister, they left two of their dead behind them."

"Was Mr. MacCallister hit?" Cindy asked anxiously.

"No, ma'am, didn't get a scratch. If you

folks are ready, we'll get on down to the city courthouse."

"But, surely, after all this, you aren't still going to have a hearing, are you?" Cindy asked.

"Of course we are going to have a hearing. The whole purpose of their coming here to shoot up the town was to try and stop the hearings, but we aren't going to let that happen, are we?"

"You are sure they are all gone?" Caldwell asked. "I don't want to be walking around outside when bullets are flying back and forth. I do have a family, you know."

"I know your family, Mr. Caldwell. You are married to a wonderful wife and you have good children, so I have no intention of putting you in danger. I'm positive they are all gone," Marshal Ferrell said. "Come on, let's go. I'll be with you every step of the way."

"I want to walk with Mr. MacCallister," Cindy said. "I saw how brave he was."

Marshal Ferrell chuckled. "He was brave all right, but as for you walking with him, that might be a little difficult."

"Why is that?"

"As you'll see when you step outside, Duff already has a woman with him."

Cindy's smile turned to a pout when she saw Meagan.

CHAPTER TWENTY-ONE

Johnny Taylor and the others didn't break gallop until they were at least three miles out of town. Then they let the horses continue on at a lope that ate a lot of ground, but was less exhausting for the animals.

"We've got to go back!" Leroy Blunt shouted in anguished anger. "That's my brother we left lyin' in the street back there!"

"Yeah, and Al Short went down too," Calhoun said. "We lost two good men and didn't get a damn one of them."

"We got the deputy," Johnny said. "I saw him go down."

"Hell, what good did that do? The deputy ain't one of the ones that is goin' to testify," Evans said.

"We got to go back!" Leroy Blunt said again.

"You can go back if you want to," Ike said.

"But like as not, both of 'em is dead, so why take a chance?"

"How do you know they are dead?" Leroy asked.

"Because the feller shootin' at us was Duff MacCallister. And he don't miss all that much."

"Then that means you don't really know whether they are dead or not. You're just sayin' that. And I say it ain't right for us to just leave 'em there," Leroy asked.

"We all took an equal chance," Ike said.

"It ain't right! It ain't right, I tell you," Leroy said.

"We're goin' to go back because Emile is still there," Johnny said. "And when we go back for Emile, why, we'll also be goin' back for Al and Jim."

"I tell you the truth, I ain't all that anxious to go back," Evans admitted. "We've been there twice now, and we've lost five men."

"Where do you get that we've lost five men?" Calhoun asked.

"Julius, he was kilt. And Emile was took. And, like Ike said, it's more'n likely, today, that Al and Jim got themselves kilt, too."

"That's only four men," Calhoun said.

"Yeah, well, I was countin' Harper as the fifth man. Even though he didn't start out with us, you said he was doin' somethin' for us when he got hisself caught."

"Yeah, I forgot about him," Calhoun said.

"Don't worry," Johnny said. "I've got an idea that ain't goin' to get nobody else kilt. At least, not no more of us."

Justice of the Peace Richard Norton stepped through a rear door and viewed his court. Norton had never read for the law, and he was neither a lawyer nor a real judge. He was a justice of the peace, and had been appointed to the position by Governor John Hoyt. Norton wasn't a tall man, but he was robust, with a square face and piercing blue eyes. He moved quickly to the bench, then sat down.

Even though this was just a preliminary hearing, there were several townspeople present.

"Be seated," he said.

The gallery sat, then watched with interest as Emile Taylor shuffled into the room, his legs hobbled with a fourteen-inch chain.

Justice of the Peace Norton looked over at the prisoner, who glared at him contemptuously.

"Mr. Taylor, are you of sufficient mind and intellect to understand what is going on here?"

"Yeah, it's a trial," Emile replied. "How

come I don't see no jury?"

"There is no jury, Mr. Taylor, because this is not a trial. This is a preliminary hearing. It is, however, adversarial."

"It's what?"

"Adversarial. That means that a prosecutor will present the case for the Territory of Wyoming, and you have a right to have an attorney to present your side. The prosecution has the burden to convince me that there is probable cause to believe that a crime was committed and that you committed it. The prosecutor may present witnesses, as well as physical and documentary evidence to satisfy this burden. Your lawyer will have the chance to make responsive arguments, to cross-examine the government's witnesses, and to present witnesses and other evidence of his own in an effort to show that probable cause is lacking."

"I ain't got no lawyer."

Justice of the Peace Norton looked over at Robert Dempster, who was sitting at the defense table.

"Mr. Dempster, did you not visit with the accused, and inform him that you are his court-appointed attorney?"

"I did, Your Honor."

"I just met him this mornin'," Emile said. "What chance do I have with him as my lawyer?"

"What chance did Danny Welch have?" someone shouted from the gallery. "He didn't have no lawyer, and this murderin' bastard shouldn't either!"

Justice of the Peace Norton banged his gavel on the bench and glared out over the gallery.

"If one more person says one more word to interrupt these proceedings, I will clear this court."

The court grew quiet.

"Mr. Taylor, on the fifth, instant, six men entered the Chugwater Bank and Trust with the intention of robbing it."

"We didn't just intend to rob it," Emile said with a proud smile. "We done it."

There was an immediate reaction to his statement from those in the gallery, but the rumbling stopped immediately when Norton fixed them with a glare.

"Let me get this straight, Mr. Taylor. You are admitting that you took part in the robbing of the Chugwater Bank and Trust?"

"Since I got shot while I was runnin' away from it, I can't hardly say I wasn't there, now, can I?"

"No, Mr. Taylor, you cannot. And I thank you for your candidness. I will now continue with the indictment. On the fifth instant, six men entered the bank with the intention of robbing it. And, as you pointed out, that intention was fulfilled — the bank was robbed. You have also confessed to being a part of that band of robbers. Do you now, before this court, repeat that confession?"

"Yeah, I robbed the bank."

"Very well, that part of the hearing can be dispensed with. You are also, Mr. Taylor, being charged with killing Mr. Daniel Welch. How do you plead to that?"

"I didn't do that."

"How do you plead?"

"What?"

"The defendant pleads not guilty to the charge of murder, Your Honor," Dempster said.

"Yeah, not guilty."

"Very well then, we will proceed with the details pertaining to the charge of murder. Mr. Prosecutor, if you would please, sir, make your case."

David Crader stood and faced Justice of the Peace Norton.

"Your Honor, Mr. Taylor has confessed that he was one of the men who robbed the bank. Mr. Welch was killed during the course of the robbery, and it is my contention that his very presence is damning enough to warrant that he be tried for

257

murder. In addition, we have witnesses who will testify that they saw him shoot Mr. Welch. Prosecution moves that he be arraigned for trial."

"Mr. Dempster, you have been appointed to defend Mr. Taylor. What is your response?"

"Hold on there," Emile said. "I told you, this here fella ain't my lawyer. My brother has done told me he is going to hire a good lawyer. I ain't goin' to be defended by someone you say is to defend me."

"At the moment, Mr. Taylor, Robert Dempster is the only lawyer available to you. You may use him, or you may choose to defend yourself."

"Don't you have to wait until I get a lawyer?"

"If you are remanded to trial, you will have the opportunity to be represented by counsel of your choice. This is a preliminary hearing. Now which will it be, Mr. Taylor? Do you want counsel? Or do you wish to defend yourself?"

"I'll defend myself."

"You are aware, are you not, Mr. Taylor, of the saying, 'one who defends himself has a fool for a lawyer and client'?"

Emile looked confused. "I don't know what that means," he said.

"That is my point, Mr. Taylor."

"You're tryin' to confuse me."

"No, Mr. Taylor, I am trying to give you good advice." Justice of the Peace Norton let out a deep breath and shrugged his shoulders. "Lord knows, I have tried. Make your defense."

"What I want to ask this here prosecutor is, how do these witnesses know it was me?" Emile asked.

"Because they saw you, Mr. Taylor," Crader replied.

"I was wearing a mask. So how do they know it was me? It could have been any of us that shot 'im. Besides which, he was goin' for a double-barrel shotgun, so whoever it was that shot him can't get hisself hung anyway, because it was self-defense."

"Mr. Taylor, there is absolutely no claim to self-defense in the commission of a felony. The killing of Mr. Welch is felony murder. Besides, it is not necessary to prove your guilt at this hearing," Justice of the Peace Norton said. "It is only necessary to determine whether or not probable cause exists to believe that the offense charged has been committed by you."

"Yeah? Well, who makes that decision? Like I said, I don't see no jury."

"As I told you earlier, this is not a jury

trial. This is a preliminary hearing. I am the one who makes the decision. And it is my ruling that probable cause does exist. Marshal?"

"Yes, Your Honor?"

"I am remanding this prisoner to your custody, to be held until arrangements can be made for a circuit judge to be present to conduct a trial."

"What about bail, Your Honor?" Dempster asked.

"Your Honor," Crader said. "Prosecution petitions the court to not grant bail. The charge is murder, and the defendant is clearly a flight risk."

"Your Honor, if bail is sufficiently high, I think that would reduce the possibility of flight," Dempster said.

"How high would you consider sufficiently high, counselor?"

"Five thousand dollars."

"It is my understanding that more than forty thousand was stolen from the bank. I think it would not be impossible for Mr. Taylor's brother to dip into that ill-gotten money to post bail. Bail is denied."

"Deputy Mullins, take the prisoner back to jail," Marshal Ferrell said.

"Yes, sir," Mullins said, taking charge of Emile Taylor.

"Your Honor, the next order of business is Vernon Harper."

"Very well, bring him in."

Marshal Ferrell went to the back of the courtroom, then returned a moment later with his prisoner. Like Emile Taylor before him, Harper's legs were shackled by fourteen-inch chains. His wrists were bound together as well.

Tall and slender, his hair, normally worn long anyway, was disheveled, some of it falling over his black eyes. His moustache was so full that it covered his mouth.

"Sit there," Marshal Ferrell ordered.

Glaring at the marshal, Harper sat where ordered.

"What is the charge?" Justice Norton asked.

"Attempted murder," Marshal Ferrell replied.

"How do you plead?" Norton asked.

"I don't have to say nothin'," Harper said.

"That's true, you don't have to say anything. Mr. Dempster, you will act as prosecutor for this case. Mr. Crader, you will be his defense. Please, gentlemen, begin."

"Your Honor, this person standing before you is said to have killed more than seventeen men," Dempster said.

"Seventeen men? Marshal Ferrell, is this

man wanted for any of these killings?" Norton asked.

"No, Your Honor. I have checked all my files, and have even telegraphed back to Cheyenne. There are no warrants out for him," Ferrell replied.

"That seems most unusual that he would be responsible for so many killings, and yet not have one reward poster out against him. However, Mr. Dempster, whether there are warrants out against him or not, what he has done in the past has no bearing on the issue before us now. The only question we have to decide is whether he attempted to murder Mr. MacCallister."

"He told MacCallister that he was going to kill him. He said that before the marshal and several witnesses."

"Did he shoot at Mr. MacCallister, or point his gun at him, or attempt to kill him with a knife, club, or any other weapon?"

"No, Your Honor," Dempster replied sheepishly.

"Mr. Crader, what have you to say?"

"Your Honor, I would like to call Francis Schumacher as witness for the defense."

"Mr. Schumacher, you used to be a deputy marshal, did you not?" Justice of the Peace Norton asked.

"That's right."

"Then you know how this is done. Since this isn't a trial, we're not goin' to be all that fancy, but I'm goin' to ask you to raise your right hand and swear to this court that you'll be telling the truth and nothing but the truth."

Schumacher raised his hand. "I will."

"All right, take a seat."

Crader waited until Schumacher was seated before he addressed him.

"Mr. Schumacher, did you see the altercation between Duff MacCallister and Mr. Harper?"

"I did."

"Would you tell the court what you saw, please?"

"MacCallister come up behind Harper and said somethin' to him. I don't know what it was 'cause I wasn't close enough to hear. But what happened was, Harper jumped up and turned around, and the next thing you know, MacCallister hit him and knocked him down."

"Who made the first move?"

"As far as I could tell, it was MacCallister."

"Thank you, no further questions."

"Mr. Dempster, do you wish to question this witness?"

"No, Your Honor. But I would like to

question Biff Johnson."

Biff Johnson was sworn in as casually as had been Francis Schumacher.

"Mr. Johnson, did you witness the altercation between MacCallister and Harper?"

"I did."

Biff told how Harper had waited for Duff all day long, and how Duff had stepped up behind him to introduce himself. He then told how Harper had attempted to draw his gun, but was knocked out.

"Then, while he was out, Duff removed all the cartridges from his pistol, and when Harper woke up again, he tried to shoot Duff."

"Tried to shoot?" Dempster asked.

"Yes, sir. He actually pulled the trigger, but of course there were no bullets in his gun. That's when Duff knocked him out again, and put him up on his horse."

"Thank you. Nor more questions, Your Honor."

"Closing, Mr. Crader?"

"Mr. MacCallister, would you take the stand, please?" Norton asked.

Duff was sworn in; then he took the stand.

"You have heard all the testimony given here today, by both Mr. Schumacher and Mr. Johnson. Is there any part of the testimony of either man that isn't true?"

"Nae, Your Honor. 'Tis all true."

"Why did you approach him as you did?"

"I believed that he was there to kill me."

"Is there bad blood between the two of you? Have you had a run-in with him before?"

"Nae, Your Honor."

"Why do you think he intended to kill you?"

"I'm told that Mr. Harper is a hired assassin. 'Tis my belief he has been hired to kill me."

"Did he say he was going to kill you?"

"Aye, Your Honor, when he was belly down across the horse, he did utter those words."

The gallery laughed.

"Before that, Mr. MacCallister. When you first encountered him, did he say he was goin' to kill you?"

"He dinnae say that. But when I called his name, he made a move for his gun."

"You say he made a move for his gun. Did he actually pull his gun from his holster?

"He was nae able to pull the gun, for I hit him too quickly."

Again, there was a scattering of laughter in the court.

"Very well, you are excused," Norton said. Norton looked back toward Crader. "Mr.

265

Crader, your closing?"

"Your Honor, while it is true that Mr. Harper said he was going to kill MacCallister, he made no such statement until he was belly down across his own horse. And I'm sure you can understand the anger and frustration one might feel under such circumstance. I believe he made that statement out of anger and duress. I respectfully petition the court to declare no cause for the charge of attempted murder."

Norton looked over toward Harper.

"Mr. Harper, with every fiber in my being, I would dearly love to find cause why you should come to trial. I believe you and your kind are the scum of the earth.

"But, in all fairness, I do not see sufficient cause to bind you over for trial. Release his shackles, Marshal Ferrell. There will be no charge against this man."

"Ha!" Harper said. "MacCallister, you . . ."

"If you so much as say one word without my permission to talk, I'll find you in contempt and you'll go right back to jail," Justice of the Peace Norton said.

"Don't say a word, Harper!" Crader demanded. "You are free to go. Don't be a fool now and make the judge change his mind."

Harper bit back whatever he was going to say. Instead, glaring at the marshal, he stuck his shackled hands out in front of him.

"Turn me a' loose," he said with a growl.

"Get out of town, Mr. Harper," Marshal Ferrell said as he began releasing the chains. "Get out of town now."

CHAPTER TWENTY-TWO

Back in Bordeaux the next day, Johnny Taylor saw Harper the moment he set foot in the Red Eye Saloon.

"You're out!" he said. "What did you do? Break out?"

"Nah, I didn't break out," Harper said. Without being invited, he reached down to pick up a bottle of whiskey that was sitting in the middle of the table occupied by Johnny and the others. He took several Adam's-apple-bobbing swallows straight from the bottle. He wiped his mouth and moustache with the sleeve of his dirty shirt.

"Then how did you get out?"

"They held a trial for me 'n' your brother. And then they let me out."

"They've already had the trial?"

"It weren't no real trial. It's what they said was a hearin'. It was a trial to see if they was going to have a trial for us. They said yeah for your brother, and put him back in jail, and they said no for me, and let me go. So, here I am."

"Why are you here?" Blunt asked.

Harper glared at Blunt, then looked back at Johnny. "Who is that?" he asked.

"He is working with me," Johnny explained. "All these men are workin' with me."

Harper took another swallow of the whiskey before he replied. "Yeah, well, I reckon I am too," he said. "I ain't done what you hired me to do yet, but I still aim to do it, and I still aim to collect the other half of the money you promised me."

"We may not need to kill MacCallister," Johnny said.

"What do you mean? I thought you wanted the son of a bitch kilt."

"I do, but my first goal is to get my brother out of jail. And I've just been talking over my idea with these men. Pull up a chair and join us. If you are going to work with us, you may as well get in on this as well."

"What is it you have in mind?"

"I aim for us to leave a little callin' card for the good folks of Chugwater," Johnny said.

"Callin' card? What kind of callin' card? What are you talkin' about?"

269

"You'll see," Johnny said. "I figure we'll drop in on the town tonight."

From the *Chugwater Defender:*

MORE VIOLENCE IN THE
STREETS OF CHUGWATER

Yesterday morning Johnny Taylor and the brigands who ride with him launched a dastardly attack. In a move as evil as that ever perpetrated by the most savage redskins, Johnny and his hellish associates rode into town with guns blazing. This was an apparent attempt to intimidate or kill the witnesses to the bank robbery and foul murder committed by Johnny and his band of outlaws.

But Johnny reckoned without the presence of Mr. Duff MacCallister, who stood as gallantly as did King Leonidas at the Battle of Thermopylae. Standing in the street all alone, MacCallister fired at the outlaws, the balls of his pistol taking devastating effect on two of the attackers. Killed were Jim Blunt and Al Short, known only because he has, of recent days, been a habitué of some of the drinking establishments within our fair city.

If the purpose of the attack was to prevent the arraignment of Emile Taylor, the brother of Johnny Taylor, it failed. Justice of the Peace Richard Norton found that there was sufficient justification to try Emile Taylor for murder.

In another hearing, Justice Norton released Vernon Harper from jail, saying that Harper's angry outburst, in which he threatened to kill Duff MacCallister, did not rise to the level of indictment.

"Whooeee, how about that?" Elmer said, giggling, and slapping his hand on his knee. He had gone into town this morning and returned with a copy of the newspaper. "You're a king, Duff. The newspaper called you a king."

"It dinnae call me a king, Elmer. It compared me to a king, a man named Leonidas."

"In my book, gettin' compared to a king is the same thing as bein' called a king."

Duff smiled. "If you say so."

"I seen Miss Parker while I was in town. She told me to tell you she was mad in love with you."

"What?" Duff gasped.

Elmer laughed again, a loud, gut-busting laugh, and he pointed at Duff.

"Oh, I wish you coulda seen your face when I said that."

"What did you say such a thing?"

"What she really said was, 'Elmer, would you please give Duff my fondest regards'? Fondest regards," Elmer said, repeating the phrase. "Now you tell me if fondest regards don't mean the same thing."

"Fondest regards is nae the same as love."

"Maybe, but she does love you. Me 'n' you both know that. And if you was honest with yourself, you'd admit that you love her too."

"I am very . . . fond . . . of her," Duff said with a laugh.

Elmer laughed as well, then pointed back to the newspaper. "I think Norton made a mistake by lettin' Harper go free, like he done."

"He dinnae have any choice. There was nae attempted murder."

"But you tol' me yourself that once you called out his name he started to go for his gun. Only you knocked him out before he could get to it."

"Aye, but that may be because he was startled by my unexpected appearance."

"Unexpected my hind end. I talked to some of the others this mornin'. Biff Johnson says that Harper had waited there for you for near 'bout the whole day. You can't wait for someone that long and be startled

272

when they finally do show up. And why was he waitin' for you, if he wasn't plannin' on killin' you?"

"You may have a point," Duff agreed.

"You mighty damn right I have a point. From what I've heard of Harper, he's a man that gets paid for killin', and to make matters worse, he's a man that enjoys his work."

"I did get that feeling from him," Duff admitted.

"It wouldn't surprise me none at all if he hadn't been hired by Johnny Taylor his ownself, just to kill you."

Percy Dillon drove a wagon for Guthrie Building and Lumber Supply company, Walt Goodman drove one for the Chugwater Mercantile Store. Even though the two men worked for different employers, they often made the trip to Cheyenne together, so they had become good friends.

Tonight they were celebrating Walt's thirty-fifth birthday in the Wild Hog Saloon. Kathy, Annie, and Betty, having learned that it was Walt's birthday, had given him a "birthday present" by coming over to the table and flirting with him without charging him the price of a drink. And, because Percy was with him, he also got to enjoy their company.

"Hey," Percy said to Annie. "Next month it's goin' to be my birthday. Are you ladies goin' to come spend some time with me then, the way you're a-visitin' Walt now?"

"I don't know," Annie said. She ran her hand through Walt's hair. "Walt is a lot prettier than you are."

"There you go, Percy, did you hear — wait a minute! Did you say I was *prettier* than Percy?"

"That's what I said, honey."

Percy laughed in loud guffaws. "Pretty! Annie thinks you are pretty!" He continued to laugh.

"I ain't no way pretty," Walt said. "Go away, if that's what you think I am."

"All right, honey, I'll leave if you want me to," Annie said with an exaggerated pout. She bent down and kissed Walt on top of his head before she and the other two girls left.

"Damn, Walt, now look what you done. You sent her away."

"I ain't pretty," Walt said, mumbling into his drink.

"Hey, look at the clock. It's damn near midnight, and me 'n' you both has got a run to Cheyenne tomorrow. We'd best be gettin' on back to the boardin' house."

"Yeah, you're right," Walt said.

Johnny, Calhoun, Evans, Harper, and Leroy were waiting in a little patch of woods just outside of town. The sounds of the town, the tinkling of a couple of pianos, periodic outbursts of laughter, and low murmur of conversation coming from both the Fiddler's Green and the Wild Hog Saloons drifted out to compete with the trilling of the night insects. From one of the houses on the outskirts of town, a baby started crying. In a nearby stable, a mule brayed.

They were waiting for the perfect opportunity and that came when two cowboys left the Wild Hog, staggering along the boardwalk, barely able to keep upright.

"All right, let's go," Johnny said. "Remember, ride in real slow. We don't want to do nothin' that might spook them."

They rode in slowly, but not quietly, because the horses' hooves made loud clopping noises.

"I tell you what, Percy, I been thinkin' about it. And I think Annie is in love with me," Walt said.

Percy laughed. "What makes you think that?"

"Well, 'cause she called me pretty."

"I thought that made you mad."

"Well, it did at first, but then I got to thinkin' about it. She more 'n likely figured that was a compliment."

The five horsemen rode on up to the two drunken men, as if totally oblivious to them, and the two men, engaged in their own conversation, paid no attention to the riders. Neither Percy nor Walt noticed it when Johnny Norton and Bart Evans dismounted no more than thirty feet behind them.

"Bullshit, Walt. Annie is no different from any of the other women who work there. They are only in love with you as long as you have money to spend on 'em," Percy replied.

"Well, I wasn't buyin' her no drinks tonight, now, was I?"

"That's just 'cause it is your birthday."

"No, I mean I can tell by the way she acts, the way she looks at me. It's like she's sayin' that she don't really want to drink with nobody else but me."

"Ha! Walt, you are as full of . . ."

That was as far as he got, because Johnny had dismounted and come up behind him. Grabbing a handful of Percy's hair, Johnny forced his head back, exposing his neck. He drew a sharp knife across Percy's neck, cutting the carotid artery. Percy made a gurgling sound, even as Walt was having his own carotid artery severed.

Johnny and Calhoun stepped back to let the two men crumple to the ground. Then, as the two men lay bleeding their lives away in the dirt of Bowie Avenue, Johnny reached down and pinned a note to the one who had stopped flopping first.

"All right," Johnny said, rubbing his hands together as if in appreciation of his own work. "Let's see what happens next."

A crowing rooster awakened Louise Teasdale the next morning. Louise was a cook at the City Café and she had to get up early every morning in order to be to the café in time to get the fire laid in the cook stove and start preparing breakfast. She yawned, stretched, then smiled as she wished she could have held on to the dream that was just now drifting away. In it, she wasn't a cook, but a pampered wife in a big house that was filled with servants who would clean and cook for her and her handsome and wealthy husband.

"That's why they call them dreams," she said, chuckling as she spoke aloud. She hurried to get dressed.

The sun was but half a disk above the eastern horizon when she left her small, one-room house and headed for work. She saw two men lying in the street, just off the boardwalk in front of her, and she shook her head. Her route to work took her right by the Wild Hog Saloon. These two men were not the first passed-out drunks she had ever encountered.

"Looks like Marshal Ferrell could at least get the drunks off the street," she said aloud. She hiked her skirt, preparing to going around the two men. That was when she saw the blood.

"What?" she asked curiously, and she leaned down for a closer look.

One of the men was lying facedown, but the one that was lying on his back had his head tipped back. His skin was a gray pallor, and his mouth and eyes were open. But the most grotesque sight was the great gaping gash in his neck. It looked as if his neck had nearly been sawed in two.

Louise's scream awakened households for two blocks around.

The double murder was the lead story in the *Chugwater Defender* that evening.

GRISLY FIND IN STREETS OF CHUGWATER

While on the way to her place of employment at the City Café, where she works as a cook, Miss Louise Teasdale discovered the bodies of Percy Dillon and Walt Goodman. Both men had been brutally murdered, their throats cut in a most foul manner.

Attached to Mr. Goodman's body was a note that read, "We will kill more of your citizens if you do not let my brother go."

Although the note was not signed, it is believed to have been written by Johnny Taylor, whose brother, Emile, having been legally indicted, is currently incarcerated and awaiting trial for murder in connection with the recent bank robbery.

When contacted, Marshal Ferrell stated that the note will have no effect on him, and that Emile Taylor will remain in jail until such disposition as shall be made of him by the court. That disposition, it is believed by all, will be a hanging, and to that end a gallows is already being built.

The two young men, known as good and dependable workers by their employers, R.W. Guthrie and Fred Matthews, had made many friends in our fair community. A kind word for all is how their friends remember them and speak of them today.

Yesterday was Mr. Goodman's birthday, and he celebrated it with his friends at the Wild Hog Saloon. It is said that they left the saloon at just before midnight, and as their bodies were discovered but two blocks from the watering establishment, it is assumed that they were murdered very soon after.

Messers Guthrie and Matthews have expressed a willingness to pay all expenses for the burial of their two employees. They invite the town to attend the funeral to say good-bye to these two young men who from this earth were untimely plucked, to be transported to a place where a more befitting abode awaits them.

CHAPTER TWENTY-THREE

Because the two men had been freight wagon drivers, their caskets were open and lying in the back of the same wagons they had driven in life. The two wagons, with Walt's wagon in the lead, were decorated with black bunting, pulled by horses that were draped with a black pall. The wagons were driven slowly through town in a funeral cortege that grew in numbers as it proceeded toward the cemetery.

At first, people were puzzled as to why so many people would want to attend the burial, then someone suggested that perhaps it was because the boys had no family of their own to mourn for them. Their graves were side by side because, as Fred Matthews said, "They were friends in life, they will be friends through eternity."

Elmer came into town for the burial. He knew both men on sight and had even had a few drinks with them. But he didn't come because he knew them. He came because he had seen a lot of men — friends, acquaintances, enemies, even perfect strangers, buried in unmarked graves a long way from home. And as the two graves were being simultaneously closed, he remembered another burial. Not a burial, really, but a committal of a body to the sea.

They were fourteen days out of Madagascar when the boy fell from the rigging and died within moments after crashing onto the deck. He was buried at sea within an hour, the sail maker having made a shroud for the committal.

The ship's company turned out for the burial, but there was no clergyman on the three-masted *Baltic Trader,* so the captain read the rites of burial.

The man they were burying had only come aboard for this cruise, joining the ship in Norfolk, Virginia. He had given his name as John Smith, but most just referred to him as "Red" because of the color of his hair. It was suspected by some, though nobody knew for sure, that he was running from the law, and had come on this cruise on as a means of escape.

"Think he's got folks somewhere?" one of the other sailors asked Elmer.

"Everybody has folks somewhere," Elmer replied.

"There ain't goin' to be nobody ever knows what happened to this fella."

"That ain't true."

"What do you mean?"

"I'll know," Elmer said.

It was one week after Dillon and Goodman were buried, and Duff and Elmer were up on the roof of the barn replacing shingles when Marshal Ferrell came riding up.

"Hello, Marshal," Elmer called down to him. "Get yourself a hammer and come on up and help."

"If there is anything you don't want, it's me climbin' around on a roof," Marshal Ferrell said. "Duff, have you got a minute?"

"Aye," Duff said, starting toward the ladder.

"Now, damn it, you two had that all cooked up, didn't you?" Elmer said. "You prob'ly told him, 'come on out tomorrow 'bout nine or so and say you need me so's I can get Elmer to finish with the roof.' "

Duff chuckled as he stepped onto the ladder to climb down. "Aye, Elmer, what can I say? Sure now, and you have it all figured out."

"I knew it, I knew it," Elmer said, though

his complaining was ameliorated by his laughter.

"Good Morning, Jerry. What brings you to Sky Meadow?"

"Johnny Taylor," Marshal Ferrell said.

"There hasn't been another killing, has there?"

"No, but the town is awfully uneasy."

"I expect it would be," Duff said.

"Duff, maybe I should have checked with you before I did this, but I was hoping that you would agree to it. And if you don't agree, I'll understand. On the other hand, if you do agree, why, then it won't take no time because it's already set."

"Here now, Jerry, and would you be for tellin' me what it is you are trying to say? Sure 'n' you're talkin' in riddles."

"I'm talkin' about deputyin'."

"Deputying?"

"Yes, deputying. In particular, I'm talkin' about you deputying."

"Marshal, there's nae need for you to appoint me a deputy. Sure 'n' haven't I always come to your aid when asked? And didn't I do the same thing for Marshal Craig, before you?"

"I'm not talkin' about being a deputy town marshal, which truth to tell don't give you much more authority than to bring in a fella for takin' a piss in the street. No, sir, I'm talkin' 'bout you bein' a deputy with some real power. I been thinkin' about this for a couple of days, so yesterday I sent a telegram to the sheriff down in Cheyenne and told him what I wanted."

"And what is it you want?"

"What I wanted was for him to make you a deputy sheriff, and that's what he's done. That gives you authority all over Laramie County."

"How can he make me a deputy? Don't I have to be sworn in?"

"You will be. I've already got things all set up for it. That is, if you are willing to accept the appointment."

"I don't know, Marshal, you know my history. 'Twas a sheriff's deputy that killed my fiancée back in Scotland. I don't know how I could bring myself to callin' myself such."

"You can call yourself anything you want, Duff," Marshal Ferrell said. "But I need your help. The town needs your help. Because I'll be honest with you, with a man like Johnny Taylor out there, I don't know where this is going to end. The town is now divided into two parts, one part wants us to hang Emile right now, and the other part wants us to let him go."

"Take the man up on his offer, Duff,"

Elmer called down from the roof of the barn. He had come down to the edge and was sitting there now, with his legs hanging down from the eves. "In the time I've known you, I've never known you to walk away from a fight. And seems to me like this Johnny fella is making it some personal. If you're worried about leavin' the place, don't be. I'll take care of things here."

"Elmer, there is much to be done out here. 'Twould not be right for me to leave you out here alone."

"Alone? Hell, Duff, this ain't no two-man operation no more, not like it was when me 'n' you first built that little ol' one room cabin. You have fourteen men workin' for you now. It ain't as if I'm goin' to be doin' physical labor all by myself. Go on. Like the marshal said, the town needs you. And I don't have to remind you that Vi and Miss Parker live in town. And I'd feel a heap better about 'em, knowin' you was there to sort of look after 'em 'n' all."

Duff nodded. "Aye, you may have a point," he said. He turned toward the marshal. "What now?"

"Come back to town with me," Marshal Ferrell said. "I can't swear you in because bein' a deputy sheriff is a county office. But Justice of the Peace Norton can. We'll go

286

see him."

"You're goin' to see the justice of the peace?" Elmer asked. "Hey, Duff, that would be a good chance for you to stop by and pick up Miss Parker on your way."

"And why would I be for doing that?"

Marshal Ferrell chuckled. "He's giving you a hint, Duff. Here, a justice of the peace can perform marriage ceremonies."

"Sure 'n' isn't that something I should discuss with Miss Parker first?"

Duff rode back to town with Marshal Ferrell. As they rode by Fiddler's Green, Marshal Ferrell asked if he wanted to stop for a beer.

"It might be good to get the dust of the ride out of our mouths," he said.

The two men dismounted then went into the saloon. Duff was surprised to see that Meagan, Fred Matthews, and R.W. Guthrie were there, along with Justice of the Peace Norton. A sign was stretched across the back wall.

CHUGWATER WELCOMES
DEPUTY SHERIFF DUFF MACCALLISTER

"Here, now, 'n' what is all this?"

"We knew you wouldn't turn the offer down," Biff Johnson said. "So we thought we'd have a bit of a celebration with the swearing-in. In celebration of the occasion, Rose cooked up a batch of haggis, taties, and neeps."

At the mention of some of his native food, Duff smiled broadly. "Did she now? Sure 'n' 'tis a foine woman you have married, Biff Johnson."

"Let's get to the swearing-in so we can celebrate," Norton suggested. "Mr. MacCallister, if you would hold up your right hand please?"

Duff did.

"Do you solemnly swear that you will faithfully perform the duties of the office of deputy sheriff for Laramie County, Wyoming?"

"I do."

"You are now a deputy sheriff."

Meagan pinned the badge onto Duff's shirt.

"You know, when Biff asked me to come over here to see you and the justice of the peace, I wasn't exactly sure what he wanted," she said quietly.

Duff looked surprised by her comment, and she laughed and put her fingers on his lips before he could say anything.

"Don't worry, I'm just teasing."

"Oh, what is the awful-tasting stuff?"

Cindy asked from the table, where such things as boiled eggs, bits of ham and cheese, cookies, and the haggis, taties, and neeps had been laid out. She had just tasted some of the latter.

"Bless her heart," Meagan said. "I'll bet she has no idea how many feathers in her cap she lost with you by that comment."

"Sure now, Meagan, and why would you be for thinking the lass had any feathers to lose?"

After a brief celebration, and congratulations from all, Duff went down to the marshal's office with Ferrell.

"I've put you a desk back there," he said. "Of course, you are sort of on your own, but I thought, just in case you wanted to check the latest reward posters, or news about any sightings, you could have a place to come."

"I appreciate it."

"Duff, have you ever heard of the town of Bordeaux?"

"It's just north of here, isn't it? I've nae been there, but I have heard of it. Why would you ask?"

"The town of Bordeaux has a reputation of being rather lawless."

"I see. And would you be for thinking that Johnny and the others might be there?"

"Not according to Marshal Cline. I sent him this telegram." Marshal Ferrell showed the telegram to Duff.

TRYING TO LOCATE JOHNNY TAYLOR STOP THINK HE MIGHT BE IN YOUR TOWN STOP HE IS WANTED FOR BANK ROBBERY STOP JERRY FERRELL MARSHAL CHUGWATER

"And this is what he sent back."

JOHNNY WAS HERE FOR SHORT TIME STOP BUT LEFT AND HAS NOT RETURNED STOP C F CLINE MARSHAL BORDEAUX

"Do you think the marshal is nae telling the truth?"

"I don't know. I've never met this fella, C.F. Cline, but I have heard of him. And from what I heard, he would seem more likely to be a snake oil salesman, or maybe even a chicken thief, than a marshal. Anyway, it was just a thought."

CHAPTER TWENTY-FOUR

"You don't want to go to Bordeaux," Elmer said that evening as he and Duff had supper together.

"Why would I nae want to go there?"

"Bordeaux is an outlaw town."

"What is an outlaw town?"

"They are towns where there is no law."

"But this town has law. It has a marshal, a man by the name of C.F. Cline."

"I know Cline."

"You know him?"

"We did a couple of jobs together back in Kansas."

"By jobs, you mean?"

"We held up a stagecoach once. And we robbed a train."

Duff chuckled. "Elmer, please tell me that we'll nae be sitting here someday when a member of the constabulary will come in, bearing a warrant for some long-ago crime."

"I can't tell you that, Duff," Elmer said.

"Though I will say that it has been so long since I done anything that would set the law after me, that ever'one has more 'n likely forgot by now."

"Have you ever been to Bordeaux?" Duff asked.

"I've never been to Bordeaux, but I've been to towns like Bordeaux . . . robbers' roosts, we used to call them."

"Marshal Ferrell says he believes Johnny might be there, but when he sent a telegram to the marshal over there, Cline telegraphed him back saying that he was nae there."

"If you ask me, a fella like C.F. Cline saying he's not there just makes me believe all the more that he would be there."

"Does it now? Then, perhaps I'll just make a visit up there and have a look around."

"I wouldn't advise that, Duff," Elmer said.

"Oh?"

"Do you know what Johnny Taylor looks like?"

"I'm nae sure I have ever encountered the gentleman."

Elmer laughed. "You seen him more than once, you've captured his brother, and you've kilt three of his men."

"Aye, but they were all masked. So I would nae recognize Mr. Taylor if he were to approach me and ask me directions."

"Right, and that's my point. You wouldn't recognize him on sight, but he damn sure knows who you are. And he has a really big reason for wanting you dead. I'd be thinkin' twice about goin' to Bordeaux, if I were you."

"And if I don't go, would you be for tellin' me how I might go about finding this man?"

"I'll go."

"What? You'll do nae such thing, Elmer Gleason. 'Tis not your job to go."

"How much are they paying you for being a deputy?"

"Why, they are nae paying me anything."

"Uh-huh. Then it's not your job either, is it?"

"Elmer, I . . ."

"I use to run in that world, Duff. and I probably still have a few friends remaining, that is them that hadn't done been carted off to prison or hanged or the like. If anyone is going to go up to Bordeaux to have a look around, it's going to be me. Don't try and talk me out of it."

"All right, Elmer, I'll nae talk you out of it."

"Damn," Elmer said. "Hell, you mean you aren't even goin' to try and talk me out of it? Just a little bit?"

"I thought you did nae want me to talk

you out of it."

"Well, I wanted you to try a little bit to talk me out of it. That way it makes me seem like more a hero when I go."

Duff laughed. "I'll ask you nae to go."

Elmer held his hand up and shook his head. "I'm thankin' you for your worry, but I'll be goin' all the same."

"Do I have to try and talk you out of it any more?" Duff asked.

"Lord no, if you ask again I just might back out. Now, tell me what you need to know."

"I want you to see if you can find this man, Johnny Taylor. All I know is his name. Also, if you can, see who the others are who are with him. I do nae mind goin' up against one or two, even more men. But if such thing is to happen, I'm sure I'd be for wantin' to know who it is that's the enemy."

"I'll get back whatever information I can find out," Elmer said.

"You're sure you don't want me to come with you? Maybe to just be there to help out, should you be needin' any."

"Don't get me wrong, Duff, but I don't want you with me. They'll recognize you, sure as a gun is iron. And if they recognize you, then see me with you, where does that leave me?"

"Aye, I see your point," Duff said. "Elmer, find out what you can, but I do nae want you to try and be a hero."

"Believe me, Duff, I ain't the hero type."

Bordeaux was a scattering of flyblown, sun-bleached, weathered, and unpainted buildings laid out on both sides of a quarter-mile-long road, which was the only street in the town. Its reputation as a "Robbers' Roost," or "Outlaw Haven" was well earned.

Marshal Cline was a lawman in name only, and visitations by law officers from elsewhere in the territory were discouraged. They were so strongly discouraged that there was a place in the town cemetery prominently marked as LAWMAN'S PLOT. Here, tombstones marked the graves of three lawmen: two deputy sheriffs and one deputy U.S. Marshal.

HERE LIES
A DEPUTY U.S. MARSHAL
WHOSE NAME AIN'T IMPORTANT
HE WASN'T WELCOME HERE

The two tombstones for the deputy sheriffs read exactly the same. It wasn't clear whether there really were three lawmen buried there or not. The very presence of

the tombstones tended to keep curious lawmen away . . . and that was their intended
purpose.

Though it had been a while since Elmer had
been in a place like Bordeaux, there was a
strong sense of familiarity to it, and an even
stronger attraction. Such towns were a part
of his heritage, and he could no more turn
his back on them than he could on the life
he was living now.

Inside the Red Eye Saloon, Kid Dingo,
Creech, and Phelps were sitting at a table
near the front window. One week ago, they,
along with Simon Reid, had robbed a
general store of two hundred and twelve
dollars and since that time had spent their
money so freely on drinks and whores that,
by now, the money was nearly gone.

"Too bad Reid ain't still cowboyin',"
Phelps said. "Takin' them cows and sellin'
'em like we done was the easiest money we
ever made."

"Except he got hisself fired," Kid Dingo
said.

"And he sure ain't done nothin' for us
since he's come here. All he does is lay
around with whores all the time," Phelps
said.

"You know what we need to do, don't you?" Creech said. "What we need to do is rob a bank. That's where the real money is."

"Banks ain't that easy to rob," Phelps said. "That's why they're called banks."

"I don't know. They're sayin' that Johnny Taylor got a lot of money from that bank down in Chugwater," Creech said.

"Yeah, and Jackson, Short, and Blunt got themselves kilt and Johnny's own brother is in jail," Phelps pointed out.

"Short wasn't killed during the bank robbery, and Blunt wasn't even a part of the holdup," Creech said.

"Hey, lookie here," Kid Dingo, pointing out the window. "Look at that old son of a bitch coming up here. What do you think he's doing in a town like this?"

"I don't know," Creech said. "Maybe he stole a pair of false teeth somewhere."

The other two laughed.

"I think I'm going to have a little fun with him," Kid Dingo said. "Watch."

"Better watch it, Kid. If he really actually stole them false teeth, he might bite you," Creech suggested.

Elmer stopped in front of the Red Eye Saloon, dismounted, then took off his long

297

duster, rolled it up, and began to tie it to the back of his saddle. As he was securing the duster, someone spoke to him.

"Old man, you may as well get back on your horse and ride out of here. We don't like strangers here."

Elmer turned to see a young man with beady eyes and a wild shock of hair. He returned to the task of tying off his duster.

"Didn't you hear what I said? Climb back up on your horse and get. An old man like you is liable to get run over by a horse or something. Don't you turn your back on me, you gray-haired old son of a bitch!"

Elmer continued to tie off the rawhide cords, without so much as an acknowledgment of the irritating young man. That was when he heard the sound of a revolver being cocked.

"Maybe I had better introduce myself," the punk said. "Folks call me Kid Dingo. I reckon that name means something to y—"

That was as far as Kid Dingo got, because quietly, and unobserved, Elmer had snaked his shotgun from the saddle sheath. And when he turned, he didn't just turn. He whirled around much faster than the kid would have expected an old man to move. The butt of his shotgun caught the kid in the jaw, and blood and teeth flew from his

298

mouth as he went down, falling face first in a pile of recent horse droppings. The kid's confrontation with Elmer had brought Creech and Phelps out of the saloon.

"Hey, old man, you goin' to leave him like that? He's facedown in horse shit. He could smother."

Elmer looked back at the kid. "Yeah, you're right," he said.

Walking over to him, Elmer kicked him in the side. Kid Dingo groaned and rolled over onto his back. His face was covered with horse dung, but he was no longer in danger of smothering. When he started back toward the saloon, Creech and Phelps moved to block his way.

Elmer, who was still carrying his shotgun, raised it. It wasn't until then that the two men noticed the barrel had been sawed off to about twelve inches.

"There are two of you," Elmer said quietly. "And I've got two barrels."

The two men stepped out of his way, and Elmer went on inside.

The clientele of the Red Eye was composed of men and women who had, long ago, stepped out of mainstream society, so while Elmer's reaction to the three young punks who had confronted him gained him enough recognition to be accepted, they weren't overly impressed by it. The more experienced of them had seen men like Elmer before, and knew that age was not the determining factor in a man's mettle.

There were at least four bar girls working the saloon, but it was difficult to tell how old they were. Their years on the line had taken so much from them that even the most artful use of face paint could not reverse the dissipation of their profession.

"What can I get for you?" the bartender asked.

"What's the cheapest whiskey you got?" Elmer asked in a gravelly voice.

"Hell, the cheapest is also the most expensive," the bartender replied.

"Really? Well, then give me the best you've got," Elmer said, putting a quarter on the bar. "I don't often get to drink the most expensive whiskey."

The others in the bar laughed. None of them realized that by most measuring standards, Elmer was a wealthy man who could, if he wished, buy this saloon, and just about every other business in town.

"What's your name?" the bartender asked as he poured the drink.

"Why do you need to know?" Elmer replied. "Are you making up a list?"

"No, just curious is all."

"That a fact? No offense, mister, but I don't like people who are curious."

"Mister, look out!" one of the bar girls shouted, and Elmer swung toward the front door with his shotgun in hand.

"You son of a bitch!" a shit-faced Kid Dingo shouted. He fired at Elmer, the bullet crashing into the bar right beside him. Elmer fired back, the roar of the shotgun sounding like an explosion. The blast of double-aught shot opened up Kid Dingo's chest and propelled him back through the batwing doors with such force that one of them was ripped from its hinges.

Even as the gun was still smoking, Elmer broke the barrel down, pulled out the expended shell, and replaced it with another.

Creech and Phelps came running into the saloon then.

"Better hold it, boys! He reloaded!" the bartender shouted.

The two men stopped. Creech pointed a finger at Elmer. "That old son of a bitch killed our friend!"

"Yeah, I did. And I'm about to kill you two as well." Elmer raised the gun to his shoulder and pulled back both hammers.

"No!" Creech shouted. He and Phelps turned, and ran from the saloon, chased by the laughter of all the patrons. A moment later, they were on their horses, galloping out of town.

Elmer took his glass of whiskey to one of the tables and sat down to peruse the room. Most of the others in the saloon were in pairs or in groups of no more than three. But at one table in the corner, he saw seven men sitting together.

"You're a little free with your gun, aren't you, mister?"

Elmer looked up at the questioner, and smiled. "Hello, Cline. It's been a good while, hasn't it?"

CHAPTER TWENTY-FIVE

Marshal Cline stared at Elmer for a long moment before recognition slowly passed across his face.

"Gleason? Elmer Gleason, is that you?"

"Well, I ain't no ghost."

"Hell, I heard you went to sea. I thought maybe you'd drowned someplace."

"Near 'bout did a couple of times. Have a seat. I'll buy you a drink. And 'cause we ain't seen each other in a long while, I'll buy you the most expensive drink in the house."

Marshal Cline smiled, then took his seat. He lifted his hand toward the barkeep. "Whiskey," he called out.

"I heard you was marshalin' up here," Elmer said. "I had to come see for myself if it was true."

"Well, you've seen," he said, taking the whiskey from the barkeeper. "What do you think?"

"I have to say that I'm damn surprised. I never thought I'd see my old friend C.F. Cline on this side of the law."

"Old friend? We may have pulled a couple of jobs together, but we never was what you would call close friends. Hell, the way I remember it, you run away to sea to keep me from killin' you."

"Is that the way you remember it?" Elmer asked, calmly and unemotionally.

"Yeah." Cline took a drink, then set the glass back down. "Hell of it is, though, I don't remember for the life of me why it is that I was about to kill you."

"Does that mean I'm safe, 'til you remember?"

Cline laughed. "I reckon it does. What'd you kill the boy for?"

"It seemed the thing to do. I mean, seein' as he was tryin' to kill me."

"Did you know him?"

"I met him about fifteen minutes ago."

"You only knew him for fifteen minutes, and he tried to kill you? How the hell did you piss somebody off enough in just fifteen minutes that he wanted to kill you?"

"It might have had something to do with the fact that I sort of knocked him facedown into a pile of horse shit."

Cline laughed again, this time so hard that

he got the attention of the others in the saloon. One of the others came over to the table.

"For a marshal just come to arrest someone for a killin', you two seem to be gettin' on pretty well."

"Johnny, this here is my old friend Elmer Gleason. Elmer, this is Johnny Taylor."

"You robbed the bank in Chugwater," Elmer said. It wasn't a question, nor was it a challenge. It was a simple statement of fact.

"How do you know that?" Johnny asked, his suspicions aroused. "Are you a lawman?"

"Hell, Johnny, ever'body in Laramie County knows you robbed that bank. And no, I ain't no lawman any more than my ol' friend C.F. Cline is a lawman."

"That's a funny way of puttin' it. Seein' as Cline is a lawman."

"Is he?"

Johnny looked at Cline, then shook his head and smiled. "I reckon you're right. He ain't no lawman. Not no real lawman, anyway. Real lawmen ain't welcome here. So, tell me, Gleason, what are you doin' in Bordeaux?"

"I come here 'cause I thought this was a place where folks didn't ask you a lot of fool questions."

"Some folks don't ask questions and some do. I got a reason for askin'. Seein' as you know I held up the bank in Chugwater, it could be that you are a bounty hunter. If you are, you're goin' to play hell collectin' on it."

"Or, it could be that your operation was so slick, and you got so much money, that I might be wantin' to join up with you for your next one."

"How do you know there's goin' to be a next one?"

"I don't see you walkin' away from a winnin' hand on the table."

"You and Mr. Gleason ought to get along, Johnny, seein' as you are in the same business," Cline said.

"You've held up banks before?" Johnny asked.

"With your marshal," Elmer answered.

"Jonesburg, Kansas," Cline said.

Johnny nodded. "All right, come on, let me introduce you to some of my pals."

Elmer stood up, but before he walked away he looked back down at Cline. "What about the man I just kilt? Do I need to be signin' any papers, or goin' before a judge, or a justice of the peace or anything?"

"You got twenty dollars on you?" Cline asked.

"Yeah, I got twenty dollars."

"Give it to me, and this will all go away."

"Twenty dollars, and I don't hear nothin' else from it? How does that work?"

"I'm not your ordinary kind of city marshal. I don't draw a salary from the city. I have to come up with my own ways of makin' money."

"I'll give you ten dollars."

"That ain't enough. I got to make a livin'."

"Twenty dollars is all I got. I ain't givin' you all I got."

"Keep your twenty dollars, Mr. Gleason," Johnny said. "I'll pay it for you."

"Well, that's mighty nice of you."

Johnny put a twenty-dollar bill on the table in front of Cline, then escorted Elmer over to meet the others with him.

"Gleason wants to join up with us," Johnny said after he introduced him to the others.

"I don't know, he's a little old, ain't he?" Evans asked.

"You might be right," Johnny replied. "I know that's what Kid Dingo thought."

The others laughed.

"Yeah, well, I don't mean nothin' by it. I was just sayin', is all."

During the entire conversation Harper had been staring at Elmer. Now he spoke for the first time. "I've seen you before, somewhere."

"I wouldn't doubt it," Johnny said. "I expect you two have run in some of the same circles."

"No, I've seen him somewhere just real recent," Harper said.

"I was wonderin' if you would recognize me."

"Then I have seen you before, ain't I?"

"Yeah, you have. But belly down on the horse like you was, I'm surprised that you seen me at all. Or anyone else for that matter," Elmer said.

"What?" Johnny asked. "What are you talkin' about, belly down on a horse?"

"I'm talkin' 'bout the last time me 'n' Harper met. Only we didn't exactly meet. I was standin' just real close whenever the marshal took him down off the horse and arrested him. I was in the court when I heard the judge let you go, too."

"Harper, you never told us nothin' about you bein' belly down over a horse. What was that all about?"

"Maybe you better let me do the tellin'," Elmer suggested. "I seen it all."

"All right, you tell us what happened,"

Johnny said.

"What happened is a man by the name of MacCallister come up behind Harper in the saloon. And without so much as a fare-thee-well, while Harper wasn't lookin' MacCallister brought a chair down on top of Harper's head, knocking him out. Then, while Harper was still unconscious, he dragged him out of the saloon and tied him belly down over his own saddle. I've seen a lot of dirty tricks in my life, but that's near 'bout the dirtiest I've ever seen."

"That the way it happened, Harper?" Johnny asked.

"Yeah," Harper said, glancing toward Elmer. The expression on Harper's face indicated his thanks for the way Elmer had told the story. "That's the way it happened all right. The son of a bitch hit me from behind."

"Then you got as much of a beef with MacCallister as I do."

"Let me add my own beef to it," Elmer said.

"What's your problem with MacCallister?"

"I had a sweet deal goin', saltin' an old abandoned mine and gettin' suckers to invest in it. Then MacCallister come along and homesteaded the land where my mine was. He dynamited the mine shut, and I was put out of business. The main reason I'm wantin' to join up with you boys is because I want to be a part of the next job you pull. But I was also sort of hopin' that I might get a chance to get back at him."

"We're goin' to take care of MacCallister all right," Johnny said. "But first things first. First thing we're goin' to do is get my brother out of jail."

Elmer shook his head. "You ever seen that jail?"

"I seen it once, in the dark."

"Well, Harper has seen it, 'cause he was in it, so I know he'll agree. That jail is built out of a double brick wall with reinforced concrete poured down between the walls. If you was to try and blow a hole in that wall, you'd have to use so much dynamite that you'd kill anyone that's inside, includin' your brother."

"Don't worry, we ain't goin' to try nothin' like that. I've got a different plan, and we've already started it," Johnny said.

"If you was in Chugwater the other day, you prob'ly already know about it," Blunt said. "We kilt two of the citizens and left 'em lyin' in the street."

"I was there."

"We plan to do that again," Johnny said.

"How many do you plan to kill?"

"I plan to kill as many as it takes, until they turn my brother loose," Johnny said. "Why? Do you have a problem with that?"

Elmer stuck his hand down into his pocket and pulled out six more shotgun shells.

"I might have to buy me a few more shells," he said.

Johnny laughed out loud, then slapped Elmer on the back. "Elmer, you're all right," he said. "After we take care of business down in Chugwater, it'll be good to have you along for our next job."

"Did you really get over thirty thousand dollars out of that robbery in Chugwater?" Elmer asked.

"Thirty? We got over forty," Calhoun said, proudly.

"Forty thousand dollars." Elmer whistled. "I ain't never seen that much money in my whole life. You boys got it on you? Could I see it?"

"Now, do you think we would be so dumb as to carry that much money on us in a place like this?" Johnny asked. "We got near all of it hid out."

"Where you got it hid?"

Johnny glared at Elmer for a moment; then he laughed. "What? Do you expect us to tell you that, so you can just waltz in and take it all yourself?"

"You can't blame a fella for tryin'," Elmer said, smiling back at Johnny. "So, how soon before we can pull another job so I can get some money like that for my own self?"

"I told you. After we get my brother out of jail. And I plan to take another step in that direction tonight."

The night insects were singing as Johnny, Elmer, and the others waited just outside of town.

"We goin' to get us another couple of drunks tonight?" Evans asked.

"No. Turns out the two we kilt didn't have no kin in town, so it didn't really make that much of a difference to anybody whether they was dead or not. I'm changin' the plans. Tonight we're goin' to raise the stakes a little."

"What do you mean?" Ike asked.

"Tonight we're goin' to make sure we kill someone that will get the attention of the rest of the town."

"You got 'ny idea who that might be?"

"Yeah, I got me a good idea," Johnny said. "They's a woman in town that runs a café. Well, not a regular café. The only thing she sells in her café is pies, but I had me a piece of pie while I was in town, and seemed like there was lots of folks come in to her place while I was there and near all of 'em knew her, and called her by name. Vi, I think it was. I figure if we kilt Vi, and left her body out in the street, it would for sure get some attention."

CHAPTER TWENTY-SIX

It was eleven o'clock at night and it was cold enough that the horses exhaled clouds of vapor, which floated away, white, in the night air. Seven men — Johnny, Evans, Calhoun, Thomas, Leroy Blunt, Harper, and Elmer Gleason — were riding toward the town of Chugwater.

"How are we going to do this?" Evans asked. Of Johnny Taylor's original gang, only Evans and Calhoun remained.

"It's easy. The pie woman lives in a little cabin out behind her pie shop, across the alley from it," Johnny said. "It's like a whore's crib."

"A whore's crib?" Calhoun said. He laughed. "Maybe she figures that if the pie business don't work out for her, she can always whore some."

"Is she good lookin' enough to whore?" Blunt asked.

"Who says a woman has to be good lookin'

to be a whore?" Ike Thomas asked. "Hell, if you had to be good lookin', there wouldn't be a whore in Bordeaux."

"You got that right," Calhoun said.

"If you men will shut up and pay attention, I'll tell you what we are going to do," Johnny said. "We'll wait 'til town is real quiet, then we'll ride in, go 'round back of her place, go into her crib, and kill her."

"More 'n likely, she'll have the door locked," Harper said.

"I ain't never seen a lock that Bart Evans couldn't pick," Johnny said. "The thing is, we need to be real quiet."

"What if she screams?"

"If we get to her fast enough, one scream won't mean much. Folks that hear it will just figure it's a whore screamin'. Whores is always screamin' 'bout first one thing then another."

"Damn," Elmer said. He stopped. "Hold it up for a moment, will you?"

"What is it?"

"My horse has gone lame. Might just be a rock in the foot, I don't know, but he's limpin' so bad I can't keep up with you. Wait up for a while." Elmer dismounted, then picked up his horse's right hind foot.

"We can't be waitin' for you. We need time to scout the town out for a bit before we do this," Johnny said.

"You can't wait on me, just for a few minutes? If I'm goin' to join up with you, I aim to be a part of this."

"What if it's a split hoof?" Johnny asked. "If your horse has a split hoof, you'll just get in the way."

"All right, I tell you what. You boys go on ahead. If it's no more'n a rock, I'll prob'ly catch up with you. If it's somethin' worse, I'll go on back to Bordeaux. That is, if he can get me back that far."

"All right, catch up with us if you can. Let's go, boys," Johnny said.

The others rode off as Elmer stayed behind to examine his horse's hind foot. He watched until the others disappeared in the dark, then he remounted and started riding hard, not by the same trail they took, but by a dry creek bed that he knew led to a spot just behind Curly Lathom's barber shop. He covered the distance in about five minutes. The dry creek bed was almost a full mile shorter route than the one being taken by Johnny and the others. In addition, Elmer had ridden as fast as he dared in the night. When he came out behind the barbershop, he figured that he had at least ten minutes before the others would reach town. The first thing he did was go directly to Vi's house. He knocked on the door.

"Vi! Vi, it's me, Elmer! Wake up!"

A moment later, Vi opened the door. She was in her nightgown and she smiled up at Elmer.

"Elmer, what are you doing here?"

"Get dressed, quick!" Elmer said. "Get dressed quick, and come with me. Don't show any light."

"Elmer, what's going on? You are frightening me."

"I mean to scare you," Elmer said. "Do what I tell you, I'll explain it all later. Now come with me — we're goin' to see the marshal."

"All right, if you say so," Vi said.

"Hurry, Vi," Elmer said. "Lock your door when you leave, as if you are still in the house."

It took Vi but a couple of minutes to pull a dress on over her nightgown. Then Elmer lifted her onto his horse, and they hurried down to Marshal Ferrell's house.

"Elmer, what's this all about?"

"I'll tell you and the marshal at the same time," Elmer said. "Just trust me."

"I do trust you," Vi replied.

The marshal's house was but two doors down from his office and the jail. With Vi standing beside him, Elmer pounded on the marshal's door.

"Marshal Ferrell! Marshal Ferrell! Wake up! Wake up!"

"I'm comin', I'm comin'. Keep your shirt on," a muffled voice responded from inside. A moment later, the door opened partially, and Marshal Ferrell peered through the crack.

"Who's there? What do you want?"

"It's me, Marshal. Elmer Gleason. I've got Vi Winslow with me."

"Vi?" the marshal said, opening the door all the way. He stood there, dimly backlit by a low-burning lantern.

"Elmer, what is it? What's wrong?"

"It's Johnny and his gang, Marshal. They're comin' in town tonight."

"Damn. If it's like the last time, you can guess what they have in mind."

"I don't need to guess," Elmer said. "I know what they got in mind. They're plannin' on murderin' Vi Winslow. That's why I brung her over here. I figured maybe she could wait here with Mrs. Ferrell while me and you take care of Johnny and his gang. That way she'll be safe."

"Yes, of course. Come in, Miss Winslow. Emma, come out here a moment, would you?"

Marshal Ferrell's wife, Emma, came into

the front room, clutching a dressing gown about her.

"Miss Winslow is going to stay here with you for a while. I've got to go out."

Before Jerry Ferrell had become the marshal, he had been a deputy marshal for Craig, so Emma was used to being married to a law officer. She asked no questions, but smiled at Vi to make her feel welcome.

"How many are there?" Marshal Ferrell asked.

"There are six of them," Elmer answered.

"Six? All right, well, at least we'll have the advantage of surprise. "You step down to the jail and tell Deputy Mullins what's going on. I'll join you soon as I get dressed."

"All right," Elmer agreed.

Less than five minutes later, Elmer, Marshal Ferrell, Deputy Mullins, and Deputy Pierce were behind the corners of buildings on the north side of town from which direction Elmer figured the night riders would come. Pierce was limping around on a bandaged leg, but he insisted upon being a part of it.

As Johnny and the others came into town, their horses' hooves clopped hollowly on the hard-packed dirt of First Street as they passed the dark stores and businesses of

Chugwater. Here and there, a very small yellow square of light shined from one of the quiet buildings. Somewhere a dog began to bark, and another, a little closer, answered his bark.

"Hey, Johnny, what's this pie woman look like?" a voice said in the darkness. "I mean, think maybe we could have a little fun with her before we kilt her?"

"What difference does it make what she looks like?" another voice answered. "Ain't you ever heard that all cats are gray in the dark?"

There was a ripple of ribald laughter from the riders.

"That's far enough, men! Throw up your hands!" Marshal Ferrell challenged.

"What the hell!" one of the men shouted gruffly.

"Let's get out of here!"

Elmer recognized the last voice as belonging to Johnny Taylor.

The riders started shooting, and Elmer, Marshal Ferrell, and his two deputies returned fire. Muzzle flashes lit up the night street, and gunshots roared as the riders turned and galloped away.

All but one.

As the horses disappeared into the darkness, and the gunshots stopped, a still form lay in the middle of the street.

And another still form lay on the porch in front of Sikes Hardware store.

"Marshal! Marshal Ferrell!" Deputy Pierce called. "It's Frankie! They kilt Frank Mullins!"

All up and down the street, lanterns were lit and brought out onto the front porch by curious residents. Now as many as half a dozen dogs were barking and at least two babies were crying.

"What is it? What happened?" someone shouted.

Within moments, several lanterns started drifting up the street as the men who were carrying them could no longer contain their curiosity.

Marshal Ferrell went over to check on Deputy Mullins, but Elmer went straight out into the middle of the street to see which one of Johnny's men had been hit.

It was Bart Evans.

Evans wasn't dead yet, though he had at least three wounds in his chest. The wounds were from double-aught buckshot, so Elmer knew he was the one who had shot him.

"Gleason?" Evans gasped. "Are you are a lawman?"

"No, I ain't no lawman," Elmer said. "But

Vi Winslow is my woman. And I'll be damn if I let you bastards kill her."

"I never did trust you anyway, you son of a . . ." Evans was unable to finish the sentence. He gasped a couple of times, and then he died.

"I would have stayed longer, and got more information out of them," Elmer said to Duff later that same day. "But the sons of bitches was plannin' on killin' Vi. Can you imagine that, Duff? They was goin' to kill Vi and leave her lyin' out in the street the way they done with Percy and Walt. I couldn't let that happen, so I come on in town ahead of 'em, and warned Marshal Ferrell."

"And 'twas the right thing you did, Elmer," Duff said.

"I just wish that I had kilt Taylor instead of Evans."

"You did what needed to be done," Duff said. "Now, at least, we know where they are. I'll be riding up to Bordeaux today to pay a call upon Mr. Taylor."

"Not by yourself, you ain't goin'," Elmer said.

"Elmer, did you nae tell me that Bordeaux was an outlaw town?"

"Yeah, that's what it is all right."

"And would you nae be recognized the

322

moment you rode into town? Especially after last night."

"I probably would," he agreed.

"And is there any doubt but that Johnny and the others know you betrayed them?"

"I'm pretty sure they have figured it out, by now."

"Then would you be for tellin' me why I would want you beside me when I rode into town? They would start shootin' the moment they recognized you."

"Yeah, all right, I see what you mean. But Duff, even as good as you are, you can't take on the whole town."

"Then I'll take but a wee bite of the town," Duff joked.

"When will you be goin'?"

"A few days yet. Young Frankie Mullins was engaged to R.W. Guthrie's daughter. That makes him a friend, and I'll nae go before his burying."

Within the next three days there were two burials, but only one funeral. Bart Evans was put in the ground on the very afternoon of the day he was killed, with only the two grave diggers present. They dug the hole, lowered the plain, unadorned pine box into the ground, then shoveled the dirt back in. He lay next to Julius Jackson, Al Short, and

Jim Blunt, and like their graves, his was marked only by a board on which his name, and nothing else, had been painted.

Three days later, the entire town turned out for the funeral of Deputy Frank J. Mullins. His mother and father lived in town, where his father owned and operated Mullins Meat Market. Harold Mullins was a former Texas Ranger and his background had been the inspiration for Frank to become a law officer.

Deputy Mullins had been engaged to Jennie Guthrie, and she was at the graveside now, wearing a black dress and veil as she stood next to Frank Mullins's mother.

At the request of Harold Mullins, Duff had agreed to play "Amazing Grace" on the pipes, and when he showed up at the cemetery he was wearing the kilt of the Black Watch, complete with the *sgian dubh,* and the Victoria Cross. The long, drawn-out, plaintive notes of the music drifted over the cemetery and into the town, so that even the very few who had not turned out for the funeral could hear the mournful chords.

When the music was completed, the Episcopal priest committed Frank Mullins's remains to the ground.

"Thou only art immortal, the creator and maker of mankind; and we are mortal, formed of the earth, and unto earth shall we return. For so thou didst ordain when thou createdst me, saying, 'Dust thou art, and unto dust shalt thou return.'

"Receive our brother Frank Mullins into the arms of thy mercy, into the blessed rest of everlasting peace, and into the glorious company of the saints in light. *Amen.*"

At the invitation of Deputy Mullins's parents, a tearful Jennie Guthrie dropped the first handful of dirt onto the casket.

CHAPTER TWENTY-SEVEN

"Here's another one," the mail clerk said to the postmaster. "It has the same handwriting, going to the same person up in Bordeaux — Andrew McCloud. And this one is just like all the others. It don't have no return address either."

"Why does that make you curious?" the postmaster asked.

"First of all, because in all the time I been here, there ain't been no more than three or four letters a month that go up to Bordeaux. But since this person started writing to Andrew McCloud, why, we been sending one or two a week up there."

"You should be glad postage has picked up. That's what pays our salary," the postmaster replied.

"Yeah, but here is the thing. There has never, in all the time these here letters have been goin' up there, been one letter that has ever come back from this McCloud person."

The postmaster laughed. "Corey, I don't know if you're playing detective or planning on writing a book about it. Don't you know we're not supposed to get personally involved with the mail? Neither snow nor rain nor heat nor gloom of night will stay us from the swift completion of our appointed rounds."

Corey put the mysterious letter in the bag that the mail courier would deliver north when he left on his route today.

Johnny Taylor was in Marshal C.F. Cline's office, and he wasn't happy.

"I thought you said Elmer Gleason was a friend of yours, that we could trust him."

"I never said you could trust him. All I said was that we had done some business together in the past."

"He's the son of a bitch that betrayed us," Johnny said. "He was workin' with the law all the time. I should have expected something when he stopped to take care of his lame horse. That horse wasn't no more lame than I was."

"How do you know he was one of the ones who ambushed you? Did you see him?"

"No, it was too dark."

"Then how do you know that he was one

of them? It could be that the town is just postin' guards now, after the killin' of those two men last week."

"I know because I just picked up a letter at the post office. We have a friend in Chugwater who has been keeping us posted."

"That's sort of risky, isn't it? Getting mail from Chugwater? You are a wanted man, Johnny. You need to be careful about doing things like that. I would think the post office would get on to that and tell the sheriff."

"The letter don't come to me, personal. It's addressed to Andrew McCloud. I got me a box down at the post office under that name."

"Ha," Cline said. "That's pretty smart. You got someone in Chugwater, huh? Who is he?"

"I ain't goin' to tell you," Johnny said. "Like you said, I've got to be careful. Especially after you set me up with Gleason, like you done."

"I didn't set you up."

"Whether you did or didn't, I don't trust you anymore."

Cline laughed. "It don't seem to me like you got much choice in the matter. As long as you are living here in Bordeaux, you have to trust me."

"That's just it. After gettin' this letter

today, I don't trust anybody anymore. We're pullin' out of here today."

"It's probably just as well," Cline said. "You and the others are getting too dangerous, even for Bordeaux. And when it gets dangerous for you, then it gets even more dangerous for me. You just have your own crimes to deal with. I got the crimes of ever' damn body in Bordeaux weighing down on me."

"You get paid well enough. Most city marshals make what? Fifty, sixty dollars a month? You're makin' two hundred dollars a month."

"It ain't like I'm not earnin' it. Most of the time I can keep the outside law out of here, by throwin' them a bone ever' now an' ag'in. But you boys have done killed how many now? Three? Four? Five?"

"Four. One in the bank, two last week, and one night before last."

"How do you know you kilt one night before last? I thought you said it was too dark to see."

"It was in the letter."

When Johnny returned to the Red Eye Saloon, the only one sitting at the table was Clay Calhoun.

"Where are the others?"

"They're gettin' ready to leave," Calhoun

said. "You did say we was goin' to be leavin' today, didn't you?"

"I did."

"Listen, uh, Johnny, me 'n' you is the only two left from the bank robbery."

"Yes."

"What I'm saying is, what about Al, Bart, and Julius's share of the robbery money? I mean it's still buried out there with the rest of the money, ain't it?"

"It's still there."

What's goin' to happen to it now?"

"What do you say that me and you split that money even between us?" Johnny asked with a smile.

Calhoun returned the smile. "Now that's an idea I like."

"I thought you would."

"What about Blunt or Thomas or Harper? You don't plan to give them none of it?"

"Why should I? They wasn't a part of the bank robbery, was they?"

"You're right," Calhoun said. "They wasn't none of them with us. Well, I'd better get ready to pull out of here. I just wanted to talk to you about this."

"You're a good and loyal man, Clay," Johnny said. "And I like to reward men that are good and loyal."

When Calhoun left, Johnny pulled out the

letter and began reading it again. He paid particular attention to the letter, because it seemed to offer a suggestion as to what to do next.

I suppose that you did not know that Vi Winslow was Elmer Gleason's special girlfriend. Now Gleason is a hero in town for warning the marshal that you were coming, and for shooting at you all as you rode into town.

I don't think killing Vi Winslow would have made the marshal let Emile go, anyway. There is only one person in town who has that much sway with the marshal. He is the only person who could sway Marshal Ferrell to free Emile. That person would be Duff MacCallister, and I know this is true because I have seen, with my own eyes, the influence Duff MacCallister is able to exert over the marshal.

Don't kill MacCallister as you have been trying to do. Killing him would be the wrong thing to do, for then you would lose the only source of persuasion you might have to be able to manipulate. If you want my idea, you will stop trying to kill MacCallister and take his girlfriend instead. His girlfriend is Meagan Parker, the woman that owns the dress-making shop. If you was to take and hold her, and threaten to kill her if he don't make the marshal turn Emile loose, Emile would be turned loose.

"Do me a favor," Marshal Ferrell told Duff, when Duff told him that he was about to ride up to Bordeaux to have a look around.

"And what would that be?"

"Don't go ridin' in there with your badge pinned to your shirt, shining in the sun. The word is that there is a one-hundred-dollar reward to anyone who kills a visiting lawmen. I don't know if it's true, or if that is just something that has been put out to discourage lawmen from visiting."

"Good advice," Duff said. "Before I leave, I'm going to have a visit with Biff Johnson. I'll be for passing myself off as a purveyor of spirits."

"The first thing you have to learn is, you aren't a purveyor of spirits," Biff said with a laugh. "You are a whiskey drummer. You got that?"

"Aye, a whiskey drummer."

"You'll need a sample satchel," Biff said. "I've got two or three here, and I'll get one all fixed up for you."

"Scotch," Duff said. "If I'm to be a purveyor of spirits, then I'll be promoting the virtues of Scotch."

"What are you going to be?" Biff challenged.

"Aye, I forgot. I'll not be purveying spirits, I'll be drumming whiskey."

Biff looked at Elmer and groaned. "He's hopeless," he said.

"Here now, frien', I ain't no kind of a purveyor, no how. I'm a whiskey drummer, and tha's a fac' pure 'n' simple," Duff said, perfectly duplicating the Western slang and accent.

"Damn, Duff," Elmer said. "Where did you learn to talk like that?"

"Sure now 'n' haven't I been listening to you for three years now?"

Elmer laughed. "It sounds like I learned you just real good."

"Elmer, the man that's running the Red Eye. Is he a real skinny man, dark hair slicked back, a little moustache, and a prominent Adam's apple?" Biff asked.

"You nailed him," Elmer said. "That's exactly what he looks like."

"What kind of hat does he wear?"

"Damndest kind of hat I've ever seen. Ain't no ordinary hat. It's a little round thing, ain't got no crown a'tall to speak of. Ain't got no brim either."

"Sounds like a beret," Duff said.

"That's exactly what it is," Biff said. "His name is Scooter Carmody."

"Scooter, yeah, I he'ered some folks call him that," Elmer said.

"Good," Biff said. "Duff, here are a few things you might want to know about Scooter. First of all, don't trust him. He will always sell out to the highest bidder, so he has to believe that you are a whiskey drummer. You also might want to know that he carries a small holdout pistol clamped inside his beret. So if he takes it off and starts to fiddle with it, be very aware."

"Good information, thank you."

"I ain't all that sure about Duff goin' over there as a whiskey drummer though," Elmer said. "I asked Carmody for the cheapest whiskey he had and he told me that the cheapest was also the most expensive that he had."

"That's 'cause he ain't seen what I got to offer him," Duff said, once again falling into the vernacular.

Again Elmer and Biff laughed.

"Elmer, my friend, would you be for giving me a quick and easy description of Johnny Taylor?"

"I'd say he's about five-feet-six, or maybe five-feet-seven-inches tall. He's a little bit taller 'n his brother, Emile, but not much. He has dark hair. He don't have a beard, but he don't shave all that much neither. But the easiest way to recognize him is his ears. He's got near half of one of 'em bit off."

"Which ear? Right, or left?"

"Right. No, left. Well, truth is, I don't exactly remember, but how many folks you plannin' on runnin' into that's got half a ear bit off?"

Duff chuckled. "You have a point," he said.

Over the next few minutes Biff identified the various whiskeys in his sample case, giving Duff a few words of description for each of them, until Duff thought he was ready.

"Oh, and one more thing," Biff said. "I know you can lose your Scottish accent. But can you talk like an Englishman?"

"Hoot, mon, ye'd have a Scot speak as a bloody Englishman?"

"Can you?"

"But of course, my good man, if the occasion warrants," Duff said. "The question is, why the bloody 'ell would I want to do such a thing?"

Elmer and Biff both laughed.

"Because most whiskey drummers I've met act like their shit doesn't stink. And the only Englishmen I've ever met act the same way."

"You're a good judge of character," Duff said. "For in my opinion, they are all like that."

"In which case, perhaps you are a purveyor of spirits, rather than a whiskey drummer."

"I've only one worry," Duff said.

"What is that?"

"There's nae a better salesman in the world than a Scotsman. What will I do when I take an order for two hundred dollars' worth of whiskey?"

"Don't worry about it. If that actually happens, I'll come up with enough to fill the order."

Duff looked at himself in the mirror behind the bar. At first glance he looked no different from any other rancher, or even cowboy for that matter, perhaps excepting that his denims and shirts were always clean.

"If I'm going to play the role of a bloody Englishman, I had best look like one," he said.

When Duff rode into Bordeaux later that afternoon, he was wearing a brown tweed suit, with a red satin vest. He was also wearing a bowler hat with a small red feather in the hatband. Although Duff was deadly accurate with a pistol or a rifle, he had never mastered the art of the quick draw. Because of that, he actually wore his pistol in a holster that had a flap that snapped down over it. And though that would make his draw even slower, should he actually attempt one, it also had the effect of putting a potential adversary off guard.

Though Duff didn't realize it, he arrived in Bordeaux almost two hours after Johnny and the others in his gang had left. They were the only ones who would have recognized him, and of that group, only Johnny and Calhoun had ever seen him at close enough quarters to be able to identify him. Though, given his disguise, perhaps even they would not have recognized him today.

Because none of Johnny's men were in town, and because Duff presented a most unprepossessing appearance as he rode in, most gave him little notice. As he was dismounting in front of the Red Eye Saloon, someone called out to him.

"Who are you, mister, and what are you doing in Bordeaux?"

Duff turned toward the man who had called out to him. Even if the man had not been wearing a badge, Duff would have recognized him as Marshal Cline from the description Elmer had given of a pock-marked face and a scarred upper lip.

"Ahh, how fortunate for me to encounter a representative of the local constabulary," Duff said in his best English accent. "Tell me, my good man, what would be the name of the gentleman who manages this pub?"

"I'm askin' the questions here," Cline said.

"Oh, yes, you did inquire as to my name, didn't you? I'm so sorry I didn't respond. My name is Richard Plantagenet, Esquire. I represent the Royal Distilleries of Great Britain, and I am making a tour through the American West to introduce our fine line of spirits. And I ask you again, sir, if you could tell me the name of the gentleman who runs the —" Duff paused and looked at the name painted on the window of the saloon, then read it aloud, not as the name of the establishment but as two separate words. "Red . . . Eye."

"His name is Carmody. Scooter Carmody. But he won't be buying anything from you. My cousin furnishes him with everything he needs."

"Oh, dear," Duff said. "Well, a bit of competition would be good for all three of us, your cousin, Mr. Carmody, and myself."

Duff took his case down, then walked into the saloon.

"Haw! Look at this, boys!" someone said, pointing at Duff. "You boys ever seen anyone dressed like this?"

"Thank you, I do try and turn out with my best when I am working," Duff said. Carrying his case over to the bar, he opened it up to display its contents.

"Now, gentlemen, if you will allow me to provide each of you with a sample of my wares."

"Hold on here!" the bartender said, angrily. "You can't come into my place and start giving away whiskey!"

"Not to worry, sir," Duff said. "You establish a price per drink, and even though these are my samples, I will pay you for each drink that is consumed."

"Wait a minute. You're telling me that you are going to give away this whiskey to my customers, but you are going to pay me for each drink you give away?"

"That is exactly what I am going to do. I am afraid that I must impose upon you for the glasses, though. I have the whiskey, I do not have the glasses."

Carmody smiled and nodded. "Yeah, okay. And I'll have the first drink."

"For you, Mr. Carmody, my best, a glass of Glenavon Special."

Chapter Twenty-Eight

The sun had set and it was almost time to close. Meagan had no customers in the store, so she was sorting patterns when she heard the tinkling bell. The bell was attached to the front door and, by its ringing, announced that someone had come in. Laying a bolt of cloth over the patterns to keep them from blowing away, she started toward the front.

Cindy Boyce was standing just inside the shop, and she smiled as Meagan approached.

"Miss Boyce," Meagan said, returning the smile.

"Please, call me Cindy. Everyone does," the pretty redhead said.

"All right, Cindy. What can I do for you?"

"You always look so — so elegant," Cindy said. "And I recall that you once said that you could make a dress for me."

"Yes, of course I can," Meagan said.

"And it wouldn't bother your business if you made one for me? I mean, me working in a saloon and all. What would the rest of your customers think of that?"

"What difference does it make what they think?" Meagan asked. "If you would like me to make a dress for you, I will be more than happy to do it."

Cindy clapped her hands in delight. "Oh, I just knew I could count on you."

"What kind of dress would you like?"

"Something elegant," Cindy said. "Something like —" She looked down into her reticule, then, with an expression of distress, started moving things around as if searching for something. "Oh dear."

"What's wrong?"

"I had a picture of what I wanted. You can make a dress from a picture, can't you?"

"Yes."

"I had a picture — I thought I brought it with me. When do you close?"

"I'm about to close now."

"Oh. I was about to go back to my room and get it and bring it to you. But, I have to be to work in just a few minutes. Oh, would you come with me and let me give it to you? I only live a couple of blocks from here. If you would come with me, I would have time to get back before I'm late for work."

"All right," Meagan said. "If I have the picture to guide me, I can start drawing out a muslin pattern for it tonight."

"Wonderful!" Cindy said.

"Let me just get my keys so I can lock up."

Meagan got her keys, then turned the CLOSED sign around just before she and Cindy stepped out of her shop onto the boardwalk out front. As Meagan was locking the door, she felt a prickly sensation as if someone was staring at her. Glancing toward the open space that separated the emporium from Fiddler's Green, she saw Francis Schumacher leaning against the wall of the saloon, staring at her.

"Mr. Schumacher?" Meagan asked.

Schumacher touched the brim of his hat, then turned and moved quickly toward the alley behind.

"That was rather frightening," Cindy said.

"It was certainly unusual," Meagan agreed.

Meagan and Cindy moved down Bowie Avenue toward Foley's Lodging House, which was on Bowie halfway between Second and Third Streets. Cindy explained that her room was on the bottom floor at the rear of the building.

"I don't have much of a view," she said.

"My back window looks out onto the alley, but it is the only thing I can afford."

Meagan followed her into the building, and down the center hall to the door that led to Cindy's room. Cindy unlocked it, then stepped inside.

"Come on in," she invited. "I'll light a lantern and . . ." Cindy paused in midsentence, then gasped. "Who are you? What are you doing in my room?"

Meagan felt strong arms grab her from behind, and before she could struggle, or even call out, a cloth with the cloying smell of chloroform was put over her nose and mouth. She felt a spinning, dizzying sensation, then nothing.

The buckboard drove slowly south on Bowie Avenue. They'd chosen a road that was mostly residential so there were less people to see them, and even fewer who paid any attention to them. If they had paid attention, they would have seen two men in the driver's seat, a pile of canvas in the back, and two more men on horseback, keeping pace with the buckboard.

When Meagan regained consciousness it took her a moment to realize where she was. She could hear horses' hooves and the sound of rolling wheels. She could also feel movement.

All right, she was obviously lying in the back of a wagon of some sort, so she knew where she was, she just didn't know why she was here.

She was also bound and gagged! My God! What was happening to her? What was going on?

Meagan started to gasp in panic, but as she did so, her head started spinning again, so she forced herself to breathe in slower, more controlled breaths.

How did she get here?

She tried to remember, but the last thing she could remember was closing her shop.

Closing her shop and seeing former Deputy Schumacher standing just outside.

Was he responsible for this?

A little more memory was coming back to her now.

Yes, she remembered. Cindy Boyce wanted her to make a dress, and Meagan had gone to Cindy's room with her to see a picture of what she wanted. Cindy had called out in surprise and fear. Someone had been waiting in the room!

That was the last thing Meagan could remember until she'd woken up in this vehicle, which she now believed, judging by its size, to be a buckboard.

"Johnny, I think the woman is awake back here," someone said.

"Any chance of her gettin' away?" another voice answered.

"Ha! Ain't a chance in hell."

"All right. Just keep an eye on her."

Meagan wanted to ask where they were going, and what they wanted with her, but she couldn't speak because she was gagged.

"What do you mean, they took her?" Deputy Pierce asked. "Who is it that got took, and who took her?"

"It was Meagan Parker. You know her. She is the lady that owns the dress emporium," Cindy said in a tearful voice. "She is the one that was taken, but I don't know who it was that took her. And it's all my fault," she added with a sob.

"Why is it your fault?"

"I had her come down to my room to see a picture of the dress I wanted her to make. But when we got there, someone was already in my room. They held a cloth that was soaked in something over her face for a bit, and she passed out. Then they took her. They told me — oh, they told me . . ." Cindy gasped and raised her hand to her mouth.

"They told you what?"

"They told me if I said anything to anyone they would come back and kill me."

Cindy started crying, and Deputy Pierce put his arms around her and drew her close to comfort her.

"You did the right thing, Cindy. Don't worry about it," Deputy Pierce said. "The marshal and I will keep an eye on you. Nobody is going to hurt you."

"Oh," Cindy said. "There is one thing. I don't know if it means anything or not but . . ."

She let the sentence hang.

"But what?"

"There was a man hanging around outside Miss Parker's shop when we came out. He was sort of hiding back in the shadows. I remember that he startled Miss Parker."

"Do you know who it was?"

"Yes, it was Francis Schumacher."

"How do you know it is Duff MacCallister?" Marshal Cline asked. He dropped three spoonfuls of sugar into his cup of coffee, stirred it for a moment, then looked back up at the man who was standing on the other side of his desk.

"How do I know?" Reid replied. "I know because until he fired me. I used to work for the son of a bitch. That's how I know."

"Well now, we do seem to have an interesting situation here," Cline said. "Johnny Taylor and his men are, even now, trying to set up a trap for him. But here he is, right in the middle of Bordeaux."

"What are you going to do about it?"

"Mr. Reid, one should never look a gift horse in the mouth," Cline said.

"What do you mean?"

"As I said, Johnny is out trying to find him right now, but here he is, dropped into our laps."

"What does that have to do with a gift horse?"

"I see it as an opportunity to make money," Cline said. "I expect Johnny would give at least a thousand dollars to anyone who killed MacCallister."

"A thousand dollars? Where would someone like Johnny get a thousand dollars?"

"Don't you know? He is the one who robbed the bank down in Chugwater. They got away with over forty thousand dollars."

"Oh, yeah," Reid said. "I'd almost forgot about that."

"So you can see why a thousand dollars wouldn't be too much to ask for."

"I reckon not. But there's somethin' else you ain't figured on," Reid said.

"What would that be?"

"Duff MacCallister ain't an easy man to deal with."

"Oh, don't be ridiculous," Cline said. "Did you see the way he was dressed when he come in here? He's a fop if there ever was one."

"I'm tellin' you, don't let them clothes fool you. I ain't never seen anyone as good with a gun as MacCallister is."

Back in the Red Eye Saloon, Duff was sitting at a table in the back of the saloon, writing out an order form. Carmody had not ordered any whiskey, and was very adamant that he had no intention of ordering any, but Duff, in playing out his role, insisted that he fill out an order form just to show Carmody what it would cost.

He was taking quite a while because as he was sitting there supposedly working on the form, he was able to pick up quite a bit of the conversation from the others. The most talkative of the group were two men who were young, loud, and obnoxious. Their names, Duff had learned a bit earlier, were Creech and Phelps.

"Where do you think they hid the money they got from that bank down in Chugwater?" Creech asked.

"What do you mean, hid it?" Phelps asked.

"I heard 'em talkin' about it," Creech said.

"If they hid it, why would they be talkin' about it? That seems like a dumb thing to do."

"Yeah, but Johnny and Clay Calhoun wasn't the ones that was talkin' about it, and they're the only ones who really know where the money is."

"How do you know they're the only ones who know?"

"I know 'cause they are the only two left from the bunch of them that robbed the bank. The ones I heard talkin' was Blunt, Thomas, and Harper. They're thinkin' they ought to get cut in on the money since the other ones is dead."

"Except for Johnny's brother. He ain't dead. He's in jail down in Chugwater. That's where Johnny and the others is now, back in Chugwater to see if they can't figure out some way to get Emile out of jail."

Duff had already learned that Johnny and the others were no longer in town, so this particular piece of news wasn't as interesting to him as was the news that the money was hidden somewhere. That was good news, actually. If the money was hidden somewhere, then that meant that most of it was probably still intact. And that meant that if he could find where the money was hidden, he could recover it for the bank.

"That's him, right there!" a man shouted. There was something familiar about the man's voice, and as he looked toward the front door, he saw Simon Reid.

"Reid?"

"You're worth a thousand dollars, Mac-Callister," Reid said. "And I aim to collect."

Cline already had his pistol out, and even as Reid was talking, Cline pulled the trigger.

The gun roared, but the bullet hit the samples case Duff had on the table, and one of the bottles burst, sending up a small shower of whiskey.

Duff ran toward the bar, leaped up on it, belly down, then rolled himself over the bar and down behind it. Three more shots followed him, two crashing into the bar and the third hitting the mirror behind the bar, breaking it into shards that hung in place but distorted the image it was reflecting.

At the first shot, Carmody, the bartender, had picked up the double-barreled Greener he kept behind the bar. Duff, who had his own pistol out now, pointed his gun at Carmody and shook his head. He made a motion for Carmody to put the shotgun down and, after Carmody did so, made a second motion telling Carmody to get out from behind the bar.

Carmody put both hands up, then scooted out from the far end of the bar.

"Don't shoot, don't shoot!" he shouted.

Creech suddenly appeared in the open space at the end of the bar. At first Duff thought Creech might just be curious, but then he saw a pistol in Creech's hand. Creech raised the gun to shoot, but Duff put one well-placed shot in Creech's forehead, and he fell back.

"Son of a bitch! He kilt Creech!" Phelps shouted.

Keeping low, Duff moved down toward the open end of the bar, picking up Carmody's shotgun as he did so. Pausing when he reached the end of the bar, he looked back into the mirror, and though it was nothing now but half a dozen hanging shards, he was able to locate his adversaries, distorted though the images were. One was toward the back of the room, taking cover behind the iron stove, and two more were in the middle of the room. They had overturned several tables and were using the tables to build a barricade of sorts.

Looking up, Duff saw that the two in the middle of the room had made the mistake of building their fort right under the big wagon wheel, from which hung a dozen gleaming lanterns. Raising the shotgun, Duff fired both barrels at the rope that raised and lowered the wagon wheel chandelier. He fired, the gun roared, and the wagon wheel dropped to the floor, right on top of the two men. The crash broke the chimneys of all the lanterns and, almost instantly, a large blaze leaped up from the middle of the floor.

Marshal Cline and Simon Reid shouted out in fear and pain and, forgetting about their guns, rolled across the floor to get clear of the widening pool of fire that had leapt up when the lanterns broke and the kerosene spilled.

"You son of a bitch!" Phelps shouted, leaping out from behind the stove with his gun blazing.

Duff fired one time, and Phelps went down.

Running from the saloon, Duff mounted Sky and rode out of town. There was no need to stay here any longer. He had already learned that Johnny and the others were gone.

Up and down the street he could hear shouts of warning and excitement.

"Fire! The saloon is on fire!"

"Get the fire brigade out!"

Someone started ringing a fire gong, and

another fire gong picked it up. By the time Duff reached the south end of town, at least three of the warning gongs were being sounded. He stopped and looked back to make certain no one was following him.

No one was following him. Nobody was even paying any attention to him. Instead, all were rushing toward the saloon, which was now totally engulfed, with flames leaping from the roof.

CHAPTER TWENTY-NINE

Meagan had no idea who had taken her, or why they had taken her, and she was on the edge of panic, fighting hard to maintain control. Because she was lying in the bottom of the wagon, and because it was dark, her vision was limited, but she did get a glance of the school just as they were leaving town so she knew they were going south. Because she couldn't see the ground, she had no way of gauging how fast they were going, though it felt as if they were doing at least five miles an hour. She tried to estimate how long she had been in the wagon, so she could guess where they might be.

She would have to stay alert, and try to escape if she saw any opportunity to do so. And if she couldn't escape, she needed do something — anything — that might improve her situation.

Her hands were tied in front, rather than behind her, and this did give her some range of motion. Her first thought was that she would try to slide off the back of the buckboard, but she put that idea aside when she realized that her feet were tied to the side of the carriage. If she tried to jump off, she would be dragged.

She began to feel around inside the buckboard, then felt a small glimmer of hope, when she found a little bag of nails. Using the point of one of the nails, she tried to untie her wrists, but the rope was too high up on her wrists, and she couldn't get to it. She thought about trying to use the nail to untie her feet, but that wasn't successful either.

Then she got an idea.

Using the point of the nail, she managed to cut out a small piece of cloth from her dress. Then, pushing the nail through that small piece of cloth, she dropped it over the side of the buckboard, hoping, praying that the men who were riding alongside wouldn't see it in the dark.

Evidently, they did not see it for no one said anything to her. Approximately ten minutes later she threw out another little flag. The average person might miss such small markers, but she had every confidence that Duff would come looking for her, and an equal amount of confidence that he would not only see the little markers, but know what they were.

"I don't have any idea what happened to her," Schumacher said.

"You were hanging around just outside the emporium," Marshal Ferrell challenged.

"I was not hanging around outside the emporium."

"Don't lie to me, Schumacher. You were seen there!" Marshal Ferrell said, angrily.

"Marshal, her shop is right next to Fiddler's Green. I had been in there most of the night, you can ask anyone. I'd been drinkin' a lot, and there was a lot of tobacco smoke inside. I was gettin' a headache so I come out for a breath of fresh air. That's all."

"Throw him in a cell, Willie," Marshal Ferrell said.

"What? You can't do that."

"Just watch me do it," Marshal Ferrell said. "When you are ready to talk, let me know."

"Talk about what? I tell you, I don't have anything to talk about!" Schumacher said.

"Come on," Deputy Pierce said. "You used to work here, you know where it is."

"This ain't right, Willie," Schumacher said. "I tell you, I didn't have anything to do with this."

Emile Taylor was asleep in his cell when Deputy Pierce brought Schumacher back to put him in the adjacent cell.

"Here," Emile said. "What's all the noise about? A man can't even sleep peaceable in his own jail cell around here."

"You know the way it works, Schumacher. Go all the way to the back of the cell and don't turn around until you hear the cell door shut."

"You're makin' a mistake, Willie," Schumacher said.

"I'm just the deputy, Francis," Deputy Pierce said, softening it somewhat by using Schumacher's first name. "I have to do what the marshal says. You know that."

"Well, the marshal is making a mistake."

"Francis, my old friend," Emile said coming over to stick his hand through the bars to shake Schumacher's hand. "What are you doing in here?"

"Somebody took Miss Parker, and the marshal thinks I had something to do with it," Schumacher replied.

"Did you?"

"No! I had nothing to do with it!"

"Who is Miss Parker, anyway?"

"She owns the dress shop."

"Some old biddy, is she?"

"She ain't old, and she ain't a biddy. She's a young, pretty woman. Duff MacCallister is some sweet on her, they say."

"MacCallister?" Emile laughed. "She's MacCallister's woman?"

"That's what folks say, and I got no reason not to believe it."

"I'll be damn," Emile said. "Then more 'n likely you did have something to do with it, only you just don't know it."

"What do you mean?"

"I mean it looks like Johnny ain't forgot about me."

Duff rode directly to his ranch from Bordeaux, arriving at about two o'clock in the morning. Going to bed, he slept until about seven, then he walked out to the cowboy's cook shack to have his breakfast.

"What do you want for breakfast, Boss?" his cook asked. Red Kirby was still called Red, though his hair had turned white long ago.

"Maybe a biscuit and a cup of coffee, though I would rather have tea if you have any."

"I can make you a cup of tea in just a moment. Would you like a piece of ham with your biscuit?"

"No, but some butter and marmalade

would be fine."

When Duff sat down, Elmer, carrying his oversized cup of coffee, came over to join him.

"I see you got out of Bordeaux alive."

"Yes, no thanks to Reid."

"Reid? You mean Simon Reid is in Bordeaux? Damn, I never run across him while I was there."

"Aye, he was there, and he gave me away to Cline. 'Twould appear that there is a one-thousand-dollar bounty on my head."

"Obviously Reid didn't collect. Did you kill the son of a bitch?"

"Nae. At least, I do nae think so. The saloon was on fire when I left. I assume Reid and the others got out."

Elmer laughed out loud and slapped his hand down on the table. "I'll be damn! You burned the saloon down?"

"Aye."

"I'll bet that was some sight to see. I just wish I had been there with you," Elmer said, still laughing.

"I must confess, Elmer, m' friend, there were a few moments there where I wished you had been with me as well."

Red Kirby brought the biscuit and tea, and Duff and Elmer continued their conversation.

"I did learn a few thing while I was there," Duff said. "Johnny and his brigands have left Bordeaux. And they have hidden out the money they took from the bank, which means if we could find it, we could take it back to the bank and greatly reduce the losses suffered by the people in town."

"That would sure ease a lot of burdens," Elmer said.

"Aye, that it would," Duff said, taking the last swallow of his tea. "I'd best get into town and tell the marshal what I've learned."

Duff didn't have to go to town, because even before he finished his breakfast, Marshal Ferrell came riding up to the ranch.

"Marshal, what are you doing out here?" Duff asked, as Ferrell dismounted. "Would you like a cup of coffee?"

"No, thanks," the marshal said. "I came to see Elmer. Actually, it was to see you, but I thought you might still be in Bordeaux."

"You look troubled."

Marshal Ferrell took a deep breath and ran his hand through his hair before he replied.

"They've got Meagan, Duff."

"What? Who has? And what do you mean by 'they've got'?"

"I assume it's Johnny Taylor. Cindy Boyce said some men came in the middle of the night and took her. I expect it has something to do with Emile Taylor being in jail, but we won't know until we hear from them."

"I do nae intend to wait to hear from anyone," Duff said. "I'm going to find Meagan."

"Duff, there's no need to be goin' off half-cocked here," Marshal Ferrell said. "We don't have the slightest idea where they went. Where would you even start?"

"Where was she taken from?" Elmer asked. "Do we know that?"

"Yes, that's the strange part of it. According to Cindy Boyce, Meagan was taken from her room."

"Whose room?"

"Cindy's room," Marshal Ferrell clarified. "Meagan had gone to Miss Boyce's room to look at a picture of a dress Miss Boyce wanted her to make."

"Then that's where we will start," Elmer said.

"Elmer, I'll nae be askin' you to get involved," Duff said.

"I'm already involved," Elmer said. "Duff, there is only one thing in the world I can do better than you, and that's track somebody. If you want to find Meagan, you don't have no choice. You have to let me come with you."

Duff smiled at his friend.

"I will be very glad to have you come along with me," he said.

It was daylight by the time the wagon reached the Chugwater Range. Meagan knew where she was now, because she recognized Chimney Rock.

They passed through an opening into a draw that was cut back into the long, flat slabs of rocks that made up the Chugwater Range. Meagan saw two guards who wanted to be seen and a couple who didn't want to be seen. The pass was long and narrow, with steep walls on either side. At one point, the canyon had been filled in from either side, creating a choke point so narrow that the buckboard was barely able to squeeze through. If Marshal Ferrell raised a posse to come after her, no matter how many there were, they could be held up here by no more than three or four well-armed men. One man might be able to get through, though it would take a very special man to try.

A man like Duff MacCallister.

"Get out of the wagon, girly," one of the

men said.

Meagan tried to answer, but because of the gag, she could only make a squeaking noise.

"Take the gag out of her mouth. You might as well untie her feet and hands too. She ain't goin' nowhere."

Megan felt a sense of gratitude that the gag was removed and that she was being untied.

"Thanks," she said, as she rubbed her wrists. They were raw from the ropes that had been tied tightly.

"Like I said, you ain't goin' nowhere." The man who spoke was relatively short, with dark hair and a deformed ear. Then, as she looked more closely at it, she realized that the ear wasn't just deformed; part of it was missing. She'd heard tell of a man who fit this description.

"You are Johnny Taylor," she said.

"So, you know who I am," Johnny said.

"What do you want with me?" Meagan asked.

One of the other men rubbed himself suggestively. "Girly, there's a lot I want with you."

"That'll be enough," Johnny said. "For our purposes now, we have to keep her alive, unhurt and . . . unsullied, as it were."

At first Meagan thought that Johnny was protecting her through some sense of honor, but his next statement shattered that illusion.

"After we get what we want from her, she will be fair game," he said.

"What do you want with me?" Meagan repeated.

"You are Meagan Parker, aren't you?" Johnny asked.

"I am."

"You are Duff MacCallister's . . . friend?" He set the word *friend* away from the rest of the sentence, giving it a suggestive meaning.

"We are friends," Meagan replied, without rising to the bait.

"Good. Because what I want is for Duff MacCallister to come after you."

"Believe me, you don't really want that," Meagan said.

"Oh, but I do, my dear. I really do."

CHAPTER THIRTY

Elmer looked around in the alley behind Foley's Lodging House. "Looks like maybe a buckboard, or a small wagon, pulled by a team of horses. More 'n likely it was a buckboard, I'd say. The wagon waited back here for quite a while. But wasn't only the wagon — they was riders back here, too."

"How do you know?"

"See them turds there? Horses takes a shit 'bout ever two hours. There's too many turds for 'em to all have come from one team. And as much as there is, you have to figure they was standing here for anywhere from half an hour to an hour. And there wouldn't be no reason for horses and a wagon to be hangin' around here in this alley, if they wasn't waitin' on somethin'. If you was to ask me, I'd say after she was took from the room, she was brought out here and put in a buckboard." Using a stick, Elmer began a closer examination of the horse apples.

"Also, these here horses ain't been stabled for a while. No oats, no hay. They been eatin' nothin' but grass for the last week or so."

Elmer started tracking the buckboard, while Duff kept pace with him.

"Looks like they was headin' south," Elmer said.

They were about a mile south of town when they found the marker from Meagan. Duff spotted it first.

"Look at that, Elmer," Duff said, pointing to a nail with a tiny bit of cloth. "That is nae accident."

"No, it ain't!" Elmer said, laughing. "That's a smart woman you've got, Duff."

"I'm goin' into town. I want the rest of you stay here and keep an eye on the woman," Johnny said.

"I'll keep more 'n an eye on her," Blunt said.

"No, you won't," Johnny replied. "You keep your hands off her. That goes for all of you. You don't do nothin' to her 'til I say you can. Like I said, I'm goin' into town to do a little horse tradin'. If we can't work somethin' out, and by that I mean if we can't get Emile turned loose, then we'll give the woman back to 'em anyway. Only if that happens, MacCallister ain't goin' to like the way he gets her back."

"Who gets her first?" Calhoun asked.

"We'll play high card for her," Johnny said. "Highest card goes first, then on down the line."

"Hell, I don't care where I am," Blunt said. "As long as I get my turn."

Megan listened to the men bartering for her with a mixture of fear and revulsion.

It was midmorning when Duff and Elmer reached Chimney Rock. Dismounting, Duff pulled his Creedmoor rifle from the saddle sheath. Then he and Elmer continued on foot until they reached a butte that extended north from the east-west Chugwater range. They climbed to the summit of the butte, lay on their stomachs, and began searching the canyon floor before them, each of them using binoculars.

"There they are!" Elmer said. "Up there in that far corner, by Needle Rock — do you see them?"

Looking in the direction Elmer pointed, Duff saw Meagan and four men. Meagan was sitting on the rocky ground just at the base of the Needle, and one man was standing right next to her. Two were standing several feet apart, and a fourth was acting as a lookout, perched on a rock about twenty feet higher than the others.

"What would you make the distance to be, Elmer? About six, or seven hundred yards?"

"At least seven hundred yards," Elmer said.

"Aye, seven hundred. That's what I was thinking as well. I'll take care of the lookout first. Then the one that is standing the closest to Meagan, then the other two."

"That's goin' to be one hell of a shot," Elmer said.

As Meagan contemplated her future, she couldn't help but be filled with trepidation. The one that the others had called Ike was standing very close to her, staring at her with eyes that were filled with lust and evil. His proximity to her was making her very nervous.

"You know what, girlie? I ain't goin' to wait on Johnny to get back," Ike Thomas said. He rubbed himself, smiling obscenely at her. "No, sir, I ain't goin' to wait at all. Start takin' off them clothes."

"I have no intention of taking off my clothes," Meagan said, trying to keep her voice as steady as she could.

Thomas pulled his pistol and pointed it at her.

"Take 'em off, or I'll shoot you and take them off of you myself."

"If you are going to touch me, I'd rather be dead when it happens, so go ahead. Shoot me."

"I ain't bluffin' you, woman."

"Neither am I," Meagan said, defiantly.

"What are you doin', Ike?" Blunt asked.

"I aim to have my way with this woman," Thomas said.

"You heard what Johnny said. We ain't supposed to touch her."

"Yeah? Well, that don't mean we can't look at her, does it? Take off them clothes, like I told you to. Me 'n' the others is goin' to get us a look at a naked woman."

"I have no intention of taking off my clothes."

"You'll either take 'em off now, when you ain't hurtin' nowhere, or I'll shoot you in the leg and take 'em off of you. That way you'll be hurtin' and naked."

"Yeah," Calhoun said. "Johnny didn't say we couldn't look at her naked. Hey, Harper, you better take a look down here. This here woman is about to give us a show."

Harper stood up and walked over to the

edge of the rock, then looked down on the others.

"Have her move out here where I can see her too. Come on, girlie, give us a . . . uhhnh!"

Harper pitched forward off the rock, then fell head first, striking his head on the rocks below. He lay motionless where he hit.

"Son of a bitch, he fell off!" Thomas said.

There was no sound for a full second. Then they could hear, in the distance, the barely audible thump of a gunshot.

"What the hell was that?" Calhoun asked.

Blunt moved quickly to Harper, then turned him over onto his back. His eyes were open, and unseeing. There was a big, dark red hole in the middle of his chest.

"Uhnn!" Thomas said, and blood, bone, and brain matter sprayed from the side of his head.

"What the hell! Somebody is shooting at us!" Blunt said.

"Who!" Calhoun shouted. "There ain't nobody here!"

This time, Calhoun heard the bullet as it came whizzing in. It struck Blunt in the middle of his chest, and he reached down to slap his hands over the wound. Looking down, even as the low, flat sound of the shot that hit him came rolling across the distance, he saw the blood spilling through his hands. He looked up at Calhoun.

"I've . . . been . . . kilt!" he gasped, just before he fell.

Calhoun started shooting wildly, pulling the trigger repeatedly until the gun was empty and all that remained were the echoes of the shots as they came rolling back.

"Where are you?" Calhoun shouted.

While Calhoun's attention was diverted, Meagan reached down and slipped Blunt's pistol from the holster.

"Who are you? Who's doin' all that shootin'?"

"I expect it is Duff MacCallister," Meagan said.

Calhoun whirled around toward Meagan. "Come here, woman!" He shouted. "I'm going to . . ." He stopped in midsentence when he saw Meagan holding a pistol. She had it aimed at him, and she had already pulled back the hammer.

"You are going to do nothing but stand there without saying so much as one word," Meagan said.

"Ha! Meagan's got the drop on him!" Elmer said. "Come on, let's go down there."

It took a few minutes to cover the distance

between the place where Duff had established his firing point, and where Meagan
was standing with her prisoner.

"Good job!" Duff said when he and Elmer
arrived. "Why, you didn't even need me."

"Oh, I wouldn't go that far. After all, you
were some help," Meagan replied, teasingly.

Elmer was wheezing and breathing hard
from the exercise of the long walk over
uneven, rocky ground.

"Clay Calhoun," Elmer said. "Where is
Johnny Taylor?"

"The son of a bitch run out on us,"
Calhoun said. "He left us here to die."

"He not only ran out on you, Calhoun, he
took all the money," Duff said.

"No, he didn't."

"Are you sure?" Duff said. "We know that
two days ago, there was a deposit of thirty-
five thousand dollars made to a bank in
Cheyenne in Johnny Taylor's name. He not
only stole from you, he stole from his own
brother. Where did he get that money, if he
dinnae get it from the money you took from
the bank in Chugwater?"

"He couldn't have done that," Calhoun
said. "This is the first time we have been
back here since we buried the money."

"You're sure? It does nae bother me —
you are goin' to jail anyway. You'll be tried

for bank robbery and murder, while Johnny Taylor goes off to Denver, or San Francisco, or some such place to enjoy his ill-gotten gains."

"I hear he's plannin' to buy a saloon in San Francisco," Elmer said. "He'll get rich as Croesus, while you 'n' his own brother will hang."

With a frustrated shout, Calhoun ran to the base of the Needle. He moved several rocks aside, then started digging with his bare hands.

"He wouldn't do that! If he did, I'll kill him with own bare hands! Half that money is mine! He promised me!"

Duff, Elmer, and Meagan watched quietly and unobtrusively as Calhoun became more and more agitated, digging faster and faster.

"Where is it? Where is it? Damn it! He had no right! He said that we would share the . . ." He stopped for second, then, with a shout of triumph, began to pull out the four rolled-up shirts, each shirt containing a share of the loot from the bank robbery.

"Ha! Here it is!" he shouted triumphantly. He held up one of the dirt-encrusted shirts. "I told you that he couldn't have come back for the money, not without me know . . ."

Calhoun stopped in midsentence as he saw the expressions on the faces of the people in whose hands his fate now rested.

"You — you knew he hadn't come back for the money, didn't you? You just said that to trick me in to showing you where the money was."

"Aye, lad, 'twas a bit of chicanery," Duff admitted.

"You bastard!" Calhoun shouted. Moving quickly and unexpectedly, he stepped toward Meagan, who had, with the arrival of Duff and Elmer, let her guard down.

Calhoun stepped around behind her, put his arm around her neck, and began to squeeze.

Duff saw Meagan's eyes begin to flutter, and he realized that Meagan could be gone in seconds, choked to death.

Then, Meagan, who was still holding the pistol, found the strength to point it at Calhoun's leg and pull the trigger. Calhoun went down, screaming in pain.

Meagan returned to Chugwater in the same buckboard that had taken her out of town, but this time she was driving it, and the person who was tied up in back was Clay Calhoun.

"We'll stop at the jail," Duff said.

"Jail! I need a doctor!" Calhoun complained. "You can't take me to jail before I see a doctor!"

"We'll send for the doctor after we get you in jail," Duff promised.

"That ain't right," Calhoun said. "It just ain't right."

When they reached the jail, Elmer continued on down the street to the doctor's office, while Duff ordered Calhoun out of the buckboard and into the jail.

"I can't walk," Calhoun said. "Can't you see I've got a bullet hole in my leg? That damn woman shot me in the leg."

Marshal Ferrell, who was in the office then, came out when he saw and heard all commotion. He arrived just in time to hear Calhoun complain that the woman had shot him in the leg.

"You are the one that shot him, Miss Parker?" Marshal Ferrell asked, surprised at the revelation.

"I am," she said.

"Why did you shoot him in the leg?"

"Because I couldn't get the gun high enough to shoot him in the head."

Duff, Marshal Ferrell, and Deputy Pierce, who had also come outside, laughed.

"Come on, Calhoun, inside with you."

"I can't hardly walk on this leg," Calhoun said. "It's hurtin' somethin' fierce."

"Well, I can fix you right up," Deputy Pierce said. "I've got a crutch inside that I'm hardly using anymore. I'll lend it to you just so's you can walk far enough for us to throw you in jail."

"Clay! What the hell?" Emile said. "What are you doing here? Where's my brother?"

"Where's your brother? I'll tell you where he is. He ran out on us, that's where he is. You, me, and him, we are the only three left alive. And he is the only one who is still free."

"Don't worry about it. Johnny will get us out. I know he will."

"You are a fool, Emile. We all were to trust him."

"He'll get us out. He told me he would, and I believe him. And if he can't get us out one way, he'll get us out another. He said if it came to it, he would hire the best lawyer he could find."

"How is he goin' to pay for that lawyer?"

Emile smiled. "What do you mean? I didn't get to see any of the money, but I've done heard that we got over forty thousand dollars from the bank holdup. There ain't a lawyer in the country you couldn't hire for two hundred dollars."

"Yeah? Well, we ain't got the money no

more," Calhoun said.

"What do you mean we ain't got the money no more? What happened to it?"

"We hid the money out, but it got found," Calhoun said without further elaboration.

"So you mean we done all this for nothin'?"

Schumacher chuckled. "Looks like you boys have been left suckin' hind tit."

"What's he doin' in jail?" Calhoun asked.

"They thought he had somethin' to do with you boys takin' the dress-makin' woman."

"What the hell made them think that? He didn't have nothin' to do with it."

Marshal Ferrell returned then and, going straight to Schumacher's cell, opened the door to let him out.

"Sorry, Francis," he said.

"You were listening?"

"Yes."

"Marshal, you are short a man without Frankie Mullins. I'd like to come work for you again, if you'll have me."

"No more roughing up the prisoners?"

"No more, I promise."

"All right, stop in the office. I'll swear you in again, and pin the badge back on."

"Thanks."

When the two returned to the office,

Marshal Ferrell opened the middle drawer of his desk, pulled out a badge, and pinned in onto Schumacher's shirt.

"Welcome back, Francis," Deputy Pierce said.

"Thanks, Willie. It's good to be back."

Within half an hour after Johnny left the canyon, he heard the gunshots. Thinking perhaps a posse had located his men, and not wanting to get caught up in the gun battle, he waited until he saw the buckboard heading back to town. The woman was driving the buckboard, and he recognized the two flank riders as MacCallister and Gleason.

Where were the others?

He waited until the buckboard was out of sight before he went back. Even before he got there, though, he knew what he was going to find. The buzzards circling overhead told him that.

As he got farther down into the canyon, the number of circling buzzards increased. Now, many of the big, black birds were diving toward something on the ground, and as he approached Needle Rock, Johnny saw what it was. There, drawn together so that they were lying side by side, were the bodies of Blunt, Thomas, and Harper. He didn't see Calhoun.

For a moment, Johnny was angry. His entire gang was gone!

Then, as he thought about it, he realized that if everyone was gone, the money they had taken from the bank was his, all his. He was rich!

With no more than a cursory glance toward the macabre scene of the three bodies, Johnny moved quickly to the base of the Needle to dig up the money.

As soon as he got there, though, he could see that there had been digging. A lot of purposeful digging.

"What the hell?" he said aloud. "What is this? Who has been digging here?"

With a feeling of anxiousness, Johnny dropped to his knees and began digging. He threw the rocks aside, and dug like a man possessed. His hands became bloodied and bruised, but that didn't slow him down as he slashed through the soil, tossing the dirt aside.

He knew within the first few minutes of digging that he wasn't going to find anything. He knew, and even as he could feel the sinking sensation in the pit of his stomach, he refused to tell himself the truth.

The money was there, it had to be! All he

had to do was dig a little faster.

Then, when he was much deeper than he knew they had gone, he stopped digging. It was now obvious, even beyond his own irrational hope. The money was not there.

"No!" he shouted, the angst-ridden word echoing and reechoing through the canyon.

Chapter Thirty-One

The night creatures called to each other as Johnny stood looking out toward Chugwater. A cloud passed over the moon, then moved away, bathing in silver the little town that rose up like a ghost before him. Several dozen buildings, half of which were lit up, fronted First Street, the main street of the town. The biggest and most brightly lit building was Fiddler's Green.

Someone was playing a guitar in one of the houses, and Johnny could hear the music all the way out in the hills. Johnny hobbled his horse, then walked into town. He didn't want to be seen and he decided his arrival would be less noticeable if he arrived on foot. He checked his pistol. It was loaded and slipped easily from its sheath.

As he started into town, he caught the smell of beans and spicy beef from one of the houses, and realized that it had been a couple of days since he had eaten well. His stomach growled in protest.

A dog barked, a high-pitched yap that was quickly silenced. A baby began to cry and a housewife raised her voice in one of the houses, launching into some private tirade about something, sharing her anger with all who were within earshot.

The sights, smells, and sounds reminded Johnny that there was another world, a world different from his own. There was a world of wives and kids, dogs and home-cooked meals — the world of his youth. His father had been a meat cutter in a meat-processing plant in Chicago, and had come home at night exhausted and reeking of the smell of blood and offal.

Johnny had turned his back on that world long ago, and though he had no intention of ever returning to it, there were times, such as this, when he had reflective moments. Pushing the contemplations aside, he continued on through the town, keeping as close to the fronts of the buildings as he could in order to stay in the shadows.

Reaching the block in which the jail was located, Johnny went between two buildings, then came out in the alley behind. He knew where he was because he had been here before, the last time he had come to see his brother.

Moving down the alley Johnny stopped behind the jail, then threw a rock in through the window into Emile's cell. A moment later, Emile's face appeared in the window.

"Johnny! I know'd it was you soon as you throw'd that rock in."

"Shhh," Johnny said. "Don't give me away."

"When are you goin' to get me out of here?"

"I'm comin' up with a plan."

"Yeah? Well, there ain't none of the plans worked yet, have they?"

Calhoun's face appeared in the window of the cell next to Emile's. "You comin' to get us out?" Calhoun asked.

"Clay, what happened after I left? Who kilt the others?"

"You won't hardly believe it, Johnny. They was all kilt by MacCallister. And he was shootin' from near a mile away."

"There can't nobody shoot someone from a mile away."

"He was damn near a mile, I tell you. Half a mile, anyway. He was so far away that you couldn't hear the gun he was shootin'. I mean one minute Harper was standin' there, and the next minute he was kilt, without even a sound. Same was for Blunt and Thomas."

"You wasn't kilt."

"No, I was lucky. I was shot in the leg, though."

"Where is the money?"

"What money?"

"What money?" Johnny repeated, almost yelling the word out before catching himself. "The money from the bank job. We left it buried there, remember? Where is it?"

"They got it," Calhoun said.

"They who? Where is it?"

"MacCallister and Gleason. They got it, only they give it to the marshal so more 'n likely it's been put back in the bank by now."

"How did they get it? It was hid, wasn't it?"

"Well, yeah, but . . ."

"How did they get it, Calhoun? How did they know where it was?"

Calhoun was quiet for a moment. Then, with a deep breath, he began to explain.

"They tricked me, Johnny. They told me you had took all the money and was goin' to run off with it. They said you already had the money. So I . . ."

"You dumb shit. You dug it up, didn't you?" Johnny said.

"You don't understand, they tricked me."

Johnny pulled his pistol and shot Calhoun in the forehead. Then, as every dog in the neighborhood erupted into a chorus of barking, Johnny turned and ran away, disappearing into the dark.

"What happened?" Deputy Schumacher shouted as he ran into the back of the jail. He saw Calhoun lying on the floor with one leg still up on his bunk. There was black hole in his forehead.

"It was someone from town," Emile said. "You remember how they was goin' to lynch me. They just come here and shot through the back winder. You got to protect me, Schumacher. I might be next."

From the *Chugwater Defender:*

CLAY CALHOUN SLAIN

KILLED IN HIS JAIL CELL

Assailant unknown

On the very night Clay Calhoun was brought in to jail, he was killed. Clay Calhoun was one of six men who robbed the Chugwater Bank and Trust on Clay Avenue between First and Second Streets.

Deputy Schumacher, who was on duty at the time of the shooting, reported that a shot awakened him in the middle of the night. Determining that the shot came from the back of the jail where the cells are located, he was confused as to how such a thing could happen, as he knew that neither of his two prisoners had a weapon.

Upon reaching the jail cell area, Deputy Schumacher saw Clay Calhoun lying on the floor, having been dispatched by a ball fired into his forehead by assailant or assailants unknown.

Emile Taylor, who was occupying the adjacent cell, testified that someone had fired from the darkness of the alley, but he could offer no description.

MURDER TRIAL TO TAKE PLACE

Emile Taylor on Trial for His Life

GALLOWS BEING BUILT

The indictment handed down, Emile Taylor must now face justice before the court of Judge Thurman J. Pendarrow. Judge Pendarrow is known as a "no-nonsense" judge whose decrees have sent many a murderer to that higher court where one day we all must be judged for our actions here in this temporal domain.

386

Taylor was one of six men who held up the Chugwater Bank and Trust on Clay Avenue. Of those six men, four are known to be dead. Only Johnny Taylor remains at large. Thanks to Duff MacCallister and Elmer Gleason, the money, except for two thousand eight hundred and twenty dollars, has all been recovered, and the bank is functioning, once more, at full capacity.

Marshal Ferrell says that this should be a warning to any other outlaw who might have designs on holding up the Chugwater Bank and Trust. The Chugwater Bank and Trust, located on Clay Avenue between First and Second Streets, is known by all to be one of the finest banks in all of Laramie County.

CHAPTER THIRTY-TWO

Emile Taylor was in shackles, and handcuffs as Deputy Schumacher escorted him from the jail to the city courthouse, where the trial was to be held. They walked by the gallows, which was under construction.

"What is that?" Emile asked.

"It's a gallows. What does it look like?" Schumacher said.

"What are you buildin' a gallows for? Ain't I supposed to be tried before you start thinkin' about hangin' me?"

"It's just a matter of convenience," Deputy Schumacher said. "If you are found guilty and Judge Pendarrow sentences you to hang, there's no sense in waitin' around for a gallows to be built. We'll already have it done, so we won't have to wait."

"What if I ain't found guilty? Ain't I supposed to be innocent until found guilty?"

Deputy Schumacher laughed. "In that case, it won't be any trouble to tear it down.

It's always easier to tear somethin' down than it is to build it up."

"Francis, how much money would it take to bribe you to let me go?" Emile asked.

"You don't have enough money," Schumacher replied.

"Don't be fooled by the fact that the money we stole has been took back to the bank. Me 'n' my brother can get more money. Lots more money. How much will it take for you to let me go?"

"You don't understand," Schumacher said. "When I say you don't have enough money — I mean no matter how much money you might have, it isn't enough. The marshal took me on and give me back my pride. I don't intend to do anything to betray him."

"I thought we was friends," Emile said.

"You thought wrong."

The courthouse was packed with people. So many had come for the trial that the courtroom spilled over and there were dozens waiting outside.

"This many people comin' to the trial?" Emile asked in surprise.

"Oh, yes. Danny Welch was a very popular man. He was a husband, father, a Sunday school teacher. You couldn't have made a bigger mistake than to kill one of our finest citizens."

Schumacher smiled. "On the other hand, look at it this way. These folks are all going to have to stand outside during the trial, but you will have the best seat in the house."

Schumacher opened the door, then pushed Emile in, in front of him. "Go on down to the front," he said. "There is a table and chair, just waiting for you."

As Emile started toward the front of the packed gallery, he could hear some of the comments from the spectators.

"I don't know why we're wastin' time holdin' a trial for the son of a bitch. We should go ahead and just hang him now."

"Why? He won't be no more dead than he'll be when we hang him after the trial."

"I reckon that's right."

Robert Dempster was setting at the defendant's table, and he stood up as Emile approached.

"I've got you again?" Emile said.

"I've studied your case."

"Yeah, well, I guess I ain't got no choice, seein' as I don't have the money to hire me a real lawyer."

"I assure you, Mr. Taylor, I am a real lawyer," Dempster said.

"Hear ye, hear ye, hear ye! This here trial is about to commence, the Honorable

Thurman Pendarrow, presidin','" Marshal
Ferrell, who was acting as the bailiff,
shouted. "Everybody stand."

The Honorable Thurman Pendarrow
came out of a back room. After taking his
seat at the bench, he adjusted the glasses on
the end of his nose, then cleared his throat.

"Would the bailiff please bring the accused before the bench?"

Marshal Ferrell walked over to the table
where Emile was sitting next to Dempster.

"Your Honor, permission to remove the
restraints on my client?" Dempster asked.

Pendarrow thought for a moment, then
nodded. "Granted," he said.

Schumacher removed the shackles and the
handcuffs. Emile rubbed his wrists for a
moment, then looked over at Dempster.
"Thanks," he said.

"All right, all the restraints are removed,"
Marshal Ferrell said with a growl. "Present
yourself before the judge."

Emile walked up to stand in front of the
judge, and Dempster went with him.

"You are accused of shooting to death Mr.
Dan Welch, during the commission of a
felony bank robbery. How do you plead?"

"We plead not guilty, Your Honor," Dempster said.

"Very well, take your seat. Mr. Crader,

you are the prosecutor?"

"I am, Your Honor."

"Make your case, Mr. Crader."

Half an hour earlier, Duff had approached the courthouse with Meagan Parker, Elmer Gleason and Vi Winslow. Elmer, Meagan, and Vi were here as spectators to this very exciting event, but Duff's role was considerably more involved. He, along with Cindy Boyce and Bernie Caldwell, were witnesses.

As soon as Duff and Elmer started into the courtroom, Deputy Pierce met them.

"Gentlemen, I will need you to turn over your guns," Pierce said.

"What for?" Elmer asked.

"It's the judge's orders. No guns in the courtroom."

Both Elmer and Duff complied, and then they, along with Meagan and Vi, went into the courtroom to find seats that would accommodate all four of them.

They were there when Schumacher brought the prisoner in, and they sat through the preliminaries until the actual trial began. It started with the two attorneys making their opening statements to the jury. Then the prosecutor called Duff to the stand.

"Mr. MacCallister, were you in the bank

during the robbery?" Crader asked.

"Aye."

Judge Pendarrow leaned over the desk and looked down at Duff. "The witness is instructed to answer questions requiring an affirmative or negative comment with yes and no. Does the witness understand?"

"Aye, Your Honor, I understand," Duff said. The gallery laughed and, quickly, Duff corrected himself. "I mean, yes, Your Honor."

"You may proceed, counselor," Pendarrow said.

"Please tell us what you saw."

Duff said that five masked men had come into the bank, announcing their intention to rob it. During the course of the robbery, one of the robbers shot and killed Danny Welch.

"Do you know which one of the robbers shot Mr. Welch?"

"I believe it was Emile Taylor."

"Would you point to Emile Taylor, please?"

Duff pointed to the defendant.

"Thank you, no further questions."

Dempster stood up, but he didn't approach the witness stand. "Mr. MacCallister, you said you believe it was my client?"

"Aye. I mean, yes."

"How could you tell? Did you not say they were all wearing masks?"

"Yes 'tis true they were all wearing masks, but one man was much shorter than the others. And it was the wee one who fired the shot."

"The wee one?"

"The shortest one," Duff clarified.

"Without the others herein present, how do you know that Mr. Taylor was the shortest?"

"I've seen them all, with and without masks. Emile Taylor is the shortest."

"No further questions."

Caldwell was the next witness, and his story concurred with Duff's story. Then Cindy was sworn in.

"Now, Miss Boyce you were in the bank, along with Mr. MacCallister and Mr. Caldwell, when the bank was robbed."

"I was."

"And would you tell the court who fired the shot that killed Mr. Welch?"

As soon as he asked the question, Crader turned away from Cindy to look at the jury, so that he might gauge their response to Cindy's answer.

"I don't know who fired the shot," Cindy said.

Cindy's response surprised Crader, but he showed no particular reaction to it.

"I know that all of the bank robbers were masked, so it is quite understandable if you can't be for certain as to which of them fired the shot. And, because this is a capital murder case, I can see why you might be hesitant to point your finger at someone if you aren't one hundred percent sure. However, maybe this will help. This whole trial is nothing but house cleaning anyway, because it doesn't really make any difference whether Mr. Taylor is the one who pulled the trigger or not. He was, by his own admission, one of those who came to rob the bank. Mr. Welch was killed during the commission of that felony. Therefore, under the law, all of the bank robbers are equally guilty of felony murder. Would that make it a little easier for you to suggest that Emile Taylor is the one who fired the shot?"

Again, Crader turned toward the jury.

"What if none of the robbers fired the shot?" Cindy asked.

This time Crader did react to the unexpected answer, and he spun around in total surprise.

"What? What do you mean, what if none of them fired the shot? Mr. Welch is dead, and he is dead by bullet wound. Of course one of them fired the shot."

"It could have been Mr. MacCallister who fired," Cindy said.

"What?" someone shouted from the gallery.

"Woman, have you lost your mind?" another shouted.

The gallery burst into angry shouts and calls, and Cindy, dropping her head, began to cry.

"Order! Order in this court!" Judge Pendarrow called, pounding his gavel on the bench before him.

Crader said nothing as gradually the court was called back to order. Then he pulled a handkerchief from his pocket and gave it to Cindy. She used it to wipe the tears from her eyes.

"Miss Boyce, would you tell the court why you think it was Mr. MacCallister's bullet?"

"I didn't say I thought it was — I said I thought it could have been. I mean with all the shooting that was going on. Remember, Mr. MacCallister killed one of the robbers, and he also shot Emile, uh, Taylor. I was so frightened, I'll be honest with you, I had no idea what was going on. I just know that I'm probably not a very good witness."

"No further questions."

"Cross, Mr. Dempster?"

Dempster stood up and this time he did approach the witness. He looked at her sympathetically.

"Miss Boyce, do you need another moment to compose yourself?"

"No, I'm all right."

"I know this has been very upsetting for you, so I will keep this as brief as I can," he said quietly. "A simple yes or no is all I need in response. I believe you are telling the court that you cannot, with absolute certainty, testify that the bullet that killed Mr. Welch came from Mr. Taylor's gun, or indeed, the gun of any of the other bank robbers. Is that what you are saying?"

"Yes."

"And I believe you are also saying that it is possible that the bullet that killed Mr. Welch could have even come from Mr. MacCallister's gun."

"I'm not saying that it did."

"I understand. You are merely saying that it could have. Is that right?"

"Yes."

"Thank you. No further questions."

"Redirect, Mr. Crader."

"No, Your Honor, but I would like to recall Duff MacCallister to the stand."

Once again, Duff took the stand.

"I remind you, Mr. MacCallister, that you

are already sworn in."

Duff nodded.

"You have heard the testimony of Miss Boyce, as to how the bullet that killed Mr. Welch might have come from your gun. Is that possible?"

"Nae. No, it is impossible."

"How can you be so sure?"

"Because I did no shooting inside the bank. My gun was in the bottom of a pot of expectorated tobacco juice at the time. I had to" — Duff grimaced, then demonstrated with his hand — "withdraw it from the fetid liquid, before I could shoot it. And they had already withdrawn from the bank before I did that."

"So, you are stating without equivocation, that you did not fire so much as one shot inside the bank?"

"Yes, that is what I'm saying."

The closing arguments were brief. Dempster pointed out that the jury had the duty to convict only if they were convinced beyond reasonable doubt that Emile Taylor had fired the fatal shot. He also reminded them that one of the witnesses couldn't even testify that the bullet had come from any of the bank robbers.

Crader looked down at the tablet he was

carrying, then read, "I was so frightened, I'll be honest with you, I had no idea what was going on. I just know that I'm probably not a very good witness." Crader looked up from the tablet. "Those are the exact words of Miss Boyce. And because of that, I am going to ask the jury to disregard her testimony in its entirety. But, even beyond that, I ask you to consider this.

"Mr. Welch was killed during the course of that bank robbery. A wrongful death, during the commission of a felony, is felony murder, and that guilt is spread equally among all those who are committing the felony. And here is the most important thing. It doesn't even matter whether one of the bank robbers energized the ball that ended Mr. Welch's life or not. It could have been Mr. MacCallister, though you heard both Mr. MacCallister and Mr. Caldwell testify that his gun was in the bottom of the spittoon. It could have been Mr. Caldwell who shot him, though he was unarmed and there has been no testimony to that effect. It could even have been Miss Boyce.

"The truth is, it simply does not matter who shot Mr. Welch. He was killed during the commission of a felony. Mr. Taylor has already confessed to being one of the bank robbers, therefore your decision is a simple one.

"Find Emile Taylor guilty, so that justice may be served."

His closing statement completed, Crader sat down, and Judge Pendarrow instructed the jury, then released them to find a verdict.

"Why did the girl lie, so?" Duff asked Meagan.

"Don't be too harsh on her, Duff," Meagan replied. "I'm sure she must have been terrified while the robbery was going on."

"It could nae have been more frightening than what you went through, lass, but you dinnae lose your wits."

"The jury is coming back!" someone shouted.

"Already? They have nae been gone but for a minute," Duff said.

"What?" someone shouted. "What's goin' on?"

It wasn't the entire jury returning — it was only Curly Lathom, the jury foreman. But as Lathom stepped into the room, it could be seen by all that Johnny Taylor was with him, and Johnny was holding a gun to the jury foreman's head.

Emile was sitting at the defense table and

when he saw his brother, he smiled and stood up. "I knew you wouldn't let me down!" he said.

"I couldn't let them hang my brother now, could I?" Johnny asked.

"Cindy," Emile called. "Go get the marshal's gun and bring it to me, would you?"

Everyone in the court looked at the young bar girl. Did she have the courage to resist Emile's demand?

Cindy walked over to the marshal, but Ferrell made no move.

"Give her the gun, Marshal, or I'll blow this man's brains out," Johnny warned.

"Just be calm, miss, and you'll be all right," Marshal Ferrell said reassuringly as he pulled his pistol and handed to her.

Taking the marshal's gun Cindy walked over to Emile. With a broad smile, she handed it to him. Then she leaned into him and kissed him. Emile put his arm around her.

"Have you missed me, darlin'?" Emile asked.

"More than you'll ever know."

Emile looked over at the marshal. "Bet you didn't know she was my girl, did you, Marshal? The whole reason she took a job in the saloon was so she could help set everything up for us."

"And keep me informed on what was going on," Johnny answered. "Thanks for the letters, Cindy. They were very helpful."

Johnny, Emile, and Cindy started to leave. But just as they got even with Duff, Marshal Ferrell, who was on the opposite side of the room, suddenly threw a chair through the window. Distracted by it, both brothers looked toward the sound.

Duff grabbed Johnny Taylor's gun and shot him, then he turned the gun toward Emile.

But Emile pulled Cindy in front of him and pointed his gun at her head.

"Drop your gun," Emile orders. "Or I'll kill her."

"But you said yourself that she's your woman," Duff said.

"I can get another woman. I can't get another life."

"No, Emile, what are you doing?" Cindy shouted in alarm. She twisted away from him and started to run.

"Damn you!" Emile shouted, shooting her at the same time Duff was shooting him.

Emile was dead before he hit the floor, but Cindy, though badly hurt, was still alive. Duff hurried to her, and dropped to one knee beside her.

How much like Skye she looked, and a

searing memory came flashing back to him.

Skye lifted her hand to his face and put her fingers against his jaw. She smiled. " 'Twould have been such a lovely wedding," she said. She drew another gasping breath, then her arm fell and her head turned to one side. Her eyes, though still open, were already clouded with death.

"I'm sorry," Cindy said, and when she spoke, the spell was broken. This wasn't Skye. "Why couldn't I have met you before I met Emile?"

"Sure 'n' it wouldn't have done you any good," Duff said. He looked over toward Meagan. "I've already found a woman."

"Just my luck," Cindy said as she took her last breath.

J. A. JOHNSTONE ON
WILLIAM W. JOHNSTONE
"WHEN THE TRUTH
BECOMES LEGEND"

William W. Johnstone was born in southern Missouri, the youngest of four children. He was raised with strong moral and family values by his minister father, and tutored by his schoolteacher mother. Despite this, he quit school at age fifteen.

"I have the highest respect for education," he says, "but such is the folly of youth, and wanting to see the world beyond the four walls and the blackboard."

True to this vow, Bill attempted to enlist in the French Foreign Legion ("I saw Gary Cooper in *Beau Geste* when I was a kid and I thought the French Foreign Legion would be fun") but was rejected, thankfully, for being underage. Instead, he joined a traveling carnival and did all kinds of odd jobs. It was listening to the veteran carny folk, some of whom had been on the circuit since the late 1800s, telling amazing tales about their experiences, which planted the storytelling seed in Bill's imagination.

"They were mostly honest people, despite the bad reputation traveling carny shows had back then," Bill remembers. "Of course, there were exceptions. There was one guy named Picky, who got that name because he was a master pickpocket. He could steal a man's socks right off his feet without him knowing. Believe me, Picky got us chased out of more than a few towns."

After a few months of this grueling existence, Bill returned home and finished high school. Next came stints as a deputy sheriff in the Tallulah, Louisiana, Sheriff's Department, followed by a hitch in the U.S. Army. Then he began a career in radio broadcasting at KTLD in Tallulah, which would last sixteen years. It was there that he fine-tuned his storytelling skills. He turned to writing in 1970, but it wouldn't be until 1979 that his first novel, *The Devil's Kiss,* was published. Thus began the full-time writing career of William W. Johnstone. He wrote horror (*The Uninvited*), thrillers (*The Last of the Dog Team*), even a romance novel or two. Then, in February 1983, *Out of the Ashes* was published. Searching for his missing family in the aftermath of a post-apocalyptic America, rebel mercenary and patriot Ben Raines is united with the civilians of the Resistance forces and moves to the forefront of a revolution for the nation's future.

Out of the Ashes was a smash. The series would continue for the next twenty years, winning Bill three generations of fans all over the world. The series was often imitated but never duplicated. "We all tried to copy the Ashes series," said one publishing executive, "but Bill's uncanny ability, both then and now, to predict in which direction the political winds were blowing brought a certain immediacy to the table no one else could capture." The Ashes series would end its run with more than thirty-four books and twenty million copies in print, making it one of the most successful men's action series in American book publishing. (The Ashes series also, Bill notes with a touch of pride, got him on the FBI's Watch List for its less than flattering portrayal of spineless politicians and the growing power of big government over our lives, among other things. In that respect, I often find myself saying, "Bill was years ahead of his time.")

Always steps ahead of the political curve, Bill's recent thrillers, written with myself, include *Vengeance Is Mine, Invasion USA, Border War, Jackknife, Remember the Alamo, Home Invasion, Phoenix Rising, The Blood of*

Patriots, The Bleeding Edge, and the upcoming *Suicide Mission.*

It is with the western, though, that Bill found his greatest success and propelled him onto both the *USA Today* and the *New York Times* bestseller lists.

Bill's Western series include *The Mountain Man, Matt Jensen, the Last Mountain Man, Preacher, The Family Jensen, Luke Jensen, Bounty Hunter, Eagles, MacCallister* (an Eagles spin-off), *Sidewinders, The Brothers O'Brien, Sixkiller, Blood Bond, The Last Gunfighter,* and the upcoming new series *Flintlock* and *The Trail West.* May 2013 saw the hardcover western *Butch Cassidy, The Lost Years.*

"The Western," Bill says, "is one of the few true art forms that is one hundred percent American. I liken the Western as America's version of England's Arthurian legends, like the Knights of the Round Table, or Robin Hood and his Merry Men. Starting with the 1902 publication of *The Virginian* by Owen Wister, and followed by the greats like Zane Grey, Max Brand, Ernest Haycox, and of course Louis L'Amour, the Western has helped to shape the cultural landscape of America.

"I'm no goggle-eyed college academic, so

when my fans ask me why the Western is as popular now as it was a century ago, I don't offer a 200-page thesis. Instead, I can only offer this: The Western is honest. In this great country, which is suffering under the yoke of political correctness, the Western harks back to an era when justice was sure and swift. Steal a man's horse, rustle his cattle, rob a bank, a stagecoach, or a train, you were hunted down and fitted with a hangman's noose. One size fit all.

"Sure, we westerners are prone to a little embellishment and exaggeration and, I admit it, occasionally play a little fast and loose with the facts. But we do so for a very good reason — to enhance the enjoyment of readers.

"It was Owen Wister, in *The Virginian* who first coined the phrase *'When you call me that, smile.'* Legend has it that Wister actually heard those words spoken by a deputy sheriff in Medicine Bow, Wyoming, when another poker player called him a son-of-a-bitch.

"Did it really happen, or is it one of those myths that have passed down from one generation to the next? I honestly don't know. But there's a line in one of my favorite Westerns of all time, *The Man Who Shot Liberty Valance,* where the newspaper editor tells the young reporter, 'When the truth becomes legend, print the legend.' "These are the words I live by."